I0584361

ENCHI LOTTA BODIES

A JORDAN MCALLISTER MYSTERY
BOOK 6

LIZ LIPPERMAN

OLIVERHEBERBOOKS

All rights reserved.

No part of this publication may be sold, copied, distributed, reproduced or transmitted in any form or by any means, mechanical or digital, including photocopying and recording or by any information storage and retrieval system without the prior written permission of both the publisher, Oliver Heber Books and the author, Liz Lipperman, except in the case of brief quotations embodied in critical articles and reviews.

PUBLISHER'S NOTE: This is a work of fiction. Names, characters places, and incidents either are the product of the author's imagination or are used fictitiously. Any resemblance to actual persons, living or dead, business establishments, events, or local entirely coincidental.

Copyright © Elizabeth R. Lipperman

Published by Oliver-Heber Books

0 9 8 7 6 5 4 3 2 1

ACKNOWLEDGMENTS

These past few years, my personal life has been a hot mess, and I feel like I need to thank a lot of people for making this book happen. First and foremost is my sister, Mary Ann Nedved, who died recently. She was my biggest cheerleader, and I know she is still passing out bookmarks in heaven.

Of course, I can't go without thanking the rest of my siblings, Don Roth, Dorothy Bennett, and Lillian Magistro. I know the other four are also cheering me on from heaven. Without them, I might never have known how to love unconditionally.

Next comes my husband, kids, and grandkids who make every day worth getting out of bed. Thanks, Dan, Brody and Abby, Nicole and Dennis, Grayson, Caden, Ellie, and Alice. I love you all so much.

And the Bunko Babes, who have been my sisters from other mothers for over thirty years and who keep me supplied with humorous wisecracks, all of which go directly into my books.

My biggest supporter is my agent, Christine Witthohn, who has made this journey way easier than it should have been, both as my voice to the editors as well as my friend. I love this woman.

And there's a group of women called the Plotting Princesses. Nothing like sitting around with writers from all different genres to plot a book. The romance writers want kisses and sex, the fantasy writers want werewolves and faeries, and the mystery writers want guns and knives. Obviously, we laugh a lot during these sessions. My advice to a blocked writer is always to kill someone.

For this book, I had several beta readers and would like to thank them for their exceptional editing –Kari Lee Townsend, Liese Sherwood-Fabre, Vicki Batman, and Chris Keniston.

And lastly to my publisher, Tanya Anne Crosby, as well as all the people at Oliver Heber Books, who go out of their way to make this process so painless. I am so grateful to have found them.

"Come on, Jordan. I'm starving. You know how much I love the Wednesday night buffet at China Cafe." Victor Rodriguez flopped down on the couch and waved his hand in the air, a not-so-covert signal for her to get off the phone. "If you make me miss the good desserts, I swear I'm gonna wring that pretty little neck of yours."

Jordan sent him a stern look that would have made another man flinch, but he simply grinned and puckered his lips in an imaginary kiss.

She turned away from him and lowered her voice. "So you're not coming home tomorrow?" She couldn't hide the disappointment in her tone.

Saturday was Cinco de Mayo, and she and the gang had big plans to eat and drink their way through the entire Mexican holiday. She'd counted on her boyfriend to party with them.

"Sorry, love," Alex Moreland said, the sadness evident in his voice. "We thought we'd finish up tonight, but the Terrazes cartel had other plans. Looks like I'll be in Harlingen for another two weeks or longer." He sighed. "I miss you so much and can't wait to see how much you miss me."

She was glad Victor couldn't see the hot flush she knew was creeping up her cheeks. He would have given her grief about phone sex. She lowered her voice even more. "You sound pretty confident that I'll be here waiting. It seems like an eternity since you left, and I do get lonely, you know."

"Not confident...hopeful."

"Are you whispering because you're talking dirty and don't want me to hear?"

Even before she turned around and glared at Victor, she knew he was probably halfway off the couch so that he could hear the conversation. He was her landlord as well as her closest friend on the planet, but the man had no filter. In spite of her annoyance, she giggled. "Shut up."

"I see Victor hasn't changed in the month since I've been gone," Alex said.

She shook her head as if Alex could see her, then turned around again and whispered into the phone. "Truth be told, I wouldn't have it any other way."

"Me neither." There was a slight pause before Alex continued, "Back to you and me, I'm hoping I can get home sooner, but right now we're playing it by ear. The time would definitely go by so much quicker, though, if I had something to take my mind off drugs and bad guys. Why don't you tell me exactly how you're going to make me feel welcomed when I get back to Ranchero."

Again, she colored before smiling. She didn't have to see his face to know that his eyes were crinkled in mischief. The man loved to tease her.

"Get home and be surprised," she fired back. "Hopefully, I won't have a harem of hot male models vying for my attention by then."

"My dream scenario," Victor shouted in the background.

"Tell Victor I'm counting on him to keep those guys away from you. And make sure they all know I'm a Fed and will hunt them down," Alex joked back. "Gotta run, love. With a little luck, I'll see you soon."

She stood with her back to Victor for a few seconds longer, savoring the warm feeling she always got when she talked with Alex. Before he'd left on the assignment to the border town, he'd told her he loved her, and to her surprise, she'd said it back to him. After her engagement with her college fiancé had ended several years before—more like blown up in her face when he'd dumped her—she'd sworn off love and romance forever.

That was before Alex Moreland had walked into her life and painstakingly broken down every wall she'd erected. Granted, the man had thought she was a diamond smuggler at the time and had only pursued her to make an arrest, but from the first moment their eyes met, there had been instant chemistry.

When her dog came up beside her and barked, she jumped. "Geez, Max, give me a heart attack, will you?"

Victor smacked the arm of the couch loudly. "He's starving, too, Jordan, and tired of listening to you talk lovey-dovey to Alex, although even I have to admit, the man's worth it. If I weren't with Michael, I might give you a run for your money with that FBI hunk."

Jordan laughed. "I would give anything to see your face if I told Michael what you just said, not to mention your other comment about the harem of men."

She bent down to kiss the dog that had saved her from certain death nearly a year ago when a very angry black bull had her in his sights. She'd been surprised when Alex had appeared at the door with the adorable white creature in tow. Seems the owner had been more than willing to give up the mischievous canine who chased cows and teased his neighbors' chickens all day. Jordan had fallen madly in love with the still-ornery dog, just like the entire gang had.

Victor frowned. "You really wouldn't tell Michael what I said, would you?"

She wasn't ready to let him off the hook just yet. "Depends. And let me repeat something you said to Rosie a while back when she had her eye on a really good-looking man. You told her he didn't bat for her team." She snickered. "I can assure you—Alex bats for mine."

Victor tsked. "Too bad. But seriously, Jordan, there isn't a more perfect man for you, and surprisingly enough, the guy adores you and all your quirky ways. You'd better hang on to him with both hands."

"Don't worry. I adore him, too." She walked into the kitchen before turning back to Victor. "Take Max out back to do his business, and I'll get his dinner ready and then change into my new jeans. They're not as tight as the ones I'm wearing, and I'll be able to eat more. Then we can get the gang and head out to China Café."

He was on his feet in two seconds. "Now you're talking. I can taste the sweet and sour soup now, and oh Heavenly Mother, all those desserts." He grabbed Max's leash from the kitchen counter, and after the dog raised his head to allow him to put it on, the two bounded out of the apartment, each knowing there would be a food reward when they returned.

As Jordan scooped out the dry dog food, she thought back to when she'd first moved to Ranchero, a lost soul who'd thought that life as she'd known it, was over. She was absolutely positive that divine intervention had led her to Ranchero, a small Texas town close to the Oklahoma border and as far away from big D and her ex-boyfriend Brett as she could get.

She wondered what had happened to the man she'd thought would be her happily-ever-after throughout the entire four years at the University of Texas. How stupid was she to have given up her own dreams to follow him around the state while he chased his? As a top graduate in the prestigious journalism program and the first female ever allowed in the male locker rooms at UT, she'd assumed that getting a job alongside her fiancé would eventually happen. But she'd made the mistake of thinking it was more important for Brett to become established before they settled into married life, and then she could join the short list of female sports columnists.

That was before Brett got a job at one of the biggest TV stations in Dallas and two months later decided the petite weather girl with a humongous store-bought chest was too tempting to pass up.

Heartbroken and disgusted for being so naive, Jordan somehow had found her way to Ranchero—jobless, broke, and too embarrassed to tell her parents and brothers about the breakup. They would have hightailed it to Dallas faster than a lion chasing a wildebeest and dragged her back to Amarillo. Even in her sad state of mind she'd known if that had happened, she would never have been able to leave the security blanket of her family. She'd probably be flipping burgers right now somewhere in her West Texas hometown.

She'd been smart enough to realize that a big part of her family's love would have involved them smothering her to protect her from every evil the world had to offer. It would've been like high school again, where many a suitor had come calling only to be met at the door by the full force of the McAllister testosterone. God only knows what her four brothers had said to those unfortunate souls because some of them had never looked her in the eye again.

So she'd ended up at the Empire Apartments, a rundown two-story building where she'd been immediately embraced by all the first-floor residents. Today, these people were her best friends and on more than one occasion, her partners in crime.

As she placed Max's bowl on the floor, she heard a faint knock at the door and wondered if Victor had locked himself out. She wrinkled her nose, trying to figure out why he hadn't just barged in like he always did.

She brushed back the lock of hair that had fallen over her eye and opened the door. "After all these years, you're finally knocking..." She stopped when she saw a middle-aged gentleman and then practically jumped into his arms. "George! What are you doing in Ranchero?"

"Hello, Jordan." George Christakis hugged her before holding her out in front of him so he could study her. "I didn't think it was possible, but you've gotten more beautiful since the cruise."

"I hate to think of you getting old, my friend, but they say the eyesight is the first thing to go," she joked, smiling up at the famous New York chef she'd met on a cruise ship several years before when they'd both judged a cooking contest. "You look the same as when you passed me the mint under the table right after I discovered I had just eaten a thymus gland."

His eyes twinkled with amusement. "I still laugh when I think about that."

Jordan suddenly remembered her manners. "Come in my friend. Can I get you a cup of coffee or a glass of iced tea?"

"I've heard you talk so much about Texas sweet tea, I can't wait to try it." He walked over to the couch and sat down. "Bet you're wondering why I'm in Ranchero."

She was about to reply when the door burst open and Max ran in, spied the stranger on the couch, then leaped on him, covering his face with monster licks.

"Terrific guard dog you have, Jordan," Victor deadpanned, stepping into the apartment. "Holy cow! George Christakis?" He walked over and bent down to hug the New Yorker. "Thank God you aren't a murderer."

After wiping the slobber from his face, George rubbed Max's neck. "And who is this beautiful creature?"

As if he knew he'd just been complimented, Max gave the man another full-face smooch.

"Max!" Jordan yelled before turning to Victor. "Do something."

"He's your dog," he fired back before looking down at George. "What's a big-time cooking channel guy like you doing in little old Ranchero?"

Jordan set the tea on the table before she shoved Max to the other side of the couch and sat down beside her guest. "He was just about to explain when you stormed in."

"Where's my tea?" Victor scowled.

She dismissed him with her hand. "Do I look like a waitress to you? Since when do you not invade my refrigerator anytime you want something?" She knew what she'd said sounded harsher than she'd meant it to, but she was starting to get nervous about why

George was here. Facing him, she asked, "Everything's okay with you, right?"

He gave her a half grin. "I've got some great news, and I wanted to share it."

Victor sat down in the chair opposite the visitor. "We love good news, so spit it out, man. Did you get another TV contract or... Oh dear Lord! Tell me you're not here to talk Jordan into judging another culinary contest with you."

Jordan narrowed her eyes and stuck out her tongue. "Don't be a wise-ass, Victor." She turned back to George with more than a little anxiety forming knots in her stomach. "That's not why you're here, is it?"

"I wish it were," he said. "I had more fun on that cruise with you and your friends than I've had in a very long time. That saying about all work and no play does make for a very dull guy." He shook his head. "And right now, I could use a few of those laughs."

"What's wrong? I'm beginning to get worried about why you left your restaurant in New York and showed up on my doorstep. You're not going to tell us you have a terminal illness or anything, are you?"

"It's nothing like that. It's true I've run into a few bumps in my personal life, but I'm not here to talk about that. My business life is booming, and I've come to invite you and your friends to help me celebrate." He paused for a reaction before adding, "Among other things."

"Go on," Jordan urged, glancing toward Victor to see if his reaction was the same as hers. Why would the successful restaurateur and wildly popular TV culinary critic come all the way to Ranchero to celebrate good news with people he'd only met once? Surely, he wasn't hoping to open a new restaurant in the small Texas town where all-you-can-eat buffets ruled.

George took another sip of his tea before speaking. "Have you heard about the new casino opening up just across the Texas-Oklahoma border?"

That got Victor's attention, and he shot up in his chair. "Don't tell me you're staying there for the Cinco de Mayo opening. I heard it was going to be huge. Too bad none of us can cough up the three hundred bucks for a room."

George grinned. "Not only am I staying there, I'm opening a smaller version of Chez Luí in the center of the casino. It won't come close to being as fancy as the New York version and will offer affordable steaks, lobsters, and the like."

"That's terrific, George. Does that mean we'll get to see more of you and maybe even meet Jeremy?" Jordan asked.

His eyes took on a sadness Jordan hadn't seen in all the time she'd been with him on the cruise ship. "I will have to make several trips down here, at least for a while until I get the restaurant on its feet. I socked a lot of money into it and can't afford to have it fail." He blew out a deep breath. "Once I get it up and running, Jeremy will take over as manager."

"Jeremy?" Jordan interrupted. "How can he run it from New York?"

George lowered his eyes. "He can't. His brother Terry is the CFO of the new casino, and Jeremy's going to stay with him until he can find a place of his own." He paused long enough for Jordan's morbid curiosity to kick in.

"Won't that be a hardship with Jeremy gone so much?" she asked, wishing almost immediately that she could take it back after seeing the sadness return to his eyes.

"Unfortunately, Jeremy and I have been at odds for the past six months, and a trial separation might be the best thing for us. He's actually the one who talked me into investing in the casino in the first place, and I felt like I owed it to him."

"What about your son? Won't he miss Jeremy?" Again, she wanted to smack herself and fully expected George to tell her his personal life was none of her business.

Instead, he took the last gulp of tea before continuing, "Jeremy and I became a couple when Henri was just a toddler. Now that he's a bona fide teenager, it seems that all Jeremy does is berate him for every little thing. Henri can't seem to do anything right in his other dad's eyes. It's caused a rift in our relationship— one that I'm not sure can be healed." He turned to make eye contact with Jordan. "I hate to admit this, but Henri couldn't hide his excitement when I told him Jeremy would be in Oklahoma for a while."

"I'm sorry, George," Jordan said. "Break-ups can be hard on everyone." She remembered back to when she got the "Dear Jane" email from Brett. She didn't think she'd ever recover, but somehow, the residents of Empire Apartments had helped her move on.

At that moment, the door opened and those same friends rushed in, all talking at once.

"Chicken and cashews are waiting, Jordan. Let's..." Ray Varga stopped short when he saw who was sitting on the couch. "Well, I'll be. If it isn't our famous New York friend. How the heck are you, George?"

George stood and hugged the newcomers one by one. "What's this about chicken and cashews? I haven't had that since the last time I visited Chinatown, and that was too long ago to remember."

Rosie leaned over and grabbed his hand. "Come on, Georgie. Let us show you how low-rent people eat on a Wednesday night."

Gripping her hand, he allowed her to pull him up. "Good heavens! I'd forgotten how stunning you are, my dear." He bent over and kissed the back of her hand. "Low rent? Never!"

"You shouldn't have done that," Victor said with a smirk. "Our Miss Rosie is a sucker for tall, dark, and handsome. Throw in good manners, and she's a pushover." He made a heart with his hands. "I'll have to remind her again that she's not your type."

Rosie smacked Victor on the arm. "You are such a turkey. You could learn a few things about how to treat a lady from this gentleman." She gave George one of her flirty smiles.

Jordan watched as her friends interacted with George and realized this was exactly why she loved them all. Rosie LaRue, the fifty-ish hippie who still wore tie-dyed T-shirts and braided her long blonde hair, was the mother figure of the group and did most of the cooking for their Friday night card games. She was also the reason Jordan's culinary column was so popular, since her awesome comfort food recipes ended up in the newspaper as gourmet food under fancy names.

For sure, the good people of Ranchero had caught on a long time ago, but apparently, they didn't care. The subscription rate at the *Ranchero Globe* had nearly tripled after Jordan took over as the Kitchen Kupboard editor, in large part due to Rosie's recipes. Although Jordan would rather be sitting in the press box covering the Grayson County College football games, being a culinary editor wasn't such a bad gig.

"So, am I invited to dine with you all?" George asked.

"Absolutely," Victor said, grabbing his arm and heading toward the door. "I'll call Michael and tell him we're leaving so he can meet us there after work. He'll be so excited to see you."

"Sounds terrific," George said. "I'm looking forward to tasting the local cuisine, plus I have something I want to talk about with everyone."

Lola Van Horn stepped forward and faced George. "Does this involve you and Jordan and gourmet food?" She rolled her eyes. "Because I'm not sure I can watch Jordan go through that again unless fried bologna and combination nachos are part of the deal."

Jordan shook her finger at Lola. "Don't you start. I've already heard all this from Victor."

Despite the teasing, she adored her friend. Lola Van Horn, the oldest of the group, owned Lola's Spiritual Readings in downtown Ranchero where she read tarot cards and performed other psychic services for some of the wealthiest people in the county. Almost as wide as she was tall, she wore Walmart caftans like they were Dior originals and sported oversized lips and tattooed eyeliner, compliments of a plastic surgeon who couldn't go a week without one of her readings. Lola and Ray Varga—a tough-as-nails, retired cop who shared more than a cup of coffee with her and was putty in her hands—were two of Jordan's favorites.

"No one in their right mind would invite Jordan back to judge a cooking contest, not even gentleman George here. So enough talk, people. The fried rice is calling." Victor shoved Jordan toward the door, and the others followed suit.

As Jordan patted Max one last time, she closed the door, wondering what her New York friend really wanted.

2

────────

As usual, China Café was packed on all-you-can-eat Wednesday night, and it took fifteen minutes before the group was led to a table for eight in the back room.

No sooner had they been seated when Victor jumped up, nearly knocking over his chair in the process. "Order me a margarita, will you, Jordan? My blood sugar's at a dangerously low level, and I need some help quickly." He hurried over to the desserts.

"Is he diabetic?" George was seated next to Jordan and watched as Victor plowed through the dessert line. "Because if he is, I'm pretty sure all those sweets are not what he should be eating. Jeremy is a type II diabetic and has sugar crashes often. The doctor recommended a glass of orange juice or milk to bring his numbers back up. Said it's not a good idea to overdo it as the blood level will spike, which can be just as dangerous."

"Diabetic? Victor?" Rosie rolled her eyes. "The man's as healthy as a horse. His only problem is his sweet tooth, which is bigger than the Grand Canyon. I swear he'd perform tricks for anyone who offered a piece of cake."

"A sweet-tooth brother. I knew there was a reason why I liked him so much. I have to hide my sugary snacks so I don't tempt Jeremy." George patted his stomach and looked up when the waiter approached the table. "Give these fine people anything they want and put it on my tab. We're celebrating."

"Don't tell Victor that. He loves free food almost as much as he loves sugar. We'll have to carry him out of here. When we went to Beef Daddy's a while back, he walked out of the place with not one, but two full doggie bags. Good thing I didn't care much for the guy who'd invited us." Jordan turned to the New Yorker. "But seriously, my friend, you don't have to do this. You're in our neck of the woods now, so let us treat you."

George flashed a smile. "What I'm about to talk about involves the opening of my new restaurant. That makes this a business meeting, and as such, it's a tax write off."

"I can't wait to hear what we're celebrating. No talking until I get back," Lola instructed before giving her drink order to the waiter then heading toward the buffet lines. "Better hurry before Victor eats everything on the dessert table," she said over her shoulder.

The others quickly joined her, and when they were back at the table, Michael showed up and waved from across the room. As he approached the table, he spied the stack of desserts on his partner's plate. "Going a little heavy on the sweets, aren't you, Victor? Thought you said you wanted to cut back."

Victor blew him a kiss. "You don't want to go there tonight, Michael. Just grab a plate and join us." He pointed to George. "We have a very special guest who really doesn't want to hear you bickering about my eating habits."

Michael's eyes lit up when he recognized the man, remembering how much fun they'd had judging the cruise's culinary contest sponsored by WTLK talk radio where Michael was one of the anchors. "George! What in the world are you doing here?"

The chef stood to hug him. "Go get some food, and I'll explain everything when we've all eaten so much that our bellies hurt." He sat back down and popped a forkful of the chicken and cashews into his mouth. "Breaking bread with good friends always puts me in a good mood—something I could use these days."

As Michael headed for the buffet, Jordan leaned close to George. "You have me worried. Are you sure everything's okay with you?" she whispered.

He held her gaze. "I'm sure. I just had a brilliant idea on the plane ride from New York and wanted to run it past all of you."

She let out a slow breath. "Guess I'll just have to wait until you're ready to talk."

He patted her hand. "I promise it's not bad news."

Jordan dipped her spring roll into the hot mustard and popped it into her mouth as she spied her non-diabetic friend on his way back to the table with more food, much to the chagrin of Michael, who was watching him like a hawk. She bit her lower lip to hold back a grin, knowing Victor was up to his old tricks again, getting Michael into an argument over food issues and then pouting until the poor guy agreed to something to make up. The entire gang knew what he was up to, except Michael, who fell for it every time.

She snickered to herself, remembering once when Victor thought he was losing weight before discovering the drawstring on his sweatpants had come undone. Everyone had laughed, except Michael, who knew it was a losing battle but couldn't help himself. Victor would always be cute and chubby and dared everyone to take him or leave him. He was, by far, Jordan's best friend as well as her co-conspirator in searching out trouble.

After several trips through the buffet line, everyone had eaten more than they should have and were now relaxing around the table with a fresh round of drinks.

Finally, George stood and raised his glass. "Although I've only recently met all of you, I consider you part of a small circle I call my forever friends. Thanks for allowing me to enjoy your company tonight."

After everybody clinked glasses, Jordan asked, "Now can you tell us why you're calling this a business meeting?"

Remembering her earlier conversation with George about his fragile relationship with his partner Jeremy, she wondered if George was going to announce his divorce plans. But why would he celebrate that? Divorce wasn't a happy time for either side.

"Yes, my impatient friend," George said, sitting back down. "I'll start by telling you why I'm here." He took a second to glance around the table. "As I told Jordan earlier, my partner and I have been having problems for the past year. Suffice it to say we don't always see eye to eye on disciplining my son Henri, who is a newly-minted teenager. That's a whole new challenge all in itself and probably a big part of the problem." He stopped to shake his head. "At any rate, Jeremy's brother Terry approached us six months ago about investing in an upscale restaurant in the center of a new casino under construction close to the Texas border."

"The Golden Arrow Casino and Resort in Ensenada?" Rosie asked. "I thought it was Indian-owned. They don't normally farm out their profitable ventures to outsiders."

"It's one of the few casinos in Oklahoma not owned by one tribe or another," George explained. "Anyway, Terry signed on as chief financial officer, and when he heard about the plans for the restaurant, he thought of Chez Luí and called Jeremy. I gave it some thought and decided not only would it be a money-maker, but it would also be a way to put some space between Jeremy and me to see if we can work things out."

"Terrific, George. Not about you and Jeremy, certainly. I'm just not so sure that the good people of Oklahoma are ready for your kind of food." Rosie pursed her lips and shook her head. "A twelve-ounce ribeye? No card-carrying Texan or Oklahoman would pass that up, but as for the rest—lamb chops and all the French stuff—no way. Give a Texas cowboy a plate of enchiladas and a frozen Blue Moscato Margarita in a huge frosted glass, and he'll think he died and went to cowboy heaven. But no lamb chops. He'd rather eat his goats."

George leaned back in his chair. "Exactly why I thought of you, Rosie. Jordan has always said your recipes are the only thing keeping her employed, and since I had a chance to experience your amazing King Ranch chicken first-hand on the cruise, I knew immediately what had to be done."

"Are you saying what I think you are?" Victor's eyes were as round as saucers now. "You want to use Rosie's recipes in your new restaurant?"

"Yes, but there's more." George turned to Rosie. "I'm here to invite all of you to the Cinco de Mayo grand opening of the casino. I'll need you, my dear, to teach my chefs how to make your scrumptious Mexican dishes since the entire weekend will be a celebration of the south-of-the-border cuisine you are so famous for. So, what do you say?"

Rosie looked like a deer caught in the headlights. "I... I'm honored you would ask, George, but I can just give you the recipes. I'm sure your professionals would be way better than I am at putting them together."

"At all those fancy foods you named earlier, maybe, but this is your wheelhouse, your specialty. My chefs have no clue about quesadillas or *chiles rellenos*," George said. "They wouldn't know a good comfort casserole if it bit them on the you-know-what."

"Let me get this straight, George. Did you just say we were all invited for the weekend?" Victor asked, his face showing more excitement than when he'd devoured the plateful of sweets.

"You did, Victor. Rosie would have to work, mind you, but only for four or five hours a day preparing the dinner menu and teaching my staff her secrets. The rest of you would be along only to support her and, naturally, to keep me company." He grinned. "As you can see, I won't fit in very well with the locals in my three-piece suits."

Ray laughed out loud. "No offense, George, but somehow I don't see you in chaps and a Stetson."

"None taken. You actually just made my point."

"There's no way I can afford those high-dollar rooms, especially on opening weekend. Heard they were going for upwards of four hundred bucks a night." Lola sighed. "Unless you have some magical lamp with a genie who'll foot the bill."

"Not a genie, Lola, but a CFO who is just as excited about my idea as I am. He thinks the locals will eat it up and knows Rosie comes with friends." George raised his eyebrows. "Think about it. A long weekend of gambling, shows, Rosie's food. All gratis except for the gambling. So, are you in or not?"

"Oh, hell yes!" Victor shouted, slapping Rosie on the shoulder. "You've turned out to be a real asset, honey-bee."

"Bite me, Victor, and don't call me honey-bee or I'll kick your patootie all the way to the casino myself. The day I showed up at the Empire was the day your apartment building finally got some class." She took a big drink of her margarita then focused on George. "And I can use whatever recipes I want?"

"Absolutely. For three days, the entire dinner menu belongs to you—entrées, desserts, appetizers, and even salads. I can't wait to see what you come up with. I might even take some of them back to New York and rename them to fit in with my menu there."

"I can guarantee you the New Yorkers, who spend way more money than I'll ever make, are going to love Rosie's casseroles," Jordan said.

"Okay then, it's settled," George said. "The first dinner will be tomorrow night. Can you make that happen, Rosie?"

"I might have to cancel my meeting with the mayor..." Rosie laughed. "Kidding. I don't even know who the mayor is. Heck, yeah, I can. I'll drive up after breakfast, settle in, and then prep everything before the dinner hour rolls around." She paused, before asking, "Can the rest of the gang come with me tomorrow?"

George leaned back in his chair before pointing to the ceiling. "Thank you, Jesus. Finally, I'm going to have some fun in my life."

Jordan frowned. "Now all I have to do is convince my boss into letting me have a few days off."

"Tell the old curmudgeon you want to review the new restaurant on site, Jordan. And mention that it's all gratis because of Rosie. Although it's a huge conflict of interest, your cheapskate editor will jump at the chance to get a first-hand scoop on the new casino," Lola suggested.

"Hmm." Jordan rubbed her chin. "Maybe I can convince him to let me be a special features reporter for one weekend instead of a culinary one. I could interview some of the key people in the casino and still talk up the restaurant."

"Good idea," Lola said. "He'll be excited he doesn't have to pay your expenses."

George called the waiter over and ordered another round for everyone. When they all had a fresh drink in front of them, he lifted his glass once again. "Here's to good friends, good food, and a lot of laughs."

"It's been so long since I gambled, I have no doubt my budget is going to take a direct hit," Jordan said.

"I'll be right beside you to keep you out of trouble, sweet cheeks," Victor said. "And if I can't, then I'll help you rob the place."

~

AROUND TEN THE NEXT MORNING, they piled into Ray's Suburban and headed north. Lola had been right when she'd predicted that Jordan's boss would jump at the chance to get a scoop on the casino opening without having to fork over one red cent for expenses. He'd tried to talk her into waiting until Friday night to go so she wouldn't have to miss work, but she'd marched into his office prepared. She convinced him that because Thursday was the grand opening, she needed to be at the casino to get the reactions of all the people coming to celebrate Cinco de Mayo weekend and hopefully, really loose slot machines.

The Golden Arrow Casino and Resort was a ninety-minute jaunt from Ranchero, and the chatter was nonstop the entire trip. Although Rosie was actually the only one who would have to work for her keep, she was the most excited of them all. She loved to cook, and the salary George had slipped into the deal provided an added incentive.

"How much money did you bring, Jordan?" Victor asked.

"Three hundred. I figure I can lose fifty a day and not have to file for bankruptcy. Without a doubt, I'll be eating bologna sandwiches all week instead of fast food, but it'll be worth it." She squinted. "Maybe I'll even surprise myself and bring a little cash home with me. Growing up with four brothers, I never got to play Candyland or any of the normal kid games. I was introduced to poker and blackjack when I was barely seven, and believe me when I tell you, my brothers showed no mercy. I had to learn quickly if I ever wanted to keep my allowance money every week."

"Good. You can teach me how to play. That way I won't be tempted to lose all my money on the slot machines," Victor said. "Maybe I'll come home a winner as well."

Lola gave him a smirk. "Anyone who goes to a casino expecting to win is just kidding themselves. There's a reason why Las Vegas is affectionately called 'Lost Wages,' and I predict the Golden Arrow will be no different."

"Wonder why they named it that since George mentioned it's not an Indian property," Ray mused as he exited the interstate and headed up the hill to the casino.

"Who knows? What I *can* tell you is that the casinos not under reservation ownership have a lot more rules and regulations to follow. As far as the name goes, I have no idea why they chose it, but the arrow signifies protection," Lola said. "I remember reading an Indian dude's tarot cards one day and an arrow showed up. He got so excited you'd have thought I'd just told him he'd won the lottery. Always wondered if he was running from some dangerous situation or something and needed protection."

"I interviewed a tribal chief on my show a few years back," Michael chimed in. "He said the deeply spiritual Native American Indians use symbols and signs from generation to generation. Besides protection, a single arrow denotes defense but can also signify deadly force, movement, or the direction of travel. When an arrow points to the left, it's supposed to ward off evil. To the right, protection, and pointing downward...peace."

"Which makes me even more curious about why the owner would use a recognized Native American symbol like an arrow if he's not of that race. Our money sure isn't protected when we go through the doors," Ray said.

"Beats me," Michael answered. "I hope there's only one arrow and not two, though."

"Why? Does that mean bad luck?" Jordan asked, suddenly interested in the conversation.

Michael shook his head. "No, it's a symbol for war."

Rosie fished a casino brochure out of her purse. "Thank God the arrow is pointing to the left on the logo."

"Too bad it doesn't mean winning money," Victor said when Ray pulled into the resort parking lot that was already nearly full just shy of the noon hour. "Holy cow! This place is rockin'. Lots of folks anxious to celebrate Cinco de Mayo."

"What exactly are we celebrating this weekend, Victor?" Lola asked. "Mexican Independence Day?"

"Not quite. Cinco de Mayo signifies the date of the Mexican army's 1862 victory over France at the battle of Puebla during the Franco-Mexican war. Independence Day was long before that."

Ray had barely slid the SUV into one of the few spots left before Victor hopped out of the car.

"Come on, I'm feeling really lucky."

~

JUST AS THE BROCHURE SHOWED, a huge golden arrow sculpture graced the entrance into the largest casino Jordan had ever seen. But if she thought the outside looked impressive, the inside nearly knocked her socks off when she finally got her first glimpse of the lobby. From the marble floor with embedded golden arrows to the gigantic crystal chandeliers sending flashes of light dancing throughout the entire area, the place took her breath away.

"Criminy! This must have set them back a few million just on the light fixtures alone," Rosie said. "And would you look at the lines at the reservation counters. We'll be here all day."

"Oh no, you won't," a familiar voice said from behind them. "You're all VIPs. Follow me." George Christakis grabbed Rosie's arm and led them to a specially marked counter. In less than thirty minutes, they were checked in.

"I'll have the bellhop take your luggage up and turn down the beds," George said, his face as excited as a kid with a new toy. "Come on. I want to show you the restaurant and introduce you to my staff."

Jordan was still staring at the huge chandeliers when she turned and bumped into a man directly behind her. Her purse went airborne, spilling its contents all over the marble floor. Embarrassed, she made eye contact with the man she'd just charged into.

"I am so sorry," he said. "I have a lot on my mind and wasn't paying attention. I didn't expect you to turn so suddenly."

"I...I...," she stuttered as she stared into the darkest brown eyes she'd ever seen. "It was my fault," she finally managed. "I have a bad habit of never looking before I take off."

He smiled up at her as he gathered the contents of her purse, and for a moment she forgot what a stud he was as a horrible thought hit her like a wrecking ball. She prayed she didn't have a tampon among the fallen items. When he handed her the purse with one hand, and then with the other, produced the feminine hygiene product, she was mortified.

Sure that her face was beet red, she held up her palms. "You never know what you'll find in a gal's purse."

"I never had sisters, but I'll take your word for it." He offered his hand. "Here's hoping you leave here with a much heavier purse." Then he turned and walked away, leaving her standing and staring as he entered the casino area.

"Holy bamboozle!" Victor said, coming up behind her. "Did you get a look at that cowboy? Levis should be paying him to strut around in those skin-tight jeans. And the boots...they had to be snakeskin. I'd be willing to bet he caught those suckers himself."

"Do I need to remind you you're taken, Victor?" Michael said, appearing out of nowhere.

Victor's expression never changed, despite just being caught ogling the backside of a very hot cowboy. "I know, Michael, but just because I'm on a diet doesn't mean I can't look at the menu." He grabbed Jordan's arm. "Come on, girlfriend, you promised to teach me how to play blackjack."

Jordan allowed him to nudge her toward the casino, wishing Alex was with them. She didn't need a menu to know he was the only entrée she wanted. And she intended to make sure he knew that when he finally did come home.

3

"This is awesome," Michael said after George led them through the door into the restaurant. "The ambiance is to die for."

The walls were painted a soft yellow and graced with gold sconces that even in broad daylight projected a warm blue shadow on the ceiling. Tables draped with what looked like expensive linens were strategically placed throughout a large room so no one would be tempted to eavesdrop on private conversation. In the center of each table was a bouquet of freshly cut flowers in blues and yellows surrounding a candle that tastefully matched the wall lanterns.

"The room is soundproofed to make sure you can relax and have a nice meal without the chatter and noise of the slot machines outside those doors," George explained.

"Wow! You've certainly classed up the place. Even a die-hard redneck will enjoy the peace and tranquility, especially if his luck is down and his wallet is lighter," Ray said. "A Chez Luí in Oklahoma... hard to believe."

"Not Chez Luí, Ray," George corrected. "Even before I told you about the kind of food we'd serve, I decided a name like that wouldn't attract a lot of casino patrons wearing cowboy boots and fringed shirts." He circled the room with his hand. "You're looking at Wild Card Steaks and Ribs." He lifted his eyebrows. "What do you think?"

"Great name. I would definitely eat here," Jordan said, turning to George. "Assuming I could afford the ribs."

"At the advice of the owners, I chose prices that wouldn't scare even the lower income clientele away, although it puzzles me why a person who can feed several hundred dollars into a machine would balk at paying twenty bucks for a world-class steak. As to your remark, Jordan, the ribs are reasonably priced at twenty dollars for a full rack." He turned and walked toward the kitchen. "Come on. You're about to see what's so exciting."

They followed him through the revolving door into a massive world of stainless steel where thirty or so kitchen workers decked out in fresh white uniforms were busy preparing the evening meal. He walked toward the largest grill Jordan had ever seen and a petite woman wearing a hat almost as tall as she was. The woman was talking to a younger girl but looked up as they approached.

"Everyone, meet Morgan O'Neil, the fabulous chef I talked into relocating from New York to run this place."

Standing just over five feet, the blonde woman looked to be in her late thirties, and although she looked older, Jordan knew instantly Morgan was someone she could be friends with, if her smile was any indication of her character. When she made eye contact and reached for Jordan's hand, it felt like they were already friends.

Morgan turned to the younger woman. "This is Ellen Farnsworth. She's a senior at the University of Oklahoma who's interning with me for the next three months." Although the OU student was at least five-eight and towered over her mentor, there was no doubt who was in charge.

George pushed Rosie to the front. "Morgan, I want you to meet Rosie LaRue, who makes the most fabulous casseroles I've ever eaten. She's here to instruct you and your staff on the art of great Mexican cuisine, which as you know, we're showcasing this weekend, along with the steak and ribs."

Morgan shook Rosie's hand. "I've heard a lot about you since George returned from the cruise. I'm looking forward to learning everything you're willing to teach me."

Rosie's face lit up with the compliment. "And I'm interested in learning your techniques, as well. As soon as I get settled in my room, I'll be back to begin preparations for tonight's menu. I've decided on spicy, green enchiladas, refried beans, and Mexican rice for the featured entree. We can offer those with beef, chicken, shrimp, or cheese, along with all the usual Mexican favorites like brisket and shrimp tacos, fajitas, and combination nachos. Since it's opening night, I was thinking we could include a free margarita to anyone who orders an entrée."

"Sounds perfect," George said. "I can't wait to try one of those myself."

"We'll get started on the basic appetizers and salads right now." Morgan waved as they all turned to leave. "See you in a bit, Rosie."

"Morgan's lovely," Rosie said to George on the way out.

"I know. I hated to give her up at Chez Luí, but I knew she'd be perfect for this place."

On their way out of the restaurant, they were met by two men accompanying a woman whose swagger gave the impression that she owned the place as she flirted with every male she passed.

When they approached the gang, the woman zeroed in on Michael. "Hey there, stranger, do I know you?"

Before Victor could react, one of the men with her stepped between her and Michael. "Not here, Arizona," he admonished before focusing on Rosie. "I'm assuming this is the woman you can't stop talking about. Is that right, George?"

Once again George pushed Rosie to the forefront. "That's right, Terry." He made a wide swath with his hand to take in the others. "And these are her incredible friends."

"You must be Jordan," the shorter of the two men said, walking toward her. "I've been dying to meet you since George told me about you and the sweetbreads on the cruise." He slapped his knee and giggled. "Chicken nuggets... Priceless."

Jordan blushed, wishing she could erase that memory from everybody's brain. Unfortunately, she knew it was destined to follow her wherever she went. She held out her hand to the man who was still laughing. He stood about five-six with dark hair, his eyes crinkled in glee. When his fingers closed around hers, his hand was so soft Jordan wondered if it would be bad manners to ask what kind of moisturizer he used. "Jeremy, I presume?"

"You would be correct, and this is my brother Terry." He pointed to the man still standing between the woman and Michael.

Taller than his brother but not nearly as handsome, Terry addressed them, "And this is Arizona Lightfoot, the lead singer of Serendipity, the casino band that plays two sets a night in the Lucky Seven Lounge around the corner."

Arizona stepped out from behind Terry and focused again on Michael. "And you are?"

Victor nearly tripped, racing to his partner's side, causing Jordan to bite her lip to hide the smile. Usually, Michael admonished Victor for flirting with other men. It was comical to watch her best friend getting a taste of his own medicine.

"He's Michael, and I'm Victor." With the smile still plastered to his face, he added, "And trust me when I say you don't want to go there, Miss Lightfoot."

The woman sent Victor a look that would have disarmed a weaker, less determined man, allowing Jordan time to give her the onceover. Dressed in a royal blue mini dress that exposed nearly all of her long, tanned legs, her eyes as dark as the curly ringlets that framed her face, Arizona was what Ray would call a serious "head turner." For a second Jordan was grateful that Alex wasn't with them here instead of chasing drug dealers in South Texas—but only for a second. On the cruise, her boyfriend had been around George's friend Emily, who was twice as gorgeous as Arizona, and he'd passed the test with flying colors.

When it looked like this would be the proverbial Mexican standoff between Victor and the lead singer, Arizona finally backed away and grabbed Terry's arm in a possessive way, suggesting they were more than colleagues. "Nice to meet everyone. Hope you'll all come to the lounge tonight. We've got a great show planned."

Terry quickly removed her hand from his arm,

giving Jordan a firsthand look at the wedding band on his left ring finger. She didn't have to see Rosie's face to know it was probably scrunched up in a disgusted look aimed at the two. Having been married to four cheaters, Rosie hated them. And from the way Arizona placed her hand back on Terry's arm, her fingertips stroking lightly in a seductive manner, you didn't have to be a gambler to bet some kind of hanky-panky was going on.

"We'll all be there, Arizona," George said, sending Terry a disapproving look of his own before turning back to the Ranchero gang. "Time for you all to have some fun. It's opening day, and I've been told the slot machines are loose and ready to make the Cinco de Mayo weekend enjoyable for all." He pursed his lips and faced Rosie. "Sorry, but you'll have to wait for your fun. I'm counting on you to dazzle my customers tonight."

"Oh, she definitely will," Lola said, walking past Arizona and "accidentally" bumping into her, nearly knocking her over. "Pardon me, dear," she said sweetly before winking at Victor.

~

"Shake a leg, Jordan," Victor hollered from the hallway.

"Victor," she admonished when she opened the door, and he and Michael rushed in past her. "Some people might be sleeping."

"At three in the afternoon?"

"A lot of high rollers sleep during the day so they can gamble all night long."

"Okay, I'll be quiet, but hurry up. Didn't you hear George say the slot machines are especially loose this weekend? I plan on making a killing on the penny games."

She eyed him carefully, unsure if he really was that naive about the penny slots or if he was just trying to jack with her. She decided on the former. "You do realize that in order to win big on those machines, you have to bet anywhere from a dollar to three dollars a pop."

He frowned. "No way."

"She's right, Victor," Michael interjected. "Nobody ever goes home a big winner betting low. I always say in order to win big you have to be willing to lose big."

"We'll see about that," Victor said, defiantly.

Remembering the only other time she was in a casino, it had been cold enough to hang meat, Jordan grabbed her lightweight sweater, then gently pushed her naïve friend toward the door. "Okay, but don't come crying to me when you hit the jackpot and your bet was only fifteen cents."

After the three of them were in the hallway, Jordan checked to make sure she had the room key before shutting the door. "Where's Ray and Lola?"

"Already down there," Michael answered. "Ray wanted to check out the blackjack tables and Lola spotted a Sex and the City penny machine she swore had her name on it."

Jordan chuckled. "She's a rabid fan of the show and watches all the reruns over and over again. Maybe Mister Big will make her day." They walked through the massive casino until they spotted Ray at a blackjack table.

He looked up just as the dealer busted. "You must have brought me luck," he said with a grin. "Sit down and take a load off. This will be the only time you'll see so many five-dollar tables. In a few hours, they'll all raise the minimum bet to ten dollars." He pointed to three empty seats at the end of the half-moon table.

"Michael and I are going to find Lola and gamble with her. We'll see you when I return with my winnings."

"Right. I can't wait to eyeball your ninety-eight-cent haul," Jordan joked as she sized up the two players at the other end of the table.

An older woman had a stack of black hundred-dollar chips in front of her. About five two or three, she seemed slightly overweight, and several pieces of turquoise jewelry decorated both hands.

The young girl sitting on the other side of her held a half-filled glass of liquor and a stack of red five-dollar chips. She signaled for the waitress to bring another cocktail.

When Victor came up behind Jordan, she said, "You go on. I'm gonna play blackjack with Ray for a little while."

She sat down on the seat between the two women, then pulled out two twenty-dollar bills and handed them to the dealer, deciding when they were gone, she'd quit. After placing her five-dollar bet, she waited for the game to begin.

Her first card was face down, and her second one was a five—not a great way to start. The woman next to her, who introduced herself as Violet, drew a six, and the younger woman who had a fifteen-dollar bet, got a ten. Ray's smile covered his face after his second card was a king, and he flipped over the bottom one, showing his blackjack. After paying Ray, the dealer dealt his last card, a six, which gave Jordan a little hope that she might not lose her five dollars. Her brothers had pounded into her head that you always had to assume the dealer's hidden card was a face card, which meant he'd have to draw against his sixteen and hopefully bust. Her brothers had also preached that when the dealer showed a bust card, you should always stand on anything over twelve. After losing her allowances too many times to count, she'd finally gotten the hang of it, even occasionally beating her brothers.

Jordan waved her hand, signaling she'd stay with her six. Violet asked for a card, got a queen, and busted. The young girl next to her mumbled, "Way to go, Gramma," under her breath.

After she stayed, the dealer turned over his first card to show the sixteen Jordan had hoped he'd have. While she waited for him to take another card, she worried Violet had screwed over the entire table by taking the face card that would have busted the dealer.

When the dealer turned over a jack, Jordan high-fived the younger girl before pulling in her five-dollar winnings. So far so good. She relaxed and sat back on the stool.

She played blackjack until Victor appeared beside her, visibly excited. He waved the slip of paper in her face to show he'd won twenty-three dollars. You'd have thought it was a new car by the way he celebrated.

"Come on. I saw George a little while ago, and he said the band would be practicing in fifteen minutes. Let's go hang out with him."

Her stash was up fifty dollars, and it seemed like a good place to stop before her luck changed. As the dealer "colored" her five-dollar chips into two green twenty-five dollar ones, she noticed Violet only had one chip left from her large stack she'd had when Jordan first sat down. Without blinking an eye, the woman pulled another stack of hundred-dollar chips from her purse and laid it on the table.

Jordan stood up, rolling her eyes when Ray glanced her way. He nodded, cocking his head toward the older woman. Why anyone who played as badly as Violet did would subject herself to losing more cash was beyond Jordan's wildest imagination. Surely, the slots would have been kinder, letting her at least win a little. She scolded herself for being judgmental. What the woman did with her Social Security check was her own business. The woman might very well be a retired doctor or lawyer and have more money in the bank than Jordan would ever see in her lifetime.

"Ray, do you want to come with us?" Victor asked, interrupting Jordan's thoughts.

He shook his head. "Thanks, but no. I'm going to play a few more hands and then try to find Lola. We might need to take a quick nap if we're going to keep up with you young 'uns."

"She's playing the slots with Michael close to the front entrance." Victor pointed in that direction. "And for the record, you two put us young 'uns to shame."

"For sure." Jordan turned toward the cashier's cage. "I need to cash out before we go, though."

Victor grabbed her arm. "Later. The band is only practicing for a short while, and I don't want to miss any of it."

"Okay. Lead the way."

She followed him toward the other side of the casino until they came to the door that led into a gigantic area with a stage and stadium-style seating that probably accommodated between nine hundred and a thousand people.

"The big-time entertainers perform here," George said, after he spied them and walked over to greet them. "Serendipity normally plays at the Lucky Seven Lounge, but tonight and tomorrow night, they'll be here. Then Saturday night, the James Brothers are performing two shows, both of which have been sold out for over three months."

"Wow! I love those guys," Jordan said, sitting down in the front row.

George sat down beside her. Of course, you'll come backstage and meet them. Maybe take a few selfies."

"Oh my gosh! I think I love you," Jordan said just as the members of the band entered the stage from behind the curtain.

When Arizona noticed them, she waved and silently mouthed, "Where's your friend?"

Jordan didn't have to look at Victor to know he was probably giving her the stink eye he used when someone crossed him. The lead singer blew him a kiss.

"Sheesh," he said. "That girl has zero gay-dar."

"Blue Moscato Margarita," George explained when the waiter handed Jordan a frozen drink. "Rosie said to tell you it's for luck. I can't wait to try it."

Leave it to Rosie to remember how much she loved those. After the last sip, Jordan licked her lips. When she swallowed it, the waiter magically appeared with another.

Jordan smiled at the guy who rewarded her with a grin of his own. "As much as I adore these and appreciate you keeping my glass full, no more after this one, please. I don't want to spend the rest of the night in bed."

She leaned back in her chair as the band began practicing, deciding that no matter how much she disliked the flirtatious Arizona, the girl could definitely sing. With two female backup singers, two guitarists, a keyboard player and a drummer, the group went through a complete set, each song sounding better than the previous one.

"See that blonde back-up singer?" George asked, leaning over to whisper. When Jordan nodded, he continued, "That's Meg Ballard. She used to be the lead singer until Arizona showed up at one of their rehearsals to try out for a backup spot."

Victor leaned over from Jordan's other side. "So how'd she grab the lead spot?"

George chuckled. "Oh, you know. The thinking is she slept her way into it."

That got both Jordan's and Victor's attention, and they huddled closer.

George pointed to the drummer, a tall lanky guy with dirty blond hair falling below his ears. "That's Kenny Glover. Serendipity is his band." He lowered his voice. "Rumor has it he and Meg were a thing before Arizona showed up and wiggled her way into the spotlight."

"How did Meg take that?" Victor asked. "Personally, I would have to kill the beotch if it was me."

Again, George laughed. "Meg pretends she's okay, but her eyes give her away. Watch the way she looks at Arizona. When I asked Terry about it, he said Meg is hopelessly in love with Kenny which is why she doesn't make waves. She knows sooner or later Arizona will tire of the drummer and move on to bigger and better things, and Kenny will come to his senses. Then she'll get back her lover and the lead singer gig."

"That might be a hard decision to make since Arizona is so good," Jordan said. She debated for a few seconds before asking the next question, knowing it was definitely none of her business but unable to stop herself. "Is Arizona having a fling with Terry, too?"

George nodded. "Terry, Luis Santiago, the casino CEO, and God only knows who else." He raised his eyebrows at Victor. "Seems she has her sights set on Michael as well, so watch her closely, my friend."

"I'm not worried. Michael knows how ruthless I can be when someone wanders uninvited into my space. Besides, Michael is one of the most level-headed men I know. No way he sees her as anything but what she really is—a tramp."

Just then the band quit, and before Arizona could come down from the stage, Victor grabbed Jordan's hand and pulled her from the chair. "Let's go. We've got just enough time to try out Rosie's Mexican food before we hit the tables again. You promised to teach me how to play blackjack, remember?"

She nodded before kissing George on the forehead. "Are you going to join us for dinner?"

He shook his head. "Too much to do. Besides, I've been sneaking bites all day, and I'm here to tell you the spicy green enchiladas are fabulous." He waved goodbye. "See you at the lounge for tonight's show."

When they were out of the theater, Victor said, "Arizona is definitely a piece of work. I can't believe she's sleeping with all those men and there hasn't been a gunfight or something. You know how crazy Southern men act over a woman."

"Somehow, she's bewitched them. I can understand why Terry's in the mix. The man is cheating on his wife and probably just enjoying the no-strings-attached arrangement. As for Kenny, as much as you hate Arizona, you have to admit the girl has pipes. So besides getting free sex, he's got an awesome lead singer for his band."

"And did George say Arizona was also sleeping with the casino owner?"

"He did, and never having met the guy, I can't speak to his motivation, but my guess is, he's just like any other guy who can't resist gratuitous sex with a woman who looks like Arizona."

"You've got a point." He picked up the pace, and she had to hurry to keep up with him. "Let's find the others. I'm starving."

4

The enchiladas tasted as George had described, but Jordan knew they would be, having pigged out on them so many times at their Friday game nights at the apartment. After two more margaritas, she felt pretty mellow and spent the next two hours after dinner teaching Victor the intricacies of blackjack. To her surprise, he learned fast, and both walked away from the table with a little more cash than when they'd sat down.

As they approached the cashier's cage and saw the long line, he groaned. "Dang! We've only got thirty minutes until the band starts. It's a ten-minute walk just to get to the concert hall."

"You'd think they'd have more staff working on opening night," Jordan said, trying to decide whether they should wait or come back after the show to cash in their chips.

Then she noticed Violet, the woman who had lost a ton of money at the blackjack table, standing two places in line ahead of them. Her curiosity got the best of her as she wondered how the woman could have any money left after playing so awful at the tables. Her first thought was maybe she'd hit it big on the machines. Then she remembered that people playing the slots got a paper receipt for cashing at various machines placed around the casino. They didn't need to stand in line at the cashier's cage.

To get a better look, she inched as close to the stocky man in front of her as she dared, and to her surprise, when it was Violet's turn, she opened her purse and a slew of black chips fell out.

"Holy—"

"Shh," Jordan interrupted Victor in mid-sentence, but her reaction was identical. She'd personally watched the woman gamble away a boatload of money, and now, black, hundred-dollar chips filled her handbag. "I sat next to her for over an hour, and trust me when I say, that lady should not be playing blackjack. She's awful."

"Maybe I should have taken lessons from her," Victor quipped. "Obviously, she picked up her game."

Jordan's jaw dropped as she watched the cashier count out seventy-five hundred-dollars. She was sure her mouth was still open when Violet passed her and smirked—almost as if to taunt her—before hurrying away. Speechless, Jordan collected her money and followed Victor to the concert hall where the others waited outside the door.

"Your enchiladas were magnificent, as usual," Victor said, kissing Rosie on the cheek when she walked over. "I almost hated sharing them with all those other people."

Rosie blushed with the compliment. "Hey, guys. Morgan and Ellen were awesome. They treated me like I was a professional. I loved every minute of it."

"Good," Jordan said. "And for the record, you are a professional in my book." She followed Ray and Lola to where George waved frantically from the front row where he'd saved them seats.

After greeting them all, he motioned for them to sit down just as a waiter arrived with a tray full of drinks. "If you want something besides Rosie's fantastic margaritas, you need to tell Joseph now so he can bring it before the show gets started."

"Will Jeremy be joining us?" Lola asked, unaware of the conversation Jordan had back in Ranchero with George about his partner and their relationship problems.

"Unfortunately, no, but maybe if we have drinks later," he said, unable to hide the sadness in his eyes.

For the next fifteen minutes, they made small talk, catching up on each other's lives. It was nice to be together with their new friend from New York.

When nine-thirty rolled around and the band still hadn't made an entrance on the stage, the crowd began to get restless, yelling for the show to start and some even banging on the tables. George looked at Jordan and shrugged, then got up to see what the holdup was when Kenny ran out from behind the curtain, heading directly toward them.

"She didn't show up," he said, his voice accentuating the panic that had widened his eyes.

"Who didn't show up?" George asked.

"Arizona. We sent someone to her room." Kenny threw up his hands in frustration. "She's not there, and her phone goes right to voicemail."

George put his hand on Kenny's shoulder. "I'm sure there's a reasonable explanation."

"She's never done this before. Arizona would rather die than miss an opportunity to open up at a casino." He shook his head. "Something's terribly wrong. I can feel it."

"Did you check with Terry?" George asked. "He might know where she is."

"We can't find him or Jeremy." Kenny threw up his hands. "What should we do?"

George thought for a moment before responding. "Do any of the backup singers know the songs well enough to take the lead?"

"Meg does," Kenny replied as a glimmer of hope spread across his face. "Actually, she probably knows them better than Arizona." He looked pleased with himself. "Okay then, let's get this show started." He turned and practically ran up the steps to the stage before disappearing behind the curtain.

"Hope he's right about Meg knowing the songs. It would be a shame to have the first show of the casino ruined because Arizona decided to go AWOL tonight," Victor remarked

"Oh, Meg knows them," George responded. "Like I mentioned earlier, until a few weeks ago she was the lead singer for Serendipity. That was before Arizona waltzed into the casino and changed everything."

"Not so good for Meg but a life saver for tonight," Lola said. "Did Kenny make the switch because Arizona is that much better?"

George shrugged. "Honestly, I haven't heard Meg sing yet, so we'll find out soon enough. But frankly, I have a feeling there was more to Kenny's decision to replace Meg with Arizona than the quality of her voice."

Victor practically fell out of his seat when he leaned over to get closer to George. "Don't stop now, or I'll have to hurt you," he quipped.

George laughed. "I know how much you like gossip, my friend. All I know is what I've already told you —that Meg and Kenny were an item before Arizona showed up. Jeremy mentioned that the security camera caught Arizona sneaking out of Kenny's room several times this week at the crack of dawn. Too bad his brother doesn't know that his mistress is sleeping with the bandleader."

"Sounds like Arizona knows how to play the game," Victor said. "We know what she wanted from Kenny. Wonder what Jeremy's brother has to offer? Maybe money?"

Again, George shrugged. "As CFO of the casino? Who knows? Terry is a big boy, and although I abhor cheaters, it's none of my business."

Just then the curtain opened, and the crowd went crazy as the band began playing *Proud Mary*. As soon as Meg opened her mouth, it was obvious she was just as good as the woman who had stolen her job.

Jordan couldn't stop staring at the new lead singer. Meg Ballard stood about five-six and could only be described as a knockout with her long blonde hair swirling around her face. Her bright red, tasseled dress moved at mach speed as she went into the signature Tina Turner routine, the crowd rising to its feet when she ran from side to side on the stage. Jordan couldn't help noticing the slight smile that was now threatening to explode into a full-blown victory grin on the back-up singer's face. She couldn't stop her own glee, thinking that karma could be a beotch. With a talent like Meg's, she should never have lost her job simply because Arizona had climbed under the sheets with the bandleader. No matter what reason Arizona gave for not showing up on stage, Kenny would still have to demote her after Meg's performance tonight.

George leaned over and whispered, "Meg's got to be glowing, knowing she's the star on opening night. Personally, I think she's better than Arizona,"

"Me too. And frankly, it isn't fair that a relationship with the boss can bump you up the ladder like it did for Arizona." Jordan made a pouty face.

George turned in his seat to face her. "Sometimes you are so innocent, and that's my favorite quality about you," he teased. "How do you think Meg got the lead singer gig before Arizona?"

Jordan's eyes widened. "You're serious?" When he nodded, she continued, "So much for the good guy coming out on top—no pun intended," she said to George who was now fighting to hold back a smile.

When the song ended and the crowd howled its approval, Jordan lowered her voice. "Guess Arizona is about to lose her boyfriend as well as the singing gig."

George snickered. "Just the gig. Meg and Kenny never stopped being an item. Although she has to know about Arizona, my money's on Meg walking away with everything after Arizona gets tired of playing house with Kenny."

Jordan took another look at Kenny, wondering how a guy like that could keep two really attractive women on a string. Slightly under six feet, his hair slid over his eyes as he pounded on the drums. Although he wasn't her type, she could see how he might be a chick magnet, given that girls did love band members of any kind. Add a bad boy persona to that, and he was probably like catnip to a roomful of playful felines.

Kenny caught her staring and winked. Quickly, she turned away and focused back on Meg, who was now doing an awesome rendition of a Donna Summers song. Judging by the reaction of the crowd, that had already demanded two encores, nobody missed Arizona. It was still a mystery why a woman who had worked so hard to get center stage would skip out without explanation on such a big day.

"Anyone want to go back to the blackjack table?" Victor asked, pulling Jordan out of the chair. "I'm feeling lucky."

"You go ahead. I need to have a conversation with Jeremy that I've been putting off for too long." George stood and hugged them before taking his leave.

"My lady and I are going to hit the sack," Ray said, putting his arm around Lola. "We'll let you young bucks close down the place."

"Casinos never close down," Rosie added. "But I have to get back to the kitchen to make sure everything's in place for tomorrow's meal." She patted Jordan's hand. "Go with Victor and win some money."

"Come on Jordan. We've only got a few more good hours before we need to hit the sack." Victor turned to his partner. "What about you, Michael? Want to play blackjack with us?"

Michael shook his head. "You two go ahead. The slots are calling my name. I'm up about fifty bucks."

"Be careful, love. They don't call them the one-armed-bandits for nothing," Victor and Jordan turned to go toward the middle of the casino and the black-jack tables. "See you back in the room," he called over his shoulder.

For the next two hours, the two of them played, not winning much but at least not losing, either. Violet, the woman who sat at the same table with them earlier, was nowhere in sight, but there was an older gentleman who was already playing with a stack of hundred-dollar chips in front of him when they sat down. He made eye contact with Jordan and introduced himself as Wally. With whitish-gray hair and one of the sweetest smiles Jordan had ever seen, he could have passed for anyone's grandfather. Although he wasn't as terrible at the card game as Violet had been, it was obvious that blackjack would never make him rich.

Every time the stack of black chips was diminished, he'd reach into his man-bag and pull out more. Like with Violet, Jordan had to work to subdue her judgy thoughts about how the man could spend that much money on a game that he rarely won. She was almost tempted to ask if the grandfatherly man wanted a little help. To her credit, she managed to keep her silence since casinos frowned on that, considering it almost as bad as card-counting.

When the long day began to take its toll on the two of them, they called it quits and headed up to their rooms, As they got closer to the lobby, she could see that there was some kind of commotion going on in front of the reservation desk. Her first thought was that the casino had overbooked and some irate person was causing a stink because there were no rooms left at the resort. But soon it became obvious that, whatever the reason, an elderly man was being restrained by two security cops as he spewed obscenity after obscenity at them.

"Let me go, you imbeciles," the man shouted. "I'm here to see Santiago, and I won't leave until he pays me what he owes me."

Victor shoved Jordan a little closer. "Oh, how I love drama."

Dressed in a flannel shirt, even though it was still in the high seventies outside, the man looked like he could have been playing tackle for some professional football team and towered over the much smaller cops. The security guards were visibly sweating as they tried to keep the guy from escaping their grip.

Salt and pepper hair—mostly salt—stuck out from under a huge hat that clearly marked him as a cowboy.

She wondered how a hat that size stayed on his head with so much twisting and turning going on.

Obviously a little drunk—probably a lot drunk—the man in restraints nearly broke free before two more men in uniform showed up and managed to corral him.

Unable to look away, Jordan watched as they led the man to the door. She had to give it to the guy. Even with four officers clutching him as they moved to the entrance, she wouldn't have been surprised to see him escape. A little part of her even hoped he did. She had no idea who this Santiago guy was, but if the older man was willing to make such a scene to get money owed to him, she couldn't help rooting for him.

Before she could dwell on all that, she noticed a hot looking guy out of the corner of her eye standing off to the side. It was the same guy she'd bumped into when they were checking in earlier that day. The obvious displeasure on his face made her wonder if maybe he was Santiago, the man who owed the older cowboy money.

"My money's on that old guy getting his due before this is all over." Victor gripped her arm and led her toward the elevators. "My bed's going to feel so good."

In her room, Jordan tried to be as quiet as she could so as not to wake Rosie up, but when she stubbed her toe on the leg of the dresser, she yelped.

Rosie shot up in the bed, and after rubbing her eyes, shook her head when she saw Jordan rubbing her toe. "I did the same thing earlier. We should probably put a chair next to that stupid thing." She patted the bed next to her. "Climb in. You must be exhausted. We have one more day to go before Cinco de Mayo. You need to make the most of tomorrow before the casino gets really busy."

Jordan sighed. "I am bushed, but I'll definitely be recharged by morning. What's on the menu tomorrow at the restaurant?"

"George specifically asked for that King Ranch chicken that I made on the cruise ship last year."

"Ooh! I love that. And you ought to make the Jalapeno Popper dip to go with it. Those cowboys will go crazy."

"Good idea. Maybe I'll make my famous Blackberry Peach Margaritas the drink of the night."

Jordan climbed into the bed and pulled up the lightweight cover. "Yum. You know how much I love those."

Rosie yawned. "As much as I love talking to you, my friend, I have to get some sleep. Betty White always said we girls need eight hours of beauty sleep."

"Nine if you're ugly, according to her," Jordan finished the famous line for her friend. "Loved that woman." She turned over to face Rosie. "There was this little old lady at the blackjack table tonight who reminded me of her. She was betting hundred-dollar chips like they were nothing."

"Was she really good?"

Jordan blew out a puff of air. "No way. I saw her lose at least a grand while I was there."

"Hope she wasn't using her Social Security check."

"Me too." Jordan raised her eyebrows in a comical way. "For now, all I can think about is getting some sleep. Tomorrow is another day, and I'm anxious to see what happens when Arizona shows up and demands her old job back."

"Men sometimes think with their little brain instead of the bigger one. Knowing the opposite sex the way I do, I'd bet money that Kenny will give her the lead back."

"I hope not. I loved Meg's voice, especially when she did Tina Turner." Jordan rolled back to face the wall. "Night, Rosie."

~

JORDAN WOKE up just in time to see Rosie sitting on the side of the bed, tying her sneakers. She wiped the sleep from her eyes and sat up "Where are you going so early, Rosie? We get to sleep in. Mini vacay, remember?"

Rosie laughed. "Ha! Maybe for you, but I've got to earn my keep."

Jordan checked the clock on the nightstand. "Geez, it's only 9 o'clock. The restaurant doesn't even open until five. So why do you have to get up so early?"

"Last night I cornered George and suggested that we open Wild Card Steak and Ribs for lunch this weekend. Said we should try it out today. Tomorrow is Cinco de Mayo, and starting this morning, the casino will be rocking when the crowds roll in. There's a lot of extra bucks to be made on food."

"And he agreed?"

"You bet he did. Our Mr. Christakis is an astute businessman, and as such, recognizes a great money-making plan when he hears it."

"Who doesn't?" Jordan asked. "Okay, I get why he would agree to this. He gets rich, but what about you? Sounds like you get the short end of the deal with having to work twice as hard."

Rosie tsked. "You know how much I love to cook, so I don't mind the extra work. Besides, I have some really great Mexican recipes that I want to share with his chef." She chuckled. "And did I mention that George is doubling my salary?"

Jordan sprang from the bed and high-fived her friend. "That's terrific, but I have never known you to take money over spending time with your friends."

"Oh pooh! I can see you guys back in Ranchero anytime. This is the opportunity of a lifetime for me." She grinned. "And did I also mention that Russell, the pastry chef, looks a lot like Paul Newman in his younger years?"

Jordan grinned. "I knew there had to be another reason other than the money, although that's a pretty good perk on its own. How old is this young buck, and have you made a move on him yet?"

"Have you met me? Heck yes, I have. We're having a drink later tonight after the dinner rush. And for the record, he's only ten or twelve years younger than me. Besides, I'm looking forward to picking his brain about some of his fantastic desserts."

"Yeah, right! Fantastic desserts, my butt. The dude has no clue how persistent you can be. I almost feel sorry for the guy." She covered her mouth to hide a yawn. "So what's on the menu today?"

"Taco Spaghetti for lunch and King Ranch Chicken with Jalapeno Popper Dip appetizers for dinner, just like you requested."

"Yes! You know how much I love your Taco Spaghetti. I'll definitely see you at lunch and dinner."

Rosie bent down to kiss the top of Jordan's head. "So are you going to gamble all day today and win some more of their money?"

Jordan shook her head. "It's supposed to hit 88° outside today. The gang's meeting up on the roof to check out the incredible pool that we've only seen on the brochure. I need to put a little color on my white body before Alex comes home."

"I could use some of that color myself," Rosie commented. "So when will we see your FBI hunk again?"

"Not sure. There was some kind of complication, and he said he had to stay in Harlingen for a few more days. I'm actually a little worried."

"Why? The man knows how to handle himself. I would trust him with my life."

"I know. It's just that the cartel he's dealing with is ruthless. I don't even want to think about what they would do if his cover is compromised. I wish I could shake the feeling that he's not telling me everything."

"I'll say an extra prayer for him tonight before I close my eyes." Rosie turned toward the door. "Need to go. Taco Spaghetti and young Paul Newman are waiting."

Jordon stayed in bed another fifteen minutes, hoping to catch a little more shut-eye, but it just wasn't to be. She kept thinking about finally verbalizing her fears about Alex to her friend. She hadn't even mentioned it to Victor, her closest friend in the world, but it was almost like talking about it might make it come true. She desperately wanted to talk to Alex right now so that he could reassure her that she was just being paranoid, but she knew that wouldn't happen anytime soon. She had to keep reminding herself of that.

Finally giving up on falling back to sleep, Jordan rolled over and reached for the phone. Breakfast in bed might just be what she needed to get her mind off Alex and what may or may not be happening in Mexico. By the time room service arrived, she'd already showered and was in her bathing suit. The plan was to meet everybody by the pool around eleven o'clock. She couldn't wait to tell them that they'd be eating Taco Spaghetti for lunch around two...and about Rosie's newest love interest. They probably wouldn't be too surprised, knowing that their friend had a soft spot in her heart for good-looking men, usually bad boys, and had been married four times—five, if you counted her marrying the same guy twice—even though the second time only lasted one weekend in Vegas.

5

The minute Jordan stepped off the elevator and got her first look at the rooftop, she caught her breath. The picture in the brochure didn't do it justice. The spacious pool covered most of the area and sported a gorgeous fountain in the center that changed colors with the beat of the pumped-in music. Oversized hot tubs graced each corner with a bar on both ends of the roof. She thought about the night she had really gotten to know George when they were judging the cooking contest on the cruise ship. They'd ended up in a Jacuzzi together, and after several drinks, she'd felt like she'd known him all her life. She hoped he'd find time to party with her and her friends again, but knowing how incredibly busy he would be getting his new restaurant off to a great start, that might not happen.

She walked to the edge of the roof and peered over at the gigantic parking lot. It wasn't even noon yet, and it was already filled to capacity. Today and tomorrow promised to be huge for the casino. Last night, she'd overheard one of the dealers say that there were no rooms left for the entire weekend as well as the following week. A brand-new gambling casino, coupled with the promise of ultra-loose slots and free drinks was too much for the average redneck to resist, she and her gang included.

She was jerked from her thoughts when she heard Victor calling her name, and she turned to see that he and the rest of her friends were already sitting in the far-right Jacuzzi, drinks in hand. She waved and headed that way.

"Hurry up, Jordan. We're over there," Victor shouted, pointing to two tables that had been shoved together a short distance from the hot tub. "Put your stuff down and climb in. I've already ordered you a margarita."

"Who drinks at 11 am?" she joked, after laying her phone and towel on the table.

She took off her cover-up and placed it over her phone to discourage anyone from sneaking up and absconding with it, then headed for the hot tub.

"There's no waiting on the clock before you drink when you're on vacation," Michael said, raising his glass in a mock salute. "Here's to the best friends in the world."

"I second that. I could really get used to this life," Ray said, scooting over to make room for Jordan.

"No kidding. You should have been in my room and seen the lumberjack breakfast that I ate in bed." Jordan stopped to sip the margarita that had arrived as she spoke. "Who said that money can't buy happiness, anyway? It wasn't—"

"Maybe not, but it sure as heck makes life a lot more fun," Victor interrupted. "So Jordan, why didn't Rosie come with you?"

Jordan bit her lip to hide her glee. "Our Rosie talked George into opening his restaurant for lunch this weekend so she could get more of her recipes out there."

"What? Does that mean she'll be working the entire time we're here?" Lola asked. "That won't be much fun for our girl."

"True, but she sees it as the opportunity of a lifetime to show off her culinary skills." Jordan leaned in to whisper, "Plus George is paying her double, not to mention she's got her eye on the pastry chef she says looks a lot like a young Paul Newman."

"Oh Lordy. I swear, she's my favorite cougar," Michael said from the opposite side of the hot tub. "So we'll get to eat lunch at the restaurant?"

"Yes. And if you're lucky—" Jordan stopped abruptly and stared at the elevator door. "Oh my God!"

"What?" Ray and Lola asked in unison.

Jordan pointed to the other side of the pool where Arizona Lightfoot had just stepped out of the elevator and was walking toward a row of chaise loungers on the opposite side of the roof. She looked like she'd just stepped out of a Playboy centerfold, decked out in an animal-print, string bikini that left very little to the imagination. Wearing a large straw hat and huge sunglasses that nearly covered her entire face, she sauntered over toward the chairs. They all watched in silence as Arizona placed her towel on the lounger and plopped down.

"Holy cow! Even I'm turned on," Victor said before Michael slapped his shoulder.

Jordan stood up. "I'm going over there. My curiosity about why she missed her opening performance last night is killing me."

"I'm going with you," Victor said, raising up from his seat.

Jordan gently pushed him back down. "No, you're not. You and Arizona have this animosity thing going on, remember?"

"Oh yeah. The witch was making eyes at Michael."

"Besides, I'm a journalist. I know how to get people to open up, even when they don't want to," Jordan said. "I'm dying to hear her story."

Victor gave her a little shove. "Well, hurry up. You know how impatient I am."

"Everyone does, Victor," Lola spoke up, then high-fived Jordan.

After drying off with her towel, Jordan put on her cover-up and headed in Arizona's direction. As she got closer, she noticed that the woman had taken off her sunglasses and was lying flat on the chaise lounge with the large hat over her entire face.

When Arizona didn't look up as she approached, Jordan closed in and touched her arm. "Hey, Arizona, we missed you last night. What happened?"

Startled, the singer shot straight up in the chair, knocking the large straw hat to the ground.

"Oh my," was all Jordan could say as she stared at the angriest looking black eye she'd ever seen.

Arizona glared at Jordan. "What? You've never seen a black eye before?"

Jordan focused on the singer's lips instead of rudely staring at her right eye. It was black and blue with tinges of red and yellow and so swollen that Arizona could barely open it.

"I grew up with four brothers. Shiners were a weekly occurrence after a rough and tough football game in our front yard, but I have to tell you, yours is probably the worst black eye I've ever seen." She sat down on the lounger next to Arizona's. "So what happened to you?"

The woman smirked. "I don't even know your name, so where do you get off coming over here and nosing into my personal business? It's not like you or your friends give three hoots about me."

She bit her tongue to keep from reminding Arizona that when she was introduced to all of them, she had no interest in anyone but Michael, much to Victor's chagrin. Instead, Jordan took the high road. "I'm sorry you feel that way. I came over here because I'd like to get to know you now."

"What's to know? I'm sure you've heard all the rumors about me."

It really was none of Jordan's business, but her brain couldn't stop her mouth in time. "Did someone hurt you?"

Arizona blew out a breath. "You probably hope that's what happened. Poetic justice that a girl like me got exactly what she deserves."

"Why would you assume that's the way I feel? As far as I'm concerned, what you do is your business. I just hate it when a bully takes advantage of another person, and I'm hoping that wasn't the case here."

The angry look on Arizona's face softened. "I slipped in the shower and hit the side of my face on the door."

Is she kidding? She'd have bruises all over her body if that had happened.

Jordan pretended to believe her. "I don't know why they don't use special flooring in the showers. You'd think they'd worry about lawsuits. I nearly slipped this morning myself." She paused. "Is that why you didn't perform with your band last night?"

"The last thing I need is for people to see me this way."

Jordan leaned in closer. "Actually, it's not as bad as

I had originally thought. If you ice it all day and use a lot of makeup, you might be able to pull it off without too many people noticing."

"You think?"

Jordan grinned. "Well, it's gonna take a heck of a lot of makeup."

For the first time since Jordan sat down, Arizona smiled. "I think I like you, Jordan. You don't seem to be as condescending and judgmental as most females our age. They take one look at me and run away as fast as they can, especially if there's a boyfriend with them."

No joke. Do you blame them? Jordan wanted to say. Instead, she kept that opinion to herself. "Some women are really insecure, but honestly, I can see why a woman would act that way. You are most definitely what my friend Ray would call a head turner."

"Yeah, well, that's overrated, if you ask me." She met Jordan's eyes. "What about you? If you had a boyfriend, would you hide him from me?"

You bet your sweet little tush. "I do have a boyfriend, but he's not with me this weekend. I have to say that when I first met you yesterday, I might've said yes. Now that I've chatted with you and gotten to know you a little better, who knows? I might not."

Arizona sat up on the lounge chair and motioned to the waiter walking toward them with a tray full of drinks. "Not sure I believe you, but for now, we'll let it go." She glanced up at the waiter. "What do you have?"

"Piña coladas, but I can bring you anything you want. The bar just opened so it may take a few minutes, though."

Arizona reached up and grabbed one of the glasses. "These will do." She handed one to Jordan then snagged another for herself. "Put it on my tab with a twenty-percent tip. Room 8013."

After Jordan thanked her, they drank in silence for a moment before Arizona asked. "So, how was the show last night?"

Pretty freaking awesome. "It was good. Fortunately, Meg did a good job with your songs."

Arizona nearly spit out her drink. "My songs? Everybody knows all about how the big bad girl from New Mexico walked in and took Meg's spot as lead singer. Those are actually her songs."

"New Mexico? I grew up in Amarillo which is right next door. How did you end up in Oklahoma?"

Arizona chugged the last of her drink and flagged down the young waiter for another. Jordan shook her head when she offered one to her.

"I'm a sissy drinker," she explained. "I'll have to go back to my room for a nap if I have another. What a waste that would be of the gorgeous sun out here today."

"To each his own," Arizona said as she took a long sip of the new drink. "To answer your question, though, I left New Mexico as soon as I turned eighteen. I was raised by a single mom who was so relieved to see me go, she didn't even bother to ask where I was going. She was raising my two younger sisters on her meager salary as a house cleaner and one less mouth to feed was a plus." She shook her head. "Not to mention that all her boyfriends were starting to pay more attention to me than to her."

"Where'd you go?"

A sad look crossed Arizona's face. "I thought I could make it big as a singer, so I headed to Los Angeles. Was that ever a rude awakening."

"You aren't the first person who went there with

stars in her eyes, only to find out there are so many people out there competing for so few jobs," Jordan said. "I've heard you sing, so I know you have the chops."

Arizona smiled again. "Thanks for saying that. Unfortunately, LA was overrun with talented singers and musicians, most of whom resorted to subway and street performances for rent money." She took another sip of the piña colada. "You know, Jordan, I've never had girlfriends–at least not ones I trusted, but you're beginning to grow on me."

"The feeling is mutual," Jordan replied, amazed that it wasn't a lie. She'd walked over here just to satisfy her curiosity about why Arizona had skipped out on the band gig the night before, and she never dreamed she could end up thinking that the woman might not be so bad after all. "So what happened in LA?"

"California was a total disaster. I ended up waiting tables like most of the wannabe actors and entertainers who didn't perform on the streets. Then I hooked up with the owner of a nightclub who came in one night for a late dinner. He couldn't quit looking at me and said he could make me a star. I bought it, hook, line, and sinker." She shook her head. "The only thing he ever did for me was to beat me so badly that I had to spend two weeks in the hospital. I knew right after that I had to quit trusting people if I was going to make it in this world."

"That had to be a really tough time for you."

"It was. But I got even. I took his fifty grand settlement money, made sure the LA Times got the story, bought a new car with his penance cash, and hightailed it out of there as fast as I could. Trust me when I tell you, I learned the hard way that I'm the only one I can count on. No matter what I have to do, I will never let anyone take advantage of me ever again."

"And you really got that black eye in the shower?" Jordan wanted to slap herself for being so insensitive, but it just came out.

Arizona took another long drink and licked her lips. "Girlfriend, I said I was starting to like you, so I'll let that slide for now. It's the trust thing, remember?"

"Sorry. Sometimes, I can't help myself." Jordan said.

Arizona stood up and put on the sunglasses that covered her face. "Tell you what. Rarely do I get to have a conversation like this with another women, but strangely enough, I enjoyed it."

"Me too," Jordan said, noticing a woman in a bright yellow dress getting off the elevator and surveying the entire pool area.

Arizona reached into her bag and handed Jordan a room key. "If you'd like, we could continue this conversation in my room after the show tonight. While I finish up, you can head that way and make yourself at home—maybe order some appetizers and break out the liquor in the mini bar. I shouldn't be too long after we pack everything up."

Not sure if that was a good idea but curious enough about what made Arizona tick, Jordan took the key. What would it hurt? The soft spot in her heart had been triggered by Arizona's story, and who knew? Maybe if she could be a friend to her for one night, it might change the singer's whole view of the world.

"I'll kill you if you ever go near my husband again."

Both Jordan and Arizona turned as the woman in the yellow dress approached, her eyes filled with venom.

"I beg your pardon," Jordan said.

"I'm not talking to you. I'm talking to this slut who thinks she can waltz in here and steal my husband." The woman poked Arizona's chest. "Not gonna happen, girly. At least not while I'm still breathing."

"Get your hand off me before I call security," Arizona said, unable to hide the fear in her voice.

The woman laughed. "I wouldn't do that if I were you. I'm close friends with the head of security. Not sure you'd like his response after hearing that you're sleeping with his friend who has three small children at home."

"Take it easy," Jordan interrupted. "I'm sure you both can talk this out civilly."

In the moment that it took for the angry woman to turn her attention away from Arizona, the singer grabbed her things and made a beeline for the elevator, leaving Jordan to deal with the irate woman.

"I'm sorry you think your husband's cheating on you," Jordan said, hating that the confrontation had dredged up her own feelings from several years back when she'd discovered her own fiancé was cheating after she'd followed him to Dallas. Even though she'd ended up in Ranchero surrounded by the best friends she'd ever had and a boyfriend who adored her, every now and then it still hurt.

Now was one of those times.

"Do you want to sit? Can I get you some water?"

When the woman shook her head, Jordan took a moment to size her up. About five-eight, she would be considered attractive by most men. Her yellow sundress showed off a nice figure and complimented her dark eyes and hair that fell in a stylish bob to just below her shoulders.

Tears were now threatening in those dark eyes.

"I'm sorry you had to be a witness to all this. It's just that I can't lose my husband, especially not to a hussy like that. I'm willing to do whatever it takes to keep that from happening."

"I get it," Jordan said. "But most of the time, men who cheat eventually wise up and realize what they're giving up at home."

She remembered when Brett found her in Ranchero and wanted to patch things up. It was too late. She had known then that she could never trust him again. She hoped that wouldn't be the same outcome for this woman.

"I don't think Terry will come to that realization. When we argued last night, he flat out said that she's like a narcotic to him."

"Terry?"

"My husband, Terry Redding."

6

"**Y**ou're Terry's wife? Terry, the resort's CFO?"

The woman looked surprised that Jordan knew her husband. "Yes. Don't tell me that you're having an affair with him, too." She lowered her head and swiped at a tear. "I never should have come here, but I had to see that woman for myself. I never dreamed she might not be his only diversion."

"Oh no. It's not like that. I only met him yesterday with his brother, Jeremy. My friends and I were invited to the casino for opening weekend by George Christakis, the owner of the casino's main restaurant. We met your husband when George was showing us around." Jordan looked away before she confessed that she'd also met Arizona then, hanging onto Terry's arm.

The woman looked up and gave Jordan a half smile. "I'm sorry I jumped to conclusions. It's just…"

Jordan touched her arm. "You don't have to apologize. I've been in a relationship with a cheater. Once you've been there, it gives you a whole different perspective of love and trust. You're suspicious of everyone around him." Jordan extended her hand. "I'm Jordan, by the way."

The woman shook her hand. "Marilee. I'm glad to meet you. So, Jordan, how did you meet George? I love that man."

She grinned. "It's a long story, but trust me, I adore him as well.

"Are you still with the man who cheated on you?"

Jordan shook her head.

"You were able to walk away?" Marilee sighed. "I don't think I'm strong enough to do that. Terry and I married right out of high school. I thought our wedding day was the best day of my life. I was already pregnant with our first child, and before we knew it, we had three toddlers under five running around the house. Other than being a mom, I have no marketable skills to speak of. I'm so clumsy that I couldn't even make it as a waitress."

Jordan's heart went out to this woman. She wanted to encourage her to dump the lying, cheating jerk she was married to, but she knew it wasn't her place—that leaving Terry now with no prior work experience and three small children probably wasn't an option.

"Like I said earlier. My guess is that Terry will grow tired of Arizona and —"

"I hate that witch." Marilee's face lit up with anger. "There's no way I can stand by and let her steal my husband, no matter what I have to do to prevent that from happening."

Just then Jordan heard Victor calling her name from across the pool.

"You know him?"

"Yes, and as you can see, he's getting pretty impatient. One of our friends is teaching George's New York chef how to cook Texas style. The restaurant is showcasing a few of her fabulous Mexican recipes for Cinco de Mayo weekend. Guess my friend across the way is starving, as usual." Jordan turned and waved at Victor. "It was nice meeting you, Marilee. I hope things work out for you and Terry."

"Oh, they definitely will," she said defiantly. "No way will I let her ruin everything. Not while I'm still breathing."

Jordan turned away from Marilee, but not before she saw the look on the woman's face. She was glad she wasn't on the receiving end of all that anger—and possibly revenge—that she assumed was behind that look.

She walked briskly to the other side of the pool where Victor and the others were waiting in the hot tub.

"Okay, start talking. What did Arizona have to say about missing the gig last night?" Victor paused and pointed to Marilee as she walked back to the elevator. "And who's that? It looked like she was not real happy with Arizona."

"You don't know the half of it," Jordan said. "I'll tell you later because I'm starving. I want to get back to my room and change so we can get to the restaurant before Rosie runs out of taco spaghetti."

"You're really going to make me wait to hear the juicy stuff?" Victor pouted. "Good Lord, girlfriend, can't you see I'm dying here?" He patted the seat next to him as Jordan climbed into the hot tub.

"Just for the record, the wait for lunch won't kill you," she said, biting her lower lip to hide a grin as Victor narrowed his eyes at her. "By the way, where's my drink?"

"If words don't come out of your mouth in the next minute, Jordan, I swear I'm gonna drown you." Then he handed her an empty glass. "And because you took so long to get back here, I finished your drink, but if you start spilling the beans, I'll get you another one. Tell us, please. Why did Arizona miss her gig last night?"

"No thanks on the drink. I had a piña colada with Arizona, so I'm already past my limit." She turned to the rest of her friends. "Did you all see that woman in the yellow dress who walked over to us?"

"Sure did, honey. Like Victor said, she didn't look too happy. What was her beef?" Lola scooted closer to Jordan to hear the answer.

"That was the wife of the man sleeping with Arizona." Jordan decided to withhold the fact that the woman's husband was Terry Redding, Jeremy's brother. She loved making Victor wait, knowing how impatient he was.

"Oh boy! That must've been pretty awkward for Arizona—and for you, for that matter," Ray said.

"It was. What made it worse was that she didn't even try to deny the affair, even before the woman volunteered that her husband had admitted it to her. After Arizona sprinted out of there, the other woman told me that when she confronted him about it, he told her that Arizona was like a drug he was addicted to."

"Ouch," Michael chimed in. "That couldn't have been easy to hear."

"It wasn't. The woman—Marilee, by the way–has three little kids at home which makes it worse." Jordan pushed Victor, who was now practically on top of her. "Geez, Victor! Give a girl some room. You're so close I can smell the liquor on your breath."

He narrowed his eyes once again. "You know I love you, but I have to say, you're getting on my last nerve. If you don't start telling us why Arizona missed her big show last night, I really am gonna drown you."

Jordan laughed out loud. "You're so easy to rile up. This almost makes up for all the times you've teased me. Almost being the operative word." She paused when he scowled. "Okay. Okay. Did you see the huge sunglasses Arizona was wearing?" She waited for a response, and when everyone nodded their heads, she continued. "She wore them for a reason."

"Because her eyes were bloodshot from a killer hangover?" Lola offered.

"Nope." Jordan wiggled her eyebrows in a Groucho Marx imitation. "She had the biggest black eye I've ever seen, and trust me when I say, that with four strapping male specimens for brothers, I've seen a lot of them, my own included."

"Wow! Did she say how she got it?" Victor moved even closer to her. If there was one thing he loved almost as much as sweets, it was gossip.

"Said she fell in the shower, which I think is total BS. I almost got her to tell me the real story, but at the last minute, she decided to keep it to herself."

"What do you think happened?" Ray asked from two seats away.

Jordan threw up he hands. "Don't know, but if I was a gambler..." She grinned. "I guess after this weekend I can't use that line anymore."

"Hurry up, Jordan. I'm going crazy," Victor said. "I know you must have some idea about what happened."

Jordan sniffed. Spas always opened up her sinuses. "Sort of. She had a hard life growing up. I found myself feeling sorry for her and almost forgiving her for sleeping with married—"

"Oh no you did not," Lola interrupted. "Don't let Rosie hear you say that. You know how she feels— how we all feel about cheaters."

Jordan blew out a breath. "I know. We think they're the scum of the earth."

"Then why did you feel sorry for her, honey?" Michael asked. "Other than the fact that you have always had a huge soft spot in your heart for underdogs —and all stray dogs, for that matter—what was it about her that made you feel empathy? More than likely, that other woman is probably going to lose her husband and the father of those three innocent kids because of Arizona."

"That's just it. Everybody has a story. Hers was really sad. Her life hasn't been easy, and sleeping her way to the top might be her only way of dealing with love, I guess."

"Still doesn't make it right."

"Definitely not, Lola. I'm just saying that not everything is black or white. Sometimes things are a little grayish." Jordan lowered her voice and told them about how Arizona was so badly beaten in California by a man she trusted. "She's fiercely distrustful of all men now and vowed to never rely on anyone but herself to get by in this world. I'm guessing that in her mind she thinks if she can make men dependent on her for sex, then she's in control."

"Until one of them slugs her," Victor said, sadly. "Is that what you think happened?"

"Unfortunately, yes. According to George, she's having sex with so many different men it would be hard to say which one took a swing at her."

"You're probably right," Ray said. "I find it incredible that she opened up to you the way she did. As a cop, I dealt with a lot of battered women, and on more cases than naught, I found that women who give all their power to men usually have a distinct distrust of other women."

"True," Jordan responded. "She said her mother nearly kicked her out of the house when she was eighteen because mom's boyfriends started paying more attention to her daughter than to her."

"She is gorgeous," Ray said before Lola punched his arm. "Not that I'm interested," he added, playfully.

"You'd better not be. Need I remind you that I communicate with the spirits, some of whom are not known to be friendly?" Lola responded, before turning her attention back to Jordan. "So, continue the story, dear." She glanced at her watch. "Oh, wait. Time is wasting, and we need to check out Rosie's taco spaghetti before it's all gone. I'm starving, and I still have to shower before lunch. You can finish your story while we're eating."

"I've told you most of what I found out. Arizona did invite me to her room after the show tonight for more girl talk, though. Even gave me her key."

"Ooh, I want to come," Victor said, excited now.

"What part of *girl* talk did you not hear?"

"Maybe I'll go with Jordan," Michael said, winking at his partner. "Remember, Arizona kinda has a thing for me."

Victor gasped. "You wouldn't."

Everyone laughed at his reaction. It was fun watching Michael tease Victor for a change, instead of the other way around.

"Of course, I wouldn't." Michael stood up. "I'm with Lola. I'm starving."

"Wait, I saved one more thing for last," Jordan said. When they all turned back to her, she continued. "Remember that woman in the yellow dress? The one who confronted Arizona about sleeping with her husband?"

They all nodded.

"Her name is Marilee Redding, Terry's wife."

"Terry? Jeremy's brother?" Ray asked.

"One and the same. She is so in love with Terry even though she knows he's cheating on her. Said her marriage was the best day of her life."

"Sheesh!" Victor exclaimed, shaking his head. "Anyone who thinks a marriage is the best day of their life has clearly never had two candy bars fall out of a vending machine."

Lola spit out the last of her margarita. "Is food the only thing you think about, Victor?" She bit her lip to hold back the laughter.

"Among other things." He gave Michael a thumb's up before turning back to Jordan. "So, how do you think that little love triangle will play out?"

"Not sure, but get this. She said she would do whatever was necessary to keep that hussy—her words, not mine—from stealing her husband."

"Criminy!" Victor said with a huff. "Nothing like burying the lead, Jordan. Maybe she's the one responsible for Arizona's shiner."

～

THE OLDER MAN opened the door and greeted the younger one with a frown. "I hear we have a problem."

"A big one. She's causing trouble again. I told you after I met her the first time that she didn't seem like a player. I should have shown her the door long before opening weekend." He walked over to the counter where a tray of glasses and several bottles of liquor were set up. After pouring himself a drink and taking a long swig, he shook his head. "She thinks she's way more important than she really is. Thinks she can intimidate me by threatening to talk to someone."

"Did you let her know how dangerous that would be?"

"I did. Not sure if it really sank in, though. She wants a bigger cut, and when I reminded her that she had nothing when we found her, it didn't faze her. She still insists that she's worth way more than what we're paying."

The older man walked over to the window and looked out. From this view he could see the massive, earth-moving equipment digging on the left side of the casino. He hoped, by the end of summer, they would have another wing ready to go. After that, they would begin construction on an eighteen-hole golf course and rows of exclusive shops. The more money they brought in, the better for all concerned, especially for him. He knew he was being tested—that if he failed, the consequences would be grave. He couldn't let that happen. Couldn't let one woman screw it up for him.

Turning back to the younger man, he asked. "Do you think it would help if I talked with her? I have a way of *convincing* people to see things my way."

"It might, but I doubt it. Said she's the one taking all the risks. She truly believes she deserves more than everyone else and has even offered to up her game for us."

"I thought you vetted everyone before the casino opened. How did you miss something like this?"

The younger man chugged his drink before walking back to the faux mini bar and pouring another. "She checked out, boss. She seemed genuinely grateful for the opportunity to earn easy money. Guess she just got greedy. Also, she came highly recommended."

"By whom?"

"Several of the others who said she would be perfect for this."

"Obviously, they lied." The older man sat down at the desk and glanced down at the opened file in front of him. "She looks good on paper."

"Don't they all? At any rate, I'll talk with her once more and let her know she's playing with fire."

The man turned the page and stared at the picture of the woman who was causing the current problem. "Do you think she's serious about going to the authorities?"

"Who knows? She's probably jerking our chain for more cash, but I'm not sure we can take the chance that she's bluffing."

"I agree. So what's our next step?"

The younger man cleared his throat. "For now let's play it by ear. I'll have that heart to heart with her tonight and see if I can get her to walk it back."

"And if that doesn't work?"

"Then we go to Plan B."

7

Quincy Parnell ate the last of his jelly doughnut before lifting the cup of strong coffee to his lips and taking a sip. As the hot liquid made its way to his stomach, a warm feeling rushed through his body. If he had a vote, whoever invented this caffeine drink deserved a Nobel Peace Prize. A cup of joe never failed to calm his nerves, even after a sleepless night like the one he'd just had.

Without a doubt, the calming effect and the heat in his belly probably had more to do with the double shot of whiskey he'd added along with his usual huge dollop of heavy whipping cream. He did love the way the liquor soothed him, although lately, it was taking more and more to achieve the same warm and fuzzy feeling. And then there was the added benefit the caffeine provided as it fought off the little guy in his head who wielded a huge sledge hammer and always showed up after a night of heavy drinking.

Today, the caffeine wasn't working so well, though. He rubbed his forehead and went looking for a pain killer to help finish off that little dude.

Glancing down at the half-empty bottle of Jack on the coffee table, he thought he might need to run into town and replenish his supply today, maybe even get an extra one, in case things got a little hairy again. Swallowing two pain killers, he washed them down with a gulp of coffee, forgetting how hot he'd made it and nearly scalding his throat.

Damn it!

He jerked his hand away in pain when the coffee spilled over as he scrambled to the sink for a drink of cold water to soothe his throat and a blast of the cold liquid to ease the burning pain on his hand. He reached into the cabinet for the packet of soy sauce leftover from last night's take-out. Somewhere he'd read that it would stop the burn from stinging and prevent bad blistering. He hoped it worked. He didn't relish the idea of one more trip to the ER only to sit through another long and boring lecture from the doctor about how alcohol was destroying his liver.

He didn't give a crap about his liver. His daddy had consumed nearly a fifth of vodka every day and lived to the ripe old age of eighty-four. He should be so lucky. But right now, he didn't care. His life was a mess, and although he wasn't entirely to blame, he did have to bear some of the responsibility.

Two years ago, he'd been doing great. When the price of beef had escalated to unbelievable prices, he'd made a killing with his 300 head of cattle. But life has a way of kicking your butt just when you think you're on top of the world. That same year, he'd lost his beloved wife, Irene, when she died of a heart attack. It had taken two years to finally come to terms with her sudden death. Although he wasn't completely over the loss, he was so lonely that he'd even sought out female companionship from a few lady friends in town.

But nothing eased the fear that he was destined to be alone for the rest of his life—that he would die alone, never having found another love even close to what he'd had with Irene.

He chuckled to himself, remembering when the church ladies all showed up at his doorstep with more casseroles than he could possibly eat in a lifetime. Several of them had even brazenly offered more than just a tray of lasagna.

And Irene had barely been in the ground two weeks.

Before all that, his 3000-acre ranch had been doing well. He'd employed thirty-five ranch hands who put in long hours to earn their keep, and he was about to hire five more able-bodied men to help with the cattle when disaster stuck, turning his world upside down.

Quincy had tried many times to teach his son the ins and outs of ranching so that he could take over when and if he ever retired. But Jake had no desire to learn the ropes, more interested in easy money than honest hard work. Part of that was Irene's fault. She'd always babied the boy, slipping him money on the side when he'd come to her as if she were his personal ATM.

She had gone to her grave thinking Quincy didn't know about the frequent handouts. Despite the fact he worried that Jake would never learn the skills to be independent, he'd loved his wife too much to call her out on it. He was afraid that without the cash she gave him, his son would've left the ranch and never returned.

Her heart surely would've been broken.

That was why it surprised him when six months after he'd buried Irene, Jake moved into the log cabin once used by a ranch foreman who had died several years before of a heat stroke. With the small house sitting about a hundred yards from the main ranch, Quincy had let his hopes run away with him about working alongside his flesh and blood on the ranch—that maybe now Jake would learn to love the ins and outs of ranching the way he did—the way his daddy, gramps, and great granddaddy had before him.

But it was not to be.

Despite many attempts to excite Jake about the ranch, his son wasn't interested. He cared more about partying with his friends, going into town nearly every night, sometimes staying away three and four days at a time. Oh, he'd heard the rumors. Who hadn't? Anyone with two eyes could see that when the kid wasn't chasing women all over town, he was a frequent flyer at the dog races in the neighboring city. Quincy figured he must be doing okay because he always seemed to have cash in his pocket and never asked for a repeat of his mother's monetary gifts.

But that wasn't all Quincy had to worry about back then. Despite his disappointment that his son would never carry on the family business, life had been going okay until eighteen months ago when his cattle started acting weird. It had begun with a group of ten cows. Some of the ranch hands had approached him and mentioned that these cows had stopped eating and were having bouts of diarrhea. By the time they'd started frothing at the mouth and having convulsions, it was too late. All ten cows were dead soon after that. Necropsies performed by the local vet indicated the cause of death was lead poisoning. Even though all the dead cows had been quarantined as soon as they'd noticed the symptoms, the other cows began to show signs of the fatal diagnosis as well.

Quincy knew all about lead poisoning, had seen it happen to a rancher down the road a few years back when he'd lost his entire herd of cattle because of it. The vet had said crankcase oil, grease from machinery, or lead plumbing and batteries were usually the cause—that cows were attracted to the oily substances and would drink or lick it freely.

Old Doc Harris had explained how the lead settled in their stomachs then formed poisonous salts, which eventually led to bleeding, depriving them of oxygen, and severely damaging their kidneys and liver. According to the vet, even a small amount of lead was enough to take down an otherwise healthy cow in a matter of hours.

Armed with that information, Quincy had gotten on his four-wheeler and searched every inch of the ranch, trying to find the cause of the poisoning but found none of the substances that could have killed the cows anywhere on his property. In the end, all but fifty cows succumbed to the poisoning, and even those who survived had to be put down after their bloodwork showed traces of the lead. Quincy couldn't afford to keep them alive, as they were no longer fit for human consumption.

Without the beef as a source of income, he'd been forced to let his ranch hands go, and for a few months, he'd lived on the small nest egg he'd saved over the years when his cattle had brought in a nice profit. But all that dried up quickly, and as much as he'd hated to do it, he'd sold half of his 3000 acres to the corporation that was building a casino in nearby Encenada to pay off his debt before the bank foreclosed on his ranch.

Though he'd managed to keep fifteen hundred acres for himself, he was undecided about what to do with it. His initial plan had been to head over to Stockman and buy several head of cattle at the auction, but he was hesitant to put more money into the business until the source of the lead could be determined. When he received the bulk of the money from the sale of half his acreage, which supposedly was tied up in government regulations for over a year and counting—BS, as far as he was concerned—he planned to hire a livestock investigator to walk his property and hopefully find and eliminate the lead. Despite his many attempts to get the casino owners to pay up—usually when he was liquored up and feeling sorry for himself—nothing had worked.

He felt like such a failure. He was glad Irene wasn't alive to see how badly he'd screwed up. He should have checked on the cows more often, especially after several of the ranch hands had warned him that some of them were showing signs of odd behavior, including grinding teeth, bobbing heads, and twitching ears.

"Take care of it," he'd told his workers. "Separate the ones you think are having a problem and give them a new bale of hay." He'd never had a problem like that with the herd before, and the only thing he could think of at the time was that the hay might be moldy.

He let out a deep breath before chugging the last of his "enhanced" coffee and made his way toward the counter to pour himself another. As he walked by the sink, he glanced out the window. The land looked so desolate without the cows grazing. Last week he'd taken the baler out and rolled twenty bales of hay he planned to sell to his neighbor. That would put a dent in some of his bills, at least until the money for the land came through.

But the cows weren't the only thing he missed. He loved working the ranch along with the hired help, loved herding the cattle when they strayed. He was looking forward to when things could go back to normal, hopefully sooner than later. He didn't do well with time on his hands. The whole idle hands being the devil's playground thing was right on the money.

The half-empty Jack Daniels bottle proved it.

He placed his cup on the counter and reached for the liquor. Before he could get the lid off, something outside the window about 400 yards out caught his eye. Reaching for the binoculars he kept on the window sill, he trained his eyes on the activity. In disbelief, he watched for a few minutes before it dawned on him what was happening.

"What the hell?"

He ran to the door, pushed it open and took another look through the binoculars. *Is that what I think it is?*

"Son of a ..."

As USUAL, Rosie's taco spaghetti was to die for. Lunch was extra special because she was able to find the time to come out and sit with them over dessert.

"Rosie, my friend. I've tasted chicken spaghetti before, but I have to say, this taco spaghetti beats it by a mile. I'm so glad Jordan called and convinced me to have lunch with you all." George leaned back in his chair. "I may never eat real spaghetti again." He shoved the last of the pecan pie brownie into his mouth. "Oh my word! I think I've died and gone to heaven. Who knew you Texans were hiding all this great food from us snooty New Yorkers? We thought that all you cooked in this neck of the woods was BBQ." He laughed. "Just kidding."

Rosie laughed with him, but you could tell she was beaming after the compliments from the famous chef himself. "The spaghetti is one of my favorites. Now it's become your chef's favorite, too. And by the way, before you head back to New York, you'll have to taste my Brisket While You Sleep. Talk about a good BBQ." She turned to Jordan. "So, what's on your agenda today, roomie? More blackjack?"

"Maybe later," Jordan replied. "I'm up about fifty bucks, and I want to try the slots. If I lose more than twenty dollars, I'm heading back to the tables to hopefully repeat my winning ways from yesterday."

"Ooh, I'll go with you to the slots," Victor said. "Michael won over a hundred big ones last night."

"I did," Michael chimed in. "Love that Texas Stampede."

"Lola and I are going to check out the shops," Ray said. "We can't afford any of the stuff on our fixed incomes, even with what she brings in from her psychic shop, but it's fun just browsing through the windows and imagining we could walk in there and buy something without checking out the price." He gave Lola a smile. "Besides, my lady and I ate so much with the lunch and delicious dessert, we need to burn off some of those calories walking around. This place is huge, so it shouldn't take us long to accomplish that."

"Definitely a lot of square footage," George said. "And they're expanding. All I can say is there must be huge profits in gambling. I'm thinking maybe I'm in the wrong business." He laughed. "Terry told me this place cost upwards of twenty billion."

At the mention of Terry Redding's name, Jordan made eye contact with Victor, who was shaking his head like he was trying to get rid of a bug that had flown into his hair. It was his way of cautioning her not to mention having met Terry's wife earlier at the pool and definitely not about revealing that said wife had confronted Arizona.

She knew he was right. Telling George would accomplish no purpose.

"Terry also mentioned the tribal casinos pull in over six billion a year," George continued.

"Holy cow! That's a lot of money for people to lose," Victor said.

"Oh, it's not all from gambling, my friend. To put it in perspective, Terry said this place has over fourteen hundred slot machines as well as about a thousand tables. But that doesn't even factor in the over two thousand rooms they're charging a fortune for." He stopped and wrinkled his brow. "Why people would pay that kind of money for a room they only sleep in is beyond me. But, as I always say, to each his own."

"No kidding," Lola said. "I'm sure none of us would have ever seen the inside of one of these rooms if it weren't for you, George. Thanks so much."

"My pleasure. But back to our discussion about the lucrative business of owning a casino. As I mentioned, it's estimated that tribal casinos pull in upwards of several billion a year. I'm not sure what they're projecting this one will make since the Indian-owned resorts operate on an entirely different set of rules than those that are privately-owned," George explained. "Terry figured they should make about two million a day— maybe even double that this weekend—with gambling and rental rooms at capacity."

"Whoa! You are in the wrong business," Ray said. "Think what you could do with all that money."

"Speaking of money, I saw the woman next to me at the slot machines cash in on a ten grand payout. Why couldn't I be that lucky?" Michael asked.

"You have to pay taxes on that kind of money, right, Ray?" Lola asked.

"Yeah. I did my homework before we came. If you win twelve-hundred dollars or more in winnings from bingo or slot machines, fifteen-hundred from Keno, or five-thousand in poker tournaments, you have to provide the casino with your Social Security number. They'll give you a form to fill out so you can file your winnings as income."

"What about blackjack?" Jordan asked, suddenly interested.

Everyone at the table laughed.

She scrunched up her face. "What's so funny about that?"

"Seriously, Jordan, do you really think you're going to get into trouble with the IRS because of the fifty bucks you won last night?" Ray asked. "The good news is, according to the article I read, you can win up to fifty grand playing blackjack without having to fill out a tax form." He patted her shoulder. "Who knows? You may get lucky."

"Ha!" Victor said. "I'll wager that nobody ever won that kind of money betting five dollars a hand like she does."

"Hush, Victor," she countered. "I won more than you did."

"That's because you didn't have *you* as a teacher like I did."

This time Jordan playfully slapped his shoulder. "You are an ungrateful turkey. I'll let you play on your own tonight, and we'll see how you do without your teacher."

"Girlfriend, you know I love you. I just like to jerk your chain every now and then." He blew her a kiss.

"Blackjack wouldn't be any fun without you by my side."

"That's what I thought." She blew the kiss back to him, before turning to George. "So do you want to meet up for dinner before the show tonight?"

"Can't. I never did have that conversation with Jeremy, and I can't put if off any longer. I need to see if there's anything left of our relationship to salvage."

"Here's hoping there is," Jordan said, sadly. "We all know how hard breakups can be on both parties."

George sighed. "Unfortunately, I hold out little hope for that, but I wanted to give Jeremy a chance to come clean, to hear his side of the story."

"Come clean? What do you mean?" Victor asked.

George took a deep breath and blew it out slowly, almost as if deciding whether to go on with the conversation or not. "I never told you before, but I found out that Jeremy was cheating on me back in New York. While I was busy running the restaurant every night, apparently, he was doing the night scene. Since he was always home by the time I was able to get away from work, I didn't even suspect, even though there were other signs—little things that should have set off warning bells." He shook his head. "Stupid of me."

"Clubbing doesn't always mean cheating. Maybe he just got bored with you gone so much," Michael said, before quickly adding, "Not that there's ever a good excuse for cheating."

"How did you find out?" Ray asked.

"My son told me."

"What? How did he know when you didn't?" Victor, who had no filter, asked.

"Victor, that's none of your business," Jordan scolded.

"It's okay. He's asking a question I've asked myself

many times. Unfortunately, Henri couldn't sleep one night and waited up for me. When he heard voices outside the door, he looked through the peep hole and saw Jeremy and another man locked in a very passionate kiss."

"Oh, George, I'm so sorry," Jordan said.

"What makes it even worse is that because of little things that Jeremy has said and done since I arrived here two weeks ago, I'm pretty sure the man followed him to Oklahoma."

8

Quincy grabbed the shotgun from the house, then ran to the garage and hopped on his four-wheeler. After backing it out of the garage, he turned it toward the scene playing out in the distance. He pushed the gas pedal down as far as he could, and the utility vehicle's front wheels jumped into the air before taking off in that direction. About a hundred yards out, he spotted what had initially caught his attention from his kitchen window.

He couldn't believe what he was seeing. Why would a bright yellow John Deere excavator be actively digging on his property? He tried to go faster, but he was already at the machine's top speed of fifty miles per hour.

"Dammit," he muttered to himself as he laid on the horn, hoping to attract someone's attention before they did any further damage to his land. But the noise from the big rig completely drowned out the sound of the loud horn.

Several other pieces of equipment were parked behind the extractor, including three loaders and a large dump truck. The earth movers had apparently been hard at work as the pile of dirt from the freshly-dug hole measured about six feet high.

Reaching for his phone, he dialed as he closed in on the activity.

"911. What's your emergency?"

"This is Quincy Parnell calling from the Parnell Ranch out on Route 151. There are five or more pieces of heavy equipment digging up my ranch. Get the sheriff out here ASAP before I do something I know I'll regret."

He disconnected and took a deep breath, trying to calm down. This had to be some kind of horrible mistake—one that would be straightened out as soon as the sheriff arrived.

He guided the UTV toward the excavator and stopped directly behind the large hole in the ground.

"If you want this friggin' machine to keep on digging, you're gonna have to go through me," he shouted to the operator who was now giving him a look meant to kill from his perch high above the ground.

After the excavator stopped in midair, three men in hard hats ran up to him.

"What do you think you're doing, old man? You trying to get yourself killed?" the shortest of the three asked, clearly irritated.

"I could ask you the exact same question." Quincy held up the trusty shotgun that had once belonged to his great grandfather. "You're on my property, and by law, I have every right to shoot you."

All three men backed away. "Hold on, Mister! We are definitely not trespassing, and we have the documents to prove it." The same man who had spoken before answered. "Please, can you lower that weapon while I get the paperwork that will explain it all?"

Quincy shut off the ignition and stepped out of his vehicle. Still wielding the shotgun, he followed the three men to the side of the big rig where they were joined by two others.

"You need to know the sheriff is on his way right now." Quincy stepped closer to the man—a boy, actually—who looked to be in his early twenties and still wet behind the ears. His own six two frame did what he intended it to—intimidated the much shorter man. "I would advise you not to do anything stupid while we wait for the good sheriff."

Just then, an older man emerged from a small trailer several yards behind the machines, probably after seeing the conflict play out from his window. The scowl on his face was proof that he wasn't a happy camper.

"What the hell do you think you're doing?" the new arrival asked, repeating the earlier question.

"And who are you?"

"John Davenport, owner of Oklahoma Drilling, Inc. in Oklahoma City." He stepped in front of the five workers. "I was contracted to build an oil well on this spot, and frankly, you are impeding my ability to do the job."

"Oh, really! And as I already told your man, you, sir, are trespassing on my property. I assure you, I have never given any thought to digging a well out here, and certainly didn't hire you or your company. Trust me when I say, there will be consequences for the damage you've caused already."

The owner turned back to his crew and whispered something. Quincy couldn't hear everything being said, but what little he did hear suggested the boss had just been told the local law enforcement agency was on the way. One of the men turned and quickly ran back to the trailer.

John Davenport stared at Quincy. "As soon as the sheriff gets here, this will be cleared up quickly, which is good. We're on a tight schedule, and we have to get back to work ASAP."

"Not gonna happen," Quincy said. He was about to raise the shotgun again when he heard a car pull up. "That should be Sheriff Peterman now. Turn off your equipment while I ride back to fetch him and bring him out here. I swear, if you lift one more piece of dirt out of my ground, you'd better hold onto your ass with both hands. I'll sue you until you're left with nothing but that hard hat on your head."

He walked back to the four-wheeler and turned the key, then made a 180 degree turn and headed back to the house. The sheriff was already out of his vehicle even before Quincy came to a complete stop, and he hopped into the passenger side of the UTV.

"You say these people are digging on your property? And you didn't authorize any of it?" he asked as soon as they were on their way back to the heavy equipment.

"No, sir, I did not. This has to be some mistake. Maybe they have the wrong ranch or something. All I know is there's going to be hell to pay for tearing up my land."

The sheriff squinted to shut out the bright sun, then pulled out a pair of dark shades from his pocket and put them on. "Let me do the talking, Quincy. We'll get to the bottom of this sooner that way."

Quincy nodded. He'd known Sonny Peterson practically all his life. Had gone to school with him. Even campaigned to help him get elected. He felt confident it wouldn't take long for the more-than-qualified man to work this out and get those city-slickers off his property.

"Sheriff," John Davenport said, as soon as Quincy and Peterson stepped out of the vehicle. "There's obviously been some kind of a misunderstanding here." He reached behind him and took a folder from the man who was still panting from running to and from the trailer. He handed it to the sheriff. "This should explain everything."

Peterson studied the contents for a few minutes before glancing up at Quincy. "This document says the land belongs to Jubilee Ranch, LLC."

"Never heard of it, and I can assure you there's no way anybody but me owns this land."

The sheriff took the legal paper, placed it on the seat of UTV and took a photo with his phone. "I'll check this out when I get back to the station." He turned to the equipment owner. "In the meantime, you'll need to shut down the operation until we can resolve this issue."

"No can do, Sheriff," Davenport said, before pointing to Quincy. "As I've explained to this gentleman, I'm on a deadline, and the legal document in your hand proves that he is not the owner. The most likely scenario is the old man doesn't remember selling the land."

Peterson shifted his focus back to Quincy. "Is that something that could have happened?"

"No way. About a year and a half ago I sold 1500 acres to the casino and kept 1500 for myself to rebuild the ranch." Quincy turned toward Davidson. "And for the record, I'd put my memory up against yours or your workers any day of the week. I did not—"

"Apparently, you are mistaken," Davenport interrupted.

Quincy glared at the owner, his eyes narrowing in a manner that should have made the smaller man back away. It didn't. "Okay, for the sake of argument, let's just say that maybe I did sell the land—which I surely did not. Do I look dumb enough to sign away the mineral rights, knowing how lucrative that might be at some later point in time? I can assure you I am not."

"I have no idea what you may or may not have done," Davenport said, defiantly. "I only know I was hired to dig a well." He glanced down at his watch. "And this delay is costing me time and money."

Quincy laughed. "That's not nearly all you'll lose after my lawyer slaps you with a lawsuit."

Sheriff Roberson stepped between the two men. "Both of you need to dial it back a notch. I'll get this figured out in the next couple of hours. In the meantime, Quincy, you stay away from this area, and you, Mr. Davidson, need to pack up and go home for the day. I'll be in touch as soon as I have answers."

"Like I said, Sheriff, no can do. I'm on a deadline."

The sheriff grinned. "In that case I have a very large jail cell waiting back in town that can house all six of you. I'm sure old man Sutton and his two rowdy sons who are sleeping off a drunken night of wild women and bar fights would love the company."

With that, he turned and climbed into the UTV beside Quincy. "I'll be in touch."

~

JORDAN WAS AWAKENED from her "power nap" by the sound of the phone vibrating on the night stand. Hoping it was Alex, she shot up in the bed and grabbed it without looking at caller ID. "Hello."

"Wow! Are you really glad to hear from me, or did I just wake you from your beauty sleep?"

She tried to hide her disappointment that it was Victor. "I thought you might be Alex." Although she didn't want to burden Victor with her fears, he was her best friend, and right now, she could use a little encouragement. "I'm trying not to worry, but he never goes this long without calling."

"Sugar, you told us he was deep undercover in Mexico. If he's successfully infiltrated whatever cartel he's chasing, there's no way he can sneak off and call. You wouldn't want to compromise him, would you?"

"Absolutely not. It just would be nice to hear his voice, if only for a minute."

Victor laughed. "I can pretend to be him and say all the gooey things you want to hear." He lowered his voice. "So, Jordan, I can't wait to feel your hands all over my body." He changed to a high-pitched girly voice. "Me neither, honey pie. Kissy, kissy, kissy."

Jordan couldn't help herself and laughed. "You are such a dork. And the answer to your original question is that yes, I *was* taking a nap. Tonight's the night I'm going to spend some time after the show with Arizona, and I want to be able to hang with her."

"Oh, yeah. Are you sure I can't go with you?"

'Unless you have estrogen running through your veins, you are definitely not invited. Although the lady sleeps around, underneath all that sexual trolling, I think she genuinely hates men."

"Well, you'd better come back with some good gossip, girlfriend." He paused for a second. "So, are you ready to hit the slots?"

"Give me about a half hour for a quick shower, and I'll meet you in front of the blackjack table from last night."

"That'll work. Michael can show us where all the Texas Stampede machines are located. That's the one he made money on last night. Me and the herd of buffalo are going to get down and dirty and win some cash."

"Sounds good. But, Victor, please tell me you're going to bet more than ten or fifteen cents a pop."

"Maybe, I will. Then again, maybe I won't. I am a little jealous that Michael won last night, and he was betting two dollars a spin. The lady next to him who hit the jackpot for ten grand was feeding the machine three dollars each time."

"My brother, Danny, who loves the slots said the slots can make your day or make you cry," Jordan said. "Sometimes you win a little. Sometimes you lose a little. I'm good with that, but it's losing big that scares the crap out of me. I'm not willing to spend the next two weeks eating bologna sandwiches and pop tarts while the casino gets richer."

"Ha! So quit ragging on me for betting under a quarter." He cleared his throat. "I hate to leave you, but the machines are calling me. I'll see you in a half hour in front of the blackjack table."

Jordan hung up and lay in the bed for a few more minutes. Even though Victor never failed to bring her out of her dark moods, this time was different. She just couldn't shake the feeling that something was not right with Alex. She picked up the phone to call his mother in case she'd heard something, then quickly changed her mind. No sense worrying Natalie. Victor was probably right. Alex would call when he could. She'd have to be content with that.

She reached into the nightstand for the two chocolate chip cookies she'd bought at the small bakery in front of the elevators the night before. As she chewed the first bite, she could feel herself breathing easier. Although the cookies were no match for Hostess Ho-Hos, her usual substitute for antidepressants, it did have a calming effect of her. After she'd devoured both of them, she hopped into the shower.

No time to waste. They only had two more days at the casino, and she was feeling lucky.

~

As soon as he walked into his office, the man behind the desk looked up from the stack of paperwork strewn across his desk. "I hope you had that conversation with our problem child. Did you straighten her out?"

He shifted to his left foot, knowing he was about to deliver bad news to his boss who was now waiting for the answer. "I spent an hour trying to scare some sense into her, but she still believes she can squeeze us for more money." He got up and walked over to the window, watching as the crowd poured into the casino, all with high hopes of breaking the bank.

Fat chance.

He walked back over to the desk. "She wants to call her own shots."

"Hmm. Now that's a problem."

"Definitely. I'll take one more run at her when I leave here to see if I can convince her that it's not in her best interest to call our bluff."

The man slammed his hand on the desk, sending the stack of papers flying across the room. "Time's up for playing nice. Do what you have to, but make this problem go away." He massaged his hand.

"Unfortunately, we still need her around a little longer, and she knows that. I'll let her know in no uncertain terms that she's not indispensable. But first, I'll try to pacify her until after the weekend."

"And then?"

"And then, we go straight to Plan B."

The man behind the desk scowled. "Make it look like an accident."

9

It was Mexican chili and cornbread night at the Wild Card Steak and Ribs restaurant, and as per usual, they all stuffed themselves on Rosie's creations.

Jordan popped the last of the jalapeno cornbread into her mouth, then shoved the empty chili bowl away from her. "Thanks to Rosie, there's no way I can get up and walk out of here. I feel like I'm gonna burst at the seams any minute now."

"Me too," Lola said. "Rosie outdid herself with the chili tonight. I don't ever remember it being this good."

"It's the same awesome chili she always makes. You're probably just starving after all the walking you and Ray did checking out the casino shopping mall," Michael said. "By the way, did you end up buying anything?"

Ray shook his head. "Lola had her eye on a leather purse, and I was gonna sneak back so I could surprise her with an early birthday present." He whistled. "I nearly dropped my teeth when the clerk rang up eight hundred dollars. For that kind of money, I could have put a down payment on a new car."

"Not in this day and age, my friend," Victor said,

reaching for another piece of cornbread. "Haven't you heard about the chip shortage? Chip production for cars, like for the GPS, are down everywhere. That means vehicle inventory is also at its lowest. My cousin in Tulsa told me he would sell a hundred cars a day if he could get his hands on them. As it is, he said there were less than fifty new cars sitting on the lot, and the number of pre-owned cars was even lower than that. And to add insult to injury, not only are new cars going for a premium, but the used ones are selling for forty percent over Blue Book." He clicked his tongue in disgust. "That eight hundred bucks would barely cover the taxes on any car right now."

"What a crock," Ray said. "Guess I'll stick with my Suburban." He glanced toward Lola. "And you, sweetheart, will have to be content with the purse I bought you for your last birthday."

"I love that purse," Lola said. "But it totally amazes me that we're bickering about an expensive purse when there are people out there in the casino right now losing that much and more every night."

"For sure," Jordan said. "That elderly woman, Violet, who sat next to me last night didn't even blink an eye when she split two queens and then lost three hundred on each of them."

"Sheesh! What was she thinking?" Lola asked, picking up the dessert menu. "All this talk about money has me craving something sweet. I think I'm gonna try the Texas sheet cake. You can't have Mexican food without a little Texas thrown in."

"Ooh, is that tonight's dessert? That's my favorite cake that Rosie makes." Jordan picked up her menu. "Yep! I'm having it, too."

"Thought you were about to pop a gasket," Victor teased. "Or were you just trying to convince us that a delicate girl like you couldn't possibly put away that much food?"

"You should talk. I don't even have to ask if you're having dessert." Jordan threw her napkin at him. "Besides, I took a beating on the slots today. I'll probably end up losing money and will have to eat sandwiches all next week. I might as well overeat here on the really good stuff."

"Too bad we can't bag up all the leftovers from the weekend. We could freeze them and use them on potluck Fridays," Lola said.

"What leftovers?" Ray chimed in. "Rosie told me they've run out of everything they've served so far. Said they were going to double the amounts for the rest of the weekend."

"I'm not surprised," Jordan said. "Rosie is a goddess in the kitchen."

She motioned for the waitress. When they'd all placed their orders for desserts, she glanced at her watch. "We have about two more hours before tonight's show. I think I'd like to take a break from gambling the rest of the night and find someplace to just sit and relax. Maybe one of those little bars on the perimeter of the casino where I can chill out. I might even have a glass of Baileys as my after-dinner drink."

Victor smirked. "You're such a sissy drinker, Jordan. Baileys is like chocolate milk"

"That is, until you stand up," Michael added. "It goes down so smooth and then wham!–the room is spinning."

Jordan huffed. "That happens to me after every drink, Michael." She reached for the dessert from the waitress, thanked her, and then shoved a huge bite of the cake into her mouth. "Oh, my Lord! I'm in chocolate heaven, not to mention that my blood sugar just shot up a hundred points."

The chatter ceased as the gang savored the rich dessert. When they were finished, they all headed toward the casino area, except for Lola and Ray, who decided they would go upstairs and watch a little TV before going to bed. Tomorrow was the last full day for all of them to enjoy their mini vacation as they were headed back to Ranchero after lunch on Sunday. The plan was to gamble most of Saturday, then take in the main event at the concert hall that night. Jordan was so looking forward to seeing the James Brothers, especially since George had promised them backstage passes.

On Sunday, Jordan had already decided she would sleep in late, have breakfast in bed, then enjoy one last meal with the gang and George. Even Rosie was planning to join them as they would be saying goodbye to the man who had made the entire weekend possible. He was leaving for New York the first thing Monday morning but mentioned that he would be coming into town several times a year to check on the restaurant and promised to drive down to Ranchero for a friendship fix when he did.

As they walked away from the dining room, they heard lively music coming from the far corner of the casino. Even with the constant ding-ding-ding of the slots, the vibrant, toe-tapping rhythm had them picking up the pace. They followed the music to a bar away from the machines and luckily, found a table close to the stage just as the band finished up and announced a short break.

Jordan ordered Baileys on the rocks and took a sip the minute the waitress set it in front of her. "Umm. I had forgotten how good these were." In a matter of minutes, she had drained the chocolate drink and quickly ordered another.

"Go easy, little girl," Michael warned again. "Remember the kickback when you stand up."

"I'm good," she said, but she was already feeling the warmth in her belly. "I should probably just sip the next one, though."

By this time the band had returned to the stage and was getting ready for their next set. The first song was a fast-paced Spanish tune that had everyone tapping their feet as they all ordered another round of drinks.

"Thought you were just gonna sip that last one, Jordan," Victor said with a grin.

"I lied." She frowned at him. "You're not the booze police, Victor, nor are you the boss of me. Mind your own business and pay attention to the rockin' music. One more drink, and I'll probably drag your sorry butt out on the dance floor."

"Hello! Have you seen me dance?" He snickered. "I look like a poodle trying to score with a female German shepherd in heat."

"True story," Michael said, just as the band ended the fast song and went straight into a slow one.

Jordan sank back into the seat and closed her eyes. "That's so pretty. Although it sounds familiar, I have no idea what he's singing about."

"It's *Muy Dentro De Mi*', a Marc Anthony song. You probably know it as 'You Sang to Me.' It was one of his more popular ones," Victor explained.

"It's about a guy who didn't realize how much he loved a girl until she sang to him," Michael said. "Our station gets requests for this one all the time. Most of the time they want to hear the Spanish version."

"I can see why. The lyrics are so romantic that

way." Jordan focused on the lead singer at the mic. She could listen to him all night.

Victor twirled around to face Michael. "Even you have to admit, that dude is hot, right, bro?"

Michael frowned. "Yes, even I will admit it."

"He's probably married with three kids," Jordan said. "Besides, Victor, as Rosie has told you many times when you got your eye on a really hot guy, why settle for ground beef when you have steak at home." She leaned over and high-fived Michael.

"Point taken. I still love the way he sings."

Jordan took a moment to size up the singer who introduced himself as Rafael Morales. About five–eleven with dark eyes and dark hair that curled below his ears, the twenty-something Hispanic man was wearing leather pants that molded to his body with perfection. The colorful shirt he wore was opened halfway down his torso, giving them a peek at rock hard abs and a muscular chest, covered in a sprinkling of chest hair.

He was definitely a hottie, and when you coupled those sexy looks with his awesome singing voice, it was a no-brainer why he probably had girls lined up for miles when he *sang* to them.

When he was finished with that tune, he stepped down from the stage and began the next song, which was almost as beautiful as the previous Marc Anthony one. Moving from table to table, he stopped at theirs and made a big deal of singing directly to Jordan.

Like every other female in the bar, she swooned, mesmerized by those beautiful, sultry, black eyes.

Yowza!

After three drinks, Jordan was feeling no pain and couldn't take her eyes off him as he finished up the song, then bent over and kissed her on the forehead.

Never having been one of those women who followed bands around the country, for the first time she understood why young girls became groupies.

"Don't ever wash your face again," Victor whispered. "He is some serious eye candy."

"Excuse me," Michael said, clearly annoyed. "What does that make me? Broccoli candy?"

"Oh, sheesh. You know there will never be anyone but you for me."

"Sometimes, I wonder." Michael said but quickly lost the frown when Victor gave him one of his naughty smiles. "It's about time we made our way over to the concert hall for tonight's show."

Jordan tried to stand up and immediately, fell back into the chair. "Holy cow! You were right about those Baileys."

Michael bent down and offered his arm. "Grab on. That's what friends are for."

She gladly accepted his arm, and because she was more than a little wobbly, she leaned into him for support. By the time they reached the concert hall, she was feeling a little better. Once seated in the front row, she waved off the waiter who had arrived with more drinks.

"Are you sure? I heard you love a certain chocolaty drink." He held up a glass of Baileys.

"Tempting. And although I do appreciate the thought, just water for me, please," she said, before adding, "and a coffee with cream and a Sweet' N Low would be terrific, as well."

As she watched him walk away, she prayed the Baileys wouldn't keep her in bed all morning with a killer headache—not on their last full day at the casino. She reached into her purse for the ibuprofen, and as soon as the waiter was back with the water, quickly swallowed two of them, just in case.

The band started the show on time with Arizona front and center. Whoever had helped with her makeup had done a good job. The black eye was barely noticeable to anyone but those who knew it was there. As usual, she was awesome. At one point she caught Jordan's eye and mouthed, "See you later."

Jordan smiled back before being distracted by the sight of Meg standing behind Arizona with the two other backup singers, her eyes hard and angry. If looks were daggers, Arizona would have keeled over long before she finished her own rendition of Tina Turner's "Proud Mary." Jordan was thankful she wasn't the recipient of all that rage, but honestly, she could understand why Meg felt that way. Not only had Arizona stolen the spotlight from her on stage, but she had also seduced her boyfriend into her bed in the process.

Who wouldn't be fuming and ready to kill?

AFTER THE SHOW ENDED, Jordan said good night to her friends, promising to fill them in after her meeting with Arizona. Although she didn't approve of the way the woman led her life, it was obvious she needed a friend. Jordan had known many women who, because of one reason or another—usually involving mommy—had trust issues with other women. Most of them gravitated toward men and used sex to control their relationships. Arizona definitely fit that bill. But no matter what happened later, she hoped Arizona would be able to walk away knowing that all females weren't out to get her.

As Jordan made her way through the lobby, she spied two EMTs pushing a gurney toward the main entrance where an ambulance awaited with flashing lights bouncing off the lobby chandeliers like strobe lights. A third EMT was holding an IV above the gurney and rhythmically squeezing an Ambu bag.

"Move aside," a loud voice commanded.

Jordan looked down just as the gurney passed her. A quick glance at the patient made her catch her breath. She recognized the woman receiving emergency treatment as Violet, the high roller who had lost a boatload of money playing beside her at blackjack the night before.

"Oh my!" she said to no one in particular.

"Jordan, right?"

She turned to see Marilee Redding, Terry's wife, whom she'd met earlier that morning at the pool. Decked out in a red, off the shoulder dress that accentuated her petite figure, and with her hair pulled off her face with only ringlets of curls on the side, Jordan almost didn't recognize her.

"You look amazing, Marilee."

"I hope so. I'm on my way to confront Arizona one last time and appeal to her not to break up my marriage." She took a deep breath before continuing, "I heard Terry isn't the only one who shares her bed, so I know she probably doesn't love him the way I do. I want to plead with her not to take my man just because she can, as the infamous Dolly Parton sings about in 'Jolene.'"

"Hope you're successful, but wouldn't it be better if you had this talk with your husband? Maybe sit down for a nice drink and let him know exactly how you feel?"

Marilee narrowed her eyes. "Like I told you earlier,

the woman is like IV heroin to Terry. According to him, she does things in bed that I will never be comfortable doing." She shook her head. "No, he'll never leave her. He's too weak. She's got to be the one to make the break, and hopefully, I can convince her to do that."

Jordan touched the woman's shoulder, trying to decide if she should tell her Arizona wouldn't be available for a chat that night—that the singer would be in her hotel room with Jordan. Something told her to keep that information to herself. Marilee would find out soon enough on her own, and maybe then, she'd have that conversation with her husband instead.

"Good luck with whatever happens tonight," Jordan said. "I'll be thinking about you." She pointed to the ambulance as the emergency technicians loaded Violet into the back and shut the door. After they pulled away, Jordan said, "I hope that woman is going to be okay."

"Doubtful," Marilee said. "I was talking to my friend who works at the concierge desk. Apparently, the old gal had too much to drink and fell in her room. Cracked her head wide open on the dresser. She wasn't breathing when housekeeping found her, and they have no idea how long she was without oxygen."

"I'm sorry to hear that. I'll say a few extra prayers for her tonight." Jordan sighed. "Wish I could talk longer with you, but I have to be somewhere. Sending good vibes your way to help you get through this. It was great running into you tonight, and once again, you look amazing."

"Thanks. I could definitely use those vibes, but first I need at least three or four shots of courage-building tequila in me. God only knows what I may do to her if Arizona acts all high and mighty and blows me off."

Jordan waved, then made her way to the casino elevator and flashed Arizona's key card to the attendant before stepping into the elevator. She was glad she was the only one on the ride up because she wasn't in the mood for small talk with strangers—something she usually enjoyed.

She couldn't put her finger on it, but for some reason she was more than a little nervous about spending time with Arizona.

When the elevator stopped on the eighth floor, Jordan dug into her purse for the room key and walked down the hallway to room 8013.

As soon as she stepped into the room, she stared, incredulously. This was not just a hotel room—it was more like a one-bedroom apartment, and the place was freakin' gorgeous. The living room was twice the size of hers back in Ranchero and decked out with what looked like very expensive furniture and decorations. It could have passed for a Presidential suite and probably cost a fortune per night. In the middle of the sitting room, there was a huge basket of fruit, candies, and nuts on the coffee table.

The perks of sleeping with the owner, Jordan thought.

She glanced down at her watch. Eleven thirty. After all the liquor she'd consumed listening to the salsa music at the bar, she wasn't sure how long she could stay awake and hoped Arizona would get there soon. She picked up the phone and ordered a couple of appetizers like Arizona had suggested, then got a bottle of water from the Mini bar.

After an hour had passed with no sign of the singer, Jordan was getting impatient. She'd already eaten half the nachos she'd ordered and several bone-less chicken wings. Now she was craving something chocolate and wishing she had one of her trusty HoHos.

She glanced toward the welcome basket, noticing several different chocolate bars sticking out of the top. Plopping down on the couch, she tucked her legs under her and rummaged through the basket, thinking that surely, Arizona wouldn't mind if she had one little candy bar. She had encouraged her to make herself comfortable and order food, after all.

Her eyes zeroed in on the tip of an Almond Joy—one of her favs—near the bottom. When she wrapped her fingers around it, she felt something hard and bent over to take a closer look.

It was a hundred-dollar poker chip. As she dug deeper, she saw more at the bottom of the huge basket.

Holy moly! There was a lot of them.

Geez! Note to self—maybe I should check out the owner, she thought. A basket of fruit was one thing, but there had to be two thousand dollars in chips down there. Just as she dug deeper, she heard a loud voice in the hall and quickly shoved everything back into the basket. The last thing she wanted was for Arizona to think she was snooping—which, technically, she was.

She arranged the basket back to the way she'd found it with most of the fruit on top. After gulping down the rest of her water, she made a quick trip to the restroom, then walked back into the bedroom and sat on the edge of the bed, expecting Arizona to come through and apologize for keeping her waiting.

But the voices had moved on further down the hall.

Fighting to keep her eyes open now, she peeked once again at her watch. Twelve-thirty and still no sign of Arizona. Jordan wished she'd been smart enough to get her phone number to find out exactly what the holdup was. She decided she would wait until 1 a.m. and then assume she'd been stood up—that the woman had gotten a better offer.

She couldn't help herself, lay down on the bed, thinking she would take a ten-minute, power nap before Arizona arrived. But her eyes were so heavy, and before she knew it, she was dead to the world.

QUINCY PARNELL WAS asleep on the couch in the living room when the doorbell jarred him awake. He attempted to sit up and was immediately sorry when the pounding in his head started. Lying back down, he glanced around the room and discovered the reason for the headache—an empty vodka bottle and a half-eaten bowl of cereal on the coffee table next to him.

He lay there for a few minutes until the doorbell rang again.

"Okay. Okay," he mumbled to himself. "Hold your horses."

Slowly, he lifted his body from the couch and made his way to the door, taking deep breaths in an effort to reduce the pain in his head. As soon as he opened it, Sonny Peterson pushed through, nearly knocking him over.

"What's so freakin' important that you had to rush out here in the middle of the night, Sheriff?" Quincy's eyes widened when a sudden thought hit him. "Has something happened to Jake?"

"Jake's fine, or at least I think he is. My wife and

her sister spent the day gambling at the new casino yesterday and ran into him there. Said he was wearing snakeskin boots that she figured must have cost him a pretty penny." Peterson shook his head. "That's not why I'm here, Quincy." He walked over and picked up the empty liquor bottle. "I swear, if you don't quit drinking this poison, you won't have to worry about the equipment in your backyard. This crap will kill you for sure."

Quincy squinted. "So why are you here? I know it's not a social visit, considering we haven't had a drink together since Irene died almost two years ago."

Peterson sat down in the chair beside the couch. "I told you then, and I'll tell you again now. The doc scared the beejesus out of me the last time I got drunk and almost shot off my foot. It was a wake-up call, and I haven't touched a drop since." He glanced toward the empty bottle. "It might be wise if you did the same thing." Pointing to his watch, he continued, "And for the record, it's going on seven p.m., not the middle of the night."

Quincy turned away so the sheriff didn't see the confused look on his face. He really did need to slow down the drinking, but he was too embarrassed about thinking it was the middle of the night to admit it.

"So it's seven. I took a nap. No big deal. I still want to know what brings you out here after your shift ended. I know you leave the station every day at five, like clockwork." He walked into the kitchen to search for something for his headache.

Peterson laid the folder in his hand on the coffee table and opened it.

"We have a big problem. This is a copy of your deed of sale to Casino International eighteen months ago. Says here you sold them 2000 acres of your property along with an additional 500 acres that went to Jubilee Ranch, Inc. If you remember, that's the company listed on the Oklahoma Drilling work order."

Quincy ran back to the living room after swallowing two ibuprofens. "No way!"

"I pulled the hospital records from when Irene died and checked your signature with the one on this bill of sales." Peterson shoved the papers toward Quincy, who was now sitting on the couch staring at the folder. "I'm ninety-nine-point-nine percent sure that's your handwriting."

Quincy grabbed the legal papers and examined them. He had a distinct way of signing the Q in his name. He focused on the signature that definitely had that same Q.

After staring at it in silence for a few more seconds, he placed it back in the folder. "It looks like my signature all right, but I promise you, I would never sign something as outrageous as selling off nearly my entire ranch. It's been in my family for several generations. The only reason I even agreed to the 1500 acres in the first place was because I had no other choice after all my cows died. Just last week I was making plans to pick up a few heifers and maybe even a bull over in Stockton as soon as I get the rest of the money from the casino sale." He glared at Peterson. "So I'll ask you again—why would I sell off that many acres? And who in the hell owns Jubilee Ranch?"

The sheriff blew out a breath. "Can't answer either of those questions, but as long as I have your attention, I may as well tell you the rest of the bad news."

"What could be worse than me losing most of my ranch?"

"Keep in mind that I'm only the messenger here." The sheriff turned the document to the last page, took a slow breath, and then pointed to the signature in the middle. "You signed away all your mineral rights along with the land."

"Bull crap! How stupid do you think I am?"

The sheriff kept his eyes on Quincy. "I know you're not stupid, my friend, but I'm pretty sure this is also your signature. Maybe you were all liquored up and didn't understand what you were signing."

"I had my lawyer read over this, and he assured me it was a good deal."

Peterson shrugged. "I can't speak to any of that. You'll have to take it up with him. I only know that without hiring a handwriting expert, it's a pretty sure bet that you are the one who signed these papers." He got up from the chair. "I'm sorry, Quincy. I wish I had better news. Unfortunately, I had to give the same information to Davenport. Ever since I left here this morning, he's been calling me nearly every hour to get permission to get on with the digging. He's planning on resuming the excavation bright and early tomorrow morning."

"Over my dead body."

The sheriff got right in Quincy's face. "Now, listen to me, my friend. You don't want to do anything foolish. I would hate to have to haul you in. I came here not only as a peace officer but also as your friend. I will do everything I can to help you find answers, but my hands are tied when it comes to this matter. You just have to trust me when I say that if there's a good outcome possible, I'll help you find it."

Quincy was stunned—couldn't believe what he was hearing. "So what can I do to keep them from destroying my property?"

The sheriff's eyes grew sad. "Unfortunately, nothing. I would suggest you get with your lawyer as soon as possible and figure this out. Maybe he can persuade the judge to issue an injunction to stop the digging until this can be further investigated. Until then, there's nothing else you can do. Legally, you are no longer the owner."

He walked over to the door before turning back. "Oh, I almost forgot. I did find out that Jubilee Ranch, Inc. used a shell company in Panama to finance the sale of the property. I have a friend in the FBI office in Tulsa trying to track it as we speak. Hopefully, he'll come up with a name, but so far, no luck."

He opened the door and walked out, calling over his shoulder. "I'll get back with you as soon as I have any other news. In the meantime, don't try to stop the digging, or you'll be the one who ends up in jail with Harvey Sutton and his alcoholic sons. We can only pray the drilling won't do much more damage while we wait."

THE SOUND of the door opening startled Jordan, and she glanced at her watch once again. 2 AM. She jumped up from the bed and straightened the pillows, hoping Arizona didn't notice. She was about to confront her and tell her this was no way to treat a friend and that they'd have to postpone the girl talk until another night when she heard a deep male voice coming from the living room.

"Check everywhere. The boss won't be happy if we can't find them."

Jordan had no idea what they were talking about. She peeked through the small crack in the bedroom door and nearly lost it when a very large man walked close to the bedroom and his jacket fell open slightly.

Hiding in plain sight was a holstered gun.

Covering her mouth to stifle a scream, she did a 360 around the room, searching for someplace to hide. She barely made it to the dark gray and blue floor-length curtains just as the door to the bedroom opened. She prayed her shoes weren't sticking out of the bottom as she fought to control her breathing and stand perfectly still.

After about fifteen minutes of drawers opening and closing, she heard another man with a lower voice talking on his phone. As the two moved around the bedroom, she held her breath, imagining them tearing the bed apart.

"We've looked everywhere, boss," the man said, apparently still on the phone. "There are no chips anywhere in the suite. She must have stashed them someplace else."

"Tell him we'll check out the concert hall in the morning, then come back and rip this place apart," the first man prompted.

It must have satisfied the boss on the other end of the line because soon after, Jordan heard the door close. Shaking now, she stayed motionless for several more minutes before getting the courage to peek around the curtain. When she was certain they were gone, she pushed the drapes aside and was about to race out of the room when she remembered the chips in the welcome basket.

Were the two men talking about the ones hidden in the bottom of that basket? Were they trying to steal them?

Jordan had no idea what that meant or why they were looking for them, but if Arizona had thought it was important enough to hide the chips, there had to be something more to the story—something Jordan didn't know and, at this point, didn't want to know. But as hard as she tried, she couldn't stop herself from thinking she needed to protect Arizona's stash from the two gun-toting thugs who would most definitely find it when they returned.

Without allowing her brain enough time to convince her it was not a good idea, she grabbed one of the pillows from the bed, ripped off the case, and rushed back to the fruit basket. Then she began pulling out all the contents onto the coffee table. When she reached the bottom and the chips, she picked up handful after handful and shoved them into the pillowcase.

Holy Crap! There was way more than she had originally thought.

After she finished, she piled the fruit and the candy back into the basket and headed for the door. Once in the elevator, her breathing returned to near normal. She had no idea exactly what she had stumbled onto, but she couldn't stop the niggling questions that kept popping into her brain.

Why were those men looking for Arizona's chips, and why had she hidden them in the first place?

And the bigger question was why were the two big guys packing heat?

For the first time since she'd come to Arizona's room, she was glad the singer hadn't shown up. Who knows what those two thugs might have done to her—and to Jordan as well?

Tomorrow, she'd return the chips and have a long talk with Arizona. Maybe then she'd find out the answers to both those questions.

11

Jordan opened the door to her room and tip-toed in, trying hard not to wake Rosie. She grinned as she watched her friend spooning the edge of the bed, obviously dead to the world. She could have set off a string of firecrackers, and Rosie wouldn't have stirred. As much as she wanted to wake her to tell her about Arizona and the poker chips, she knew the poor woman had been on her feet most of the past two days and desperately needed to sleep. She couldn't feel too sorry for her friend, though, because she knew Rosie was in her glory, cooking with real chefs and basking in all the praise from George and his customers.

Jordan hid the pillowcase containing the chips behind the curtain, then pulled the covers back and crawled in, convinced that sleep would be a long time coming. How could she possibly sleep when the horrible encounter with the two thugs in Arizona's room kept replaying over and over in her head? She had no idea why the men had been looking for the poker chips or how they even knew they were there. What she did know was that she was extremely lucky to have escaped that scenario still breathing.

Tomorrow, she'd find Arizona and give her the

chips. The longer they were in her possession, the chances of her running into the two thieves again increased. She would hand over the chips, then advise Arizona to report the break-in to security and cash in the chips before any other gun-toting, mobster wannabes broke into her hotel room again.

Jordan glanced at the clock. It was already after three. She prepared herself for a restless night, but she shouldn't have worried. As soon as her head hit the pillow, she fell fast asleep. Whatever was going to happen later that morning would have to wait.

JEREMY REDDING AWOKE with a start when his phone rang. Glancing at the clock on the nightstand, he frowned. Who in the world thought it was a good idea to call him before seven? This was a casino, for heaven's sake. People didn't shell out ridiculous amounts of money for rooms here just to be in bed by midnight. That was when the crowds thinned out and serious gamblers were just waking up, ready to gamble the entire night away.

He picked up the phone and saw that it was George—George, who knew he never woke up before nine every morning, even back in New York. He answered in a hurry, worried that something must be wrong. "George, is everything okay?"

A few seconds elapsed before George responded. "I'm sorry, Jeremy. I know you like to sleep in late, but it's important that I talk to you before my meeting with your brother later this morning. What I have to say to you can't wait."

Oh boy, Jeremy thought. *Here comes another beatdown. Hadn't they said enough yesterday when they had their discussion?* He frowned. Calling it a discussion was a stretch. It had been more like an interrogation. He hoped George didn't go down that road again.

"I thought we got everything sorted out over drinks yesterday," Jeremy said, bracing for a replay of their earlier conversation.

"Why would you think that? So much was left unsaid. You know the only thing I've ever asked of you was that you be honest with me, no matter how much whatever you had to say might hurt to hear. I have always told you how much I hate liars."

"Why do you think I was lying to you? You asked if I had a lover, and I told you no. After all our years together, that should have been the end of the conversation."

He looked over at the man snoring softly beside him, wondering why George was questioning him about this now. They'd been so careful. His soon-to-be ex couldn't possibly know about the affair that had been going on for several months.

"If that's the way you want to play this, that's fine. I didn't want to bring Henri into our personal problems, hoping the two of us had enough respect for each other to tell the truth, but I can't think of any other way to do this." George paused when his voice cracked. "Our son saw you kissing your lover in the hallway outside our door."

Jeremy gasped. He had gone out of his way to hide the new relationship.

Except for the one time when they'd both had too much to drink, and his lover insisted on seeing where he lived. It had been well after two in the morning, and the teenager should have been asleep. He mentally slapped his head for letting his guard down. Once inside the apartment, at least, he'd remembered to erase the video from the outside camera. The possibility that Henri might have seen them never entered his mind.

It was important that he keep up the deception a little longer, especially now that he was so close to getting what he wanted. On Monday George would fly back to New York, and Jeremy would be able to establish himself as the manager of the casino with a six–figure salary. Gradually, like all other long-distance relationships, the flame would burn out, and the marriage would come to an end naturally. Jeremy had hoped he and George could remain friends after that, because eventually, his plan was to buy out George's share of Wild Card Steak and Ribs.

For now, he still needed George's financial help. He was counting on the frequent trips to and from no-where Oklahoma taking a toll on the already overworked chef. Ever since George signed the contract to produce a new show on the cooking channel, there just never seemed to be enough time or energy for anything else. What little time he managed to find away from his busy schedule was spent almost exclusively with Henri. Usually, he didn't leave the restaurant in Manhattan until the wee hours of the morning, always apologizing and promising that things would get better once the new venture took off.

But they never did, and that was one of the reasons Jeremy had begun frequenting some of the more popular clubs in New York and eventually seeking out extramarital companionship. He hadn't gone looking to cheat. It just happened.

The minute he'd set eyes on the new man in his life, Jeremy knew things would never be the same for him—that he could never go back to the way it was.

But he wasn't ready to confess that to George just yet.

"Henri must've been mistaken," he lied.

"Really, Jeremy, you know Henri. Why would he make up a story like that?"

"I have no idea. Lately, he's been antagonistic toward me, though. You must have noticed." Just then the man in his bed opened his eyes and sat up. Jeremy quickly put his finger to his lips to silence him.

"The two of you have not been getting along lately. I do know that. At first, I thought it was just Henry being a teenager and you not reacting well to the changes." George blew out a slow, frustrated breath before continuing, "I want to believe you, Jeremy, but you give me no real reason to do that. We aren't even sleeping in the same room here, for heaven's sake."

"Only because I knew how busy you would be with opening weekend at the restaurant. I've been putting in long hours with my brother, watching how he keeps the books, then spending the evenings in the restaurant learning the business. We're both busting our butts to make our dreams come true. The last thing either of us needs right now is less sleep than we already get." Jeremy glanced toward the bed as his lover was now sitting up and smiling at him.

God help him! At this moment, he didn't care about anything else but spending the rest of his life with that man. Whatever happened between him and George would be worth it. He was so lucky to have found love like this at a time when he'd been feeling totally neglected in New York. He held the phone away and whispered, "It's George," to his lover.

"Jeremy, are you still there?" George sounded annoyed.

"Yes, sorry. I thought I heard a knock at the door," Jeremy lied once again.

"I don't want to fight about this anymore, at least not right now. I'm already late for my meeting with Terry. It's probably for the best that you stay here in Oklahoma when I go back to New York. It will give us time to rethink the relationship." George was unable to keep the sadness out of his voice.

Jeremy barely heard him as he watched his bed-mate get up and walk toward him. When the man moved closer and whispered something in his ear, Jeremy nearly lost it and quickly moved away. "I agree, George. Today is Cinco de Mayo. We're both going to be running around like two crazy men if the projections for the huge crowds coming today are even half true. Let's take a breather from all this heavy stuff and plan on sitting down over lunch on Sunday when things calm down. That way, we can use the whole day to start thinking about how we can resurrect our commitment to each other."

After George agreed, Jeremy hung up, sad that he had to lie to his partner of so many years, yet not willing to let go of the man standing beside him. They needed to be extra careful for two more days, then George would be gone, and the world would be theirs to conquer.

Two more days.

Jeremy wasn't sure he could make it that long.

JORDAN WOKE up alone in the bed. She looked over at the clock on the nightstand, wondering how she could have slept in with so much on her mind. Her plan was to eat before taking a shower and heading up to Arizona's room. That should give the singer enough time to get moving so she could explain why she'd reneged on the girl-talk they had planned.

She picked up the phone and ordered room service—a breakfast burrito, hash browns, an English muffin with jelly, and two cinnamon rolls.

For some reason Jordan was really anxious about telling Arizona what had gone down earlier that morning. She wasn't sure if the singer would be happy that her stash of poker chips had been saved or that Jordan had discovered them in the first place. And how would she react when she heard about the two men who had broken into her room? Did she know them?

Jordan forgot all that for a moment when Room Service appeared with the big breakfast she'd ordered. Today, she would definitely need the sugar load when she confronted Arizona.

She savored every bite, almost like it might be her last meal. After a quick shower, she dressed, then grabbed the pillowcase with the poker chips in it from behind the curtain before heading out the door. Since Rosie was already gone by the time Jordan woke up, she hadn't been able to tell anyone about Arizona's chips. She definitely needed to find the time to sit down with Ray as soon as she could. As an ex-cop, he would know exactly how to proceed, even if Arizona pooh-poohed the idea of the two men checking out her room and searching for her money. But first, she needed to return the chips to the woman.

Something didn't pass the smell test here, but Jordan couldn't quite put her finger on anything that made sense.

After knocking on Arizona's door several times with no response, Jordan used the key she'd given her and cautiously opened the door slightly. When there was still no response after calling her name, she figured Arizona was probably in the shower and hadn't heard her come in. Pushing the door completely open, she walked into the room and nearly fainted. Arizona's clothes were sprawled all over the living room floor, along with the dresser drawers and the empty gift basket. The contents of the basket were half on the coffee table and half on the floor. Batting was hanging out of the couch cushions that had been slit down the middle, and the Mini bar was ajar with the small liquor bottles scattered all around, some even leaking all over the carpet.

Holy crap!

She walked into the bedroom where the scene was virtually the same—only in there it was the mattress that had been slit from one end to the other while the feathers from the pillows covered the floor.

"Arizona?" she called, knowing the woman probably wasn't there. Just in case, she checked out the bathroom.

Where could she be?

Obviously, the two men had made good on their promise to tear up the place. She wondered what they would do next since they didn't find the chips that she carried in the pillowcase.

She made a split-second decision to get out of there as quickly as she could before the two thieves returned. This was no longer something she could handle by herself. After closing the door, she sprinted to the elevators. When she got to her room, she ran past it and frantically knocked on Ray's door, praying he hadn't already gone down to the casino.

Her nerves finally got the best of her and she trembled. *What had she gotten herself into?*

~

"WHAT DO you mean you didn't find the chips?" the older man asked, clearly annoyed with the two men standing in front of him, their eyes staying focused on the floor

"There's no way they were in that room. We completely tore it apart. Like I suggested last night, she must have hidden them someplace else," the taller of the two said, finally making eye contact.

"Hmm. The woman doesn't have many friends to speak of. She's not an easy one to like. Where could she have stashed the chips?"

This time the shorter man looked up before responding. "I guess we could check out Redding's office. Everyone knows she was sleeping with him, even his wife, who showed up after the show and confronted Arizona right after we did. The conversation looked heated, and I saw her slap Arizona in the face. She was half the size of Arizona, but she charged right in, catching Arizona off-guard. Looked like she was mad enough to kill." He laughed. "Anyway, it was probably her husband who gave Arizona the chips in the first place."

The boss frowned and shifted positions in the chair behind his desk. "Redding wasn't the only one playing house with her. Rumor has it she was also in bed with our CEO."

"That dip-rod? How could anyone find him attractive?"

This time the boss looked up and smiled. "Money talks. It can make super models climb into bed with fat old men. Arizona was all about how much she could squeeze out of people." His expression turned serious. "That aside, I don't have to tell you the kind of trouble we'll all be in if someone else finds those chips."

Both men nodded. "We'll keep looking, boss."

The man behind the desk thought for a few minutes before glancing up at his employees. "Call down to the hotel operator and have her check to see if there were any phone calls made from that room last night. It's a long shot but worth a try."

"On it," the shorter guy said as he pulled out his phone. After a brief conversation with the hotel operator, he turned to his boss and grinned. "I always knew you had good instincts. A call was made to Room Service shortly after eleven. I'll find out who signed for the delivery."

The two men waited in silence while the third one questioned someone in the kitchen.

"Not sure you understand. I don't care how busy you are, and no, you will not get back to me with this. The request is coming from someone with a much higher pay grade than either you or me. It would be in your best interest to find the time now. I'll wait."

Within minutes, he thanked her and turned back to the other two. "Jackpot. A woman named Jordan McAllister signed for the food."

The boss cursed under his breath before turning to the multiple computer screens behind him. When he found the one from the hallway outside Arizona's room, he pushed rewind. "What time were you in her room initially?"

"A little after two," the short man answered.

"And what time did you return?"

This time the taller one responded, "About eight fifteen."

The boss leaned closer to the screens. "Okay, that gives us a window. Arizona swore the chips were in her room, and I believe her. I'll go back to around nine the night before." He pushed the start button and the three of them stared at the screen.

At exactly ten-thirty-five, they watched a woman use a key and enter Arizona's room.

All three shouted in unison "Gotcha."

"Find out what room she's in," the boss said before smiling at the image now frozen on the screen. "Hello, Jordan McAllister. You and I are about to get better acquainted."

12

As soon as Ray opened the door, Jordan pushed past him.

Still in his pajamas, he gave her a questioning look. "Is something wrong, kiddo? You look like you just saw a ghost."

After apologizing for waking him up, she blurted, "I couldn't wait any longer to talk to you. I'm worried about Arizona." When he looked confused, she added, "You know, Arizona Lightfoot, the lead singer of the band Serendipity?" After he nodded, she continued. "I think something may have happened to her. That someone might have harmed her. They looked—"

"Slow down." Ray held up his hand to stop her from continuing. "You're rambling, and I can barely understand you. Who are *they*?"

Just then Lola sat up in bed, and when she saw Jordan, she waved. "Hey, sweetie, what are you doing here so early? I thought we all said we were gonna sleep in so we could party all day today without a nap. Victor said..." She stopped when Ray sent her a stern look.

"Jordan is upset because she thinks something

happened to Arizona, the singer from that band we listened to last night," he explained.

Lola shrugged, a slight grin on her face. "Can't say I'm surprised. You know what they say about karma."

Jordan ran over to the bed. "No, Lola, this isn't karma. Karma is when you copy someone's answers on a test, and the instructor finds out. Then you find out that person got an A and you flunked out. This is way worse than that. I think something really bad happened to her."

Lola's grin disappeared. "Why would you think that, honey? Did she tell you she was worried about something last night when you two had your little female-bonding thing?"

"Let's allow Jordan to speak, Lola," Ray said, softly. "She's about to tell us why she's so worried. I'm gonna call room service and order some coffee, although by the look on Jordan's face, I should also order some of that chocolate liquor that makes her feel so good. She definitely needs something a little stronger than plain old caffeine." He reached for Jordan's hand and led her to one of the chairs. "I've got you covered, little girl."

While he was placing the order, Jordan collected her thoughts, trying to remember every little detail.

When Ray hung up, he sat on the edge of the bed and faced her. "Okay, now tell us why you think Arizona might be in trouble."

"I went to her room last night and waited on her like she said, but she never showed up."

Lola tsked. "Again, that doesn't surprise me. Arizona is all about Arizona. She—"

"I know," Jordan interrupted. She handed the pillowcase full of poker chips to Ray. "I took these from her room."

He opened the pillowcase, pulled out one of the chips, and whistled. "There must be at least 300 of these. Does she know you have them?"

"I don't know. Like I said, she never showed up."

"So why did you take them from her room, Jordan? She's gonna think someone has stolen them," Lola said, just as there was a knock at the door. "That must be room service. No talking until I get back." She got out of bed, walked over to the door, and opened it.

Nothing more was said until all three had a steaming cup of coffee with a little dollop of Bailey's in it, just as Ray had promised. As soon as the milky liquid hit her stomach, Jordan felt her entire body relaxing. She was safe in this room. She was with an ex-cop, for heaven's sake. If there was anyone she trusted with her life, it was Ray.

And Alex. Just thinking about him sent cold chills up her spine. She still hadn't heard from him, though, and she worried he might also be in trouble. She decided to call Natalie Moreland later that day. His mother may have heard from him or had information that would ease her worries.

She leaned back into the chair and took another big swig of the coffee. Then she told her friends about the two men who had come to Arizona's room the night before to look for the poker chips.

"How do you know they were looking for these particular chips?" Ray asked, his persona changing from Ray the friend to Ray the cop.

"I heard them talking on the phone to someone, apparently their boss. They told him they couldn't find the chips and they'd have to come back in the morning to tear up the place." Jordan stopped and turned to face Ray. "They had guns."

"Oh my gosh!" Lola said. "Did they hurt you?"

Jordan shook her head. "I was hiding behind the curtains, terrified they would see my shoes."

"Did you have the poker chips then?"

Again, she shook her head. "No, but I knew where they were." She told him about finding the chips earlier when she went digging in the welcome basket for a candy bar.

"They never checked there?"

"No, they were in a hurry. As soon as they left, I put the chips into a pillowcase and got out of there as fast as I could." She stopped to chug the rest of the alcohol-laced coffee. "The hallway was empty, so I'm pretty sure no one saw me."

"Are you forgetting about all the cameras surveilling the halls? You can be sure one of them captured your pretty face going in and out of Arizona's room."

Jordan gasped. "I totally forgot about the cameras." She frowned. "Oh God, Ray, do you think they'll come after me?"

He leaned over and patted her hand. "For now we're gonna assume that they don't have access to the security tapes. Maybe they were just two small-time punks who saw Arizona win all that money and followed her to her room. Then when they knew she wasn't there, they came back looking to score big."

"I wish that were true, but like I said, they talked to someone like he was the boss and told him they would be back to tear her room apart. Would two yahoos like that risk breaking into her room a second time?"

Ray groaned. "You're right. It doesn't sound like two drunks after easy money. I was just trying to make you feel a little less afraid." He stood up "Do you feel up to telling the head of security exactly what you just told us? He might be able to warn Arizona and maybe even put one of his men outside her room until they find the two armed intruders."

"Too late," Jordan said, "They've already been back and demolished the room."

Ray narrowed his eyes. "And how would you know that?"

"I went back this morning to talk to Arizona."

"You went back there?" Lola asked. "Honey, what were you thinking?"

"I wanted to give the chips back to her and make sure she was all right."

"And was she?" Ray asked.

"I don't know. She wasn't there, and the room looked like a category five tornado had blown through it." Jordan got up and refilled her coffee cup but declined Ray's offer of another shot of liquor. "I want to be stone-cold sober when we talk to the security guy."

"That's probably wise since we saw what happened to you when you drank too much yesterday." He got up and headed toward the bathroom. "Okay, then. Wait here while I take a shower and get dressed, and then you and I can pay the man a visit. I won't be long."

After he was out of the room, she and Lola sat quietly, each in their own thoughts, until Lola got out of bed and walked over to her closet. She handed Jordan a large, multi-colored, Vera Bradley bag that still had the price tag dangling from the strap. "Ray surprised me with this last night. Apparently, he bought it on sale at one of the stores in the casino mall and decided to give it to me now, since he had to pass on the eight-hundred dollar one. Truth be told, I like this one a whole lot better than the more expensive one." She handed the bag to Jordan. "You can't walk around carrying a pillowcase full of poker chips all day long. Put them in here."

"No way, Lola. I can't use your purse before you do. This pillowcase will be fine." She tried to give the colorful purse back to her friend.

Lola pushed the bag away. "Nonsense. You can break it in for me."

Jordan thought it over. Lola was right. She would look really conspicuous walking through the casino with a pillowcase filled with casino chips. "Are you sure?"

"Absolutely," Lola assured her just as Ray emerged from the bathroom.

"Let's go, Jordan. And let me do the talking."

"For once in my life, I'll be glad to keep my mouth shut. I'll only speak when I'm asked a direct question. And even then, I'll defer to you when I can."

"Good girl." Ray grinned. "Technically, one could conclude that you were breaking and entering. We wouldn't want the security chief to get any big ideas when he hears your story."

"Arizona gave me her key. Remember?" Jordan protested.

"That was for your visit last night, and she might not have told anyone. This morning is a whole different story. And the fact that she's missing might also get him thinking that you may have had something to do with her disappearance, if in fact, she really is missing and not drunk and sleeping it off in one of her lovers' beds."

Jordan's eyes widened. "If I wasn't convinced before, I am now. For sure, I'm not opening my mouth."

Ray bent down and kissed her forehead. "That's what I wanted to hear. There's still the security tapes, though. He'll definitely see you going in and coming out of Arizona's room last night as well as this morning." He opened the door and made a sweeping motion with his arm to allow her to go ahead of him, like the gentleman that he was.

"I'll need to think about this on the way down there and come up with some plausible excuse why you went back this morning and why you have the chips in your possession," he said as they walked to the elevator.

"Think fast, Ray. I'm counting on you to keep me out of jail—and alive."

~

QUINCY PARNELL HAD to park in the last two rows of the casino lot.

Geez! It's not even eleven in the morning. Don't these people have better things to do than to spend all day gambling?

That reminded him of Jake and the way he gambled at the dog tracks every weekend. He vowed to sit down and try to talk some sense into his son the next time he saw him. He remembered the sheriff telling him that his wife had seen Jake at the casino the day before and that it looked to her like he was wearing expensive boots. Quincy wasn't surprised his son had spent time at the casino, given his love and probable addiction to gambling. Maybe the expensive boots meant he'd hit it big at the dog races, which would not be a good thing. All the big gamblers Quincy had ever known only bet more when they won and usually ended up further in the hole.

He climbed into the casino shuttle van, glad he didn't have to walk all the way to the front door. Lately, his arthritis had been giving him fits.

When they got close to the entrance, he glanced over to the west parking lot that had been closed off. Huge tents had been set up, and there was a flurry of activity going one. No wonder he'd had to park so far back.

When the driver noticed him looking in that direction, he said, "Getting ready for Cinco de Mayo. There will be all kinds of activities and Mexican food all day long over there."

Quincy had completely forgotten that today was a holiday. Irene had always insisted they drive up to Tulsa where the city put on a real carnival-like celebration in true Mexican style every year on this day. He used to argue with her that it was too long of a drive for a few hours, but they'd always had so much fun, coming home exhausted but happy. He hadn't been back since his wife died. Going there without her just didn't seem like fun anymore.

Nothing did.

"Here you go. Hope you win big in there," the driver said, as he pulled up to the entrance.

Quincy tipped the driver and stepped out. "Thanks."

Does anyone ever really walk out of here with money in their pockets?

He pulled his Stetson over his eyes, hoping not to be recognized, and walked through the casino doors straight to the concierge desk. "Where would I find the office of the CEO?"

The young man behind the counter looked up from the computer. "Upstairs, sir, but you can't go up there without an appointment."

Quincy thought for a moment. "He's expecting me," he lied.

The man stared at Quincy, sizing him up, before

he picked up the phone and dialed a number. "Mr. Santiago, there's a gentleman here who says you're expecting him. I don't see any visitors listed on your calendar today. Should I send him up?"

Quincy kept his eyes on the picture behind the counter, not wanting to appear too anxious.

"Mr. Santiago wants to know who you are."

"Tell him Quincy Parnell's here to talk about the money I'm still owed for the sale of my land to this casino."

The young man turned his back slightly and reported verbatim what Quincy had said. After a few seconds of silence, he addressed Quincy once again. "Mr. Santiago said you'll need to call his secretary and make an appointment. There's no way he can squeeze you into his busy schedule with all the Cinco de Mayo celebrations going on today."

Quincy grabbed the phone from the concierge. "Look here, Santiago, to be clear, I'm not asking. Either you take a few minutes out of your busy schedule and address my problem, or I'm going to the police with this. You promised I would get my money a long time ago. As it is, I have yet to get even half of it. And now I find out that somehow you managed to steal more of my land than I agreed to sell."

The concierge tried to grab the phone out of Quincy's hand, but didn't even come close to being successful. Quincy was a foot taller than the young man and had him by at least eighty pounds.

Quincy continued, "It would be in your best interest to send one of your lackeys down here to escort me to your office."

"Like I told you, Parnell, today isn't the day to have a conversation about this. I'll have my secretary call you to set up an appointment later on this week," the CEO said.

Quincy tried counting to ten in an effort to keep his blood pressure from going through the roof. Failing miserably, he screamed into the phone. "This is the last time I'm going to warn you. This won't end well if you continue to play games with me."

"I'm sorry you feel that way, but I will have to tell you again that my schedule is busier than usual today. I hope you understand. I would hate to ask my security guards to escort you out the door like the last time."

Infuriated now, Quincy pulled out his trump card. "I guess I'll just have to pay a visit to the FBI and find out why Jubilee Ranch, a shell company that more than likely is illegal and off the books, is digging up my freakin' backyard."

There was silence on the line before Santiago responded. "Someone is on the way down," he said, unable to hide the anger in his voice.

"I thought so," Quincy said. "If I'm not in your office in five minutes, I'm outta here and on my way to Tulsa. I hear the FBI has a brand new building, and I'm sure they'd love to hear about Jubilee Ranch." He chuckled. "Tick, tock, Santiago."

13

A young man in a navy suit, presumably a member of the casino security team, punched in a code, and the door opened. Quincy followed him to a large escalator leading to the upper level. At the top, he got his first glimpse of an open room that looked like it probably sat above at least one third of the casino. The entire back wall was covered with screens, all showing various areas of the gambling arena below.

He whistled softly to himself. *A lot of cash must have gone into this room alone.*

Three employees with their backs to him sat in a row of chairs directly in front of the computers, their eyes never straying from the screens, not even when the newcomers walked directly behind them. Another group of employees sat in front of what Quincy assumed was a one-way glass window with a bird's eye view of the entire casino floor below.

He followed the security cop to a room in the back, where he was led to a chair facing a large desk with a huge window behind it. He sat down and took a moment to size up Luis Santiago, the CEO he'd met when they'd finalized the land sale a year and a half ago. The man was a little intimidating with his jet-black hair slicked back to expose a diamond earring in his right ear lobe. Dressed in a pin-striped suit and a matching bowtie, the man could have been cast as a very believable, Hispanic Marlon Brandon in The Mexican Godfather, if they ever made that one.

When he looked up and smiled, Quincy couldn't help it and smiled back, imagining him saying, "I'm gonna make you an offer you can't refuse."

"It's nice to see you again, Mr. Parnell. I hope we can work this out and not involve lawyers or federal agents, as you threatened."

"I hope so, too," Quincy said, a little disappointed that he hadn't repeated the famous line. He was curious what kind of offer he would have made.

He glanced away for a minute and stared at the view of the parking lot from the window, trying to decide how to approach this. His wife had always said you could catch more flies with honey than with vinegar, but he'd never been able to control his anger—had always relied on intimidation himself when he was mad.

And right now, he was in a foul mood and ready to kick ass and take names.

"Let's start with my money. Is there a reason I've only received a third of what I was promised?"

Santiago opened the folder in front of him. "As you know, initially, there was a problem involving the government regulations with the sale. I thought you understood that."

"I did, but it's been long enough for you to work out all those issues. What's the hold up now?"

Santiago pointed to the folder. "This document very clearly states that the second payment would be made when construction of the golf course and the additional hotel rooms begin. We—"

"And when will that be?" Quincy interrupted.

"As you are aware, right now there are shortages on just about everything. Production has been delayed. The price of lumber and virtually all construction items, as well as labor costs, have skyrocketed through the roof."

"It doesn't seem fair that you have nothing to lose while you wait. I'm the one with unpaid bills and a ranch to run."

Santiago glanced down at the folder. "I'm sorry, Mr. Parnell, but you signed this agreement that clearly states those terms. And you also agreed the final payment wouldn't be due until the completion of that project."

Quincy narrowed his eyes. "No one in their right mind would sign a one-sided deal like that."

Santiago turned the open folder around and shoved it toward Quincy. "See for yourself."

After reading the terms of the sale, Quincy flipped to the signature page, sure someone had forged his name. To his dismay, that was not the case. Although it was definitely his handwriting, this was not the paperwork he and his lawyer had agreed to.

"There must be some mistake."

"Again, the proof's right in front of you." Santiago got up and walked over to the counter and poured himself a drink, then offered one to Quincy.

As much as he could use a stiff one right now, Quincy shook his head. He wasn't ready to make nice with this man until he got everything straightened out. "I'll need a copy of this document before I leave so my lawyer can go over it with a fine-tooth comb. In the meantime, there's another issue we need to discuss."

Santiago held up his hand to silence him, then picked up the phone. "Geraldine, can you make a copy of this land sale for Mr. Parnell?"

Quincy waited until Santiago's secretary appeared, picked up the folder, and then left the room before he approached the other thing weighing on his mind. "For now, I'll give this a rest until my lawyer gets back to me. In the meantime, I'll need you to explain who Jubilee Ranch, Inc, is and why they're part of the deal. I sold my land to Casinos International, not some shell company located in Panama."

Santiago shrugged. "I have no knowledge of any shell company. The agreement was for 2000 acres and was financed by Casinos International, just as you said."

"The deal was for 1500 acres and not two thousand."

Santiago stood and walked back to the counter to pour himself another drink. Again, Quincy refused the offer to join him, despite the fact that he desperately needed a shot of alcohol at the moment.

Maybe even the whole bottle.

When Santiago returned to his desk, he sat down and took a long swig of the liquor before making eye contact with Quincy. "I can only refer you to the signed documents that very clearly state that 2000 acres were sold to us."

"For now, I'll have to take a wait-and-see attitude. But what about Jubilee Ranch? Who are they, and why are they digging up my land beyond the 2000 acres?"

"No idea. You might want to take that up with your son."

"My son? What does he have to do with all this?"

"Maybe nothing. All I know is you sold Casinos International 2000 acres and signed off on staggered payments. If you remember, your son was instrumental in getting this deal done."

For once in his life, Quincy was speechless. Yes, Jake had been the one to initially come to him with an offer from the casino. He'd said they wanted to buy 1500 acres to build a golf course in a few years and were willing to pay much higher than the going rate for land. At the time, Quincy had gone through all his savings and only had a couple hundred dollars in the bank to live on. He figured with the 1500 acres he had left, he could fence his cattle closer to the ranch house and away from the golf course.

So why did the paperwork for the sale say he had sold the casino more of the land than he had agreed to sell? And why had the sheriff verified that a shell company owned another five hundred acres?

He couldn't get his head around the fact that Santiago had suggested his son might have information about this. Sure, Jake had brokered the deal, explaining that he would get a finder's fee and that Quincy would be able to keep the ranch out of foreclosure. But this was just crazy. Someone was definitely trying to put the screws to him, and he was not about to let that happen.

Not as long as he still had breath in his lungs.

He considered what he should do next. He wasn't sure he wanted to hear more—couldn't handle hearing how his own flesh and blood might have had something to do with this—but he couldn't leave without at least trying to find the answers. "I know my son was instrumental in brokering this deal, but why would you think he had anything to do with Jubilee Ranch?"

Santiago took a slow drink of his whiskey. "Probably nothing. All I know is what I've already told you.

You might ask him yourself today. He's here at the casino for the Cinco de Mayo celebration."

Quincy was surprised. "Does he work here?"

"Not in any official capacity, but he did help us out before we opened. And I've been told he's sweet on a girl he met here—a singer from one of the bands, I think."

That made sense. Women seemed to flock to Jake, and he rarely turned any of them down.

Quincy stood when the secretary returned with the copies for him. "I'll get back with you after I figure this out." He walked to the door with the paperwork.

"Looking forward to straightening this out once and for all," Santiago said. "In the meantime, stop by Geraldine's desk on the way out. I'll have her give you a pass for all the wonderful Mexican food and drinks you can consume today, plus a hundred-dollar bonus card to gamble with."

Feeling defeated and helpless, Quincy could only nod as he walked out, his mind still on his son. He should have known. Gambling and women were Jake's Achilles' heel. And probably would eventually be his downfall.

But what could he possibly have to do with Jubilee Ranch?

~

THE CONCIERGE LED Jordan and Ray through the door and up the escalator to the upper level. Jordan's attention was drawn to all the screens on the back wall, all showing various parts of the casino in real time. She wondered if anyone would look through these tapes and see her going to Arizona's room.

They walked past several doors before the

concierge stopped at one located in the very back marked SECURITY. He knocked first, then opened it wide enough to allow Ray and Jordan to pass by him.

The first thing Jordan noticed was that the man behind the massive desk looked nearly as big as the desk itself. Sam Waterford, according to the placard on his desk, was definitely unnerving, as he looked up and smiled at them—a smile that seemed to be painted on his face and didn't match the cold, dark eyes that never left her face.

It was not hard to understand why he had this job.

He motioned for them to sit in the chairs facing him. "Ronald says you wanted to see me—that there's something you want to discuss." A lock of his thick gray-white hair fell over his eye, and he quickly brushed it back as he finally took his eyes off Jordan and shifted his attention to Ray. "So how can I help you?"

Jordan was about to say she was worried about Arizona when Ray spoke up. "My friend here was supposed to meet with one of the members from the band last night, and they never showed."

Waterford opened a notebook on his desk and jotted something down before glancing back up. "And why are you worried about that? No one else has called about a missing band member." He stood up, reached over the desk and offered his hand. "I'm Sam Waterford, by the way. Head of security."

Ray leaned forward, shook Waterford's hand, and then introduced himself. "Ray Varga and this is Jordan McAllister. We're worried about–"

The man turned to Jordan. "You were supposed to meet up with this person last night? What time?"

"After the show," Jordan responded, uncomfortable now under Waterford's scrutiny.

"So that would have been around ten thirty or so?"

Jordan opened her mouth to respond, then quickly shut it when Ray sent her a warning with his eyes.

"Around that time," Ray responded.

"And what makes you think something may have happened to Miss Lightfoot? Is it possible she just forgot she was supposed to meet up with you?"

Ray stiffened in his chair. Jordan knew her friend well enough to know that he was just about to give Waterford a taste of Ray, the cop.

"What makes you think it's Miss Lightfoot we're worried about?"

Waterford frowned before a slight grin covered his face. "You're not the first person to come by today with concerns about the woman." He opened a file on his desk. "One of the band members tried to reach her today, and when there was no response, she called me."

"Thought you said you hadn't heard anything about Miss Lightfoot's possible disappearance," Ray pressed.

"I wasn't sure we were talking about the same woman," Waterford responded.

"And when you got that first concerned call, did you send any of your men to Arizona's room to check things out?"

The security chief stared at Ray, his face showing that he was clearly unhappy with the way he was being questioned. "I sent a couple of my guys up there immediately after the call, even though I felt sure they'd find her there, sleeping off a night of partying."

Jordan was stunned by the nonchalant way he had reacted to a possible problem at the casino, but again, before she could respond, Ray beat her to the punch.

"And was she?" When Waterford looked confused, he added, "Was Arizona asleep in her bed?"

Waterford's expression never changed. "My men said it looked like she hadn't slept in the bed. Probably hadn't even gone to her room after the show."

Ray glanced at Jordan and shook his head, as if to tell her he had this going forward. "Well, it sounds like we're worrying about nothing. You're probably right in thinking that she simply met up with someone and totally forgot about her meeting with Jordan."

The security chief turned to Jordan once again. "And can I ask why you were meeting her so late at night? Are you friends?"

Jordan took her cue from Ray who was again shaking his head. "I wouldn't call us friends. I only met her yesterday by the pool, and before she left, she asked if I wanted to meet her in her room after the show and continue our girl talk."

"And did you?" His eyes continued to stare as if he already knew the answer.

"When I knocked at the door, no one answered. Since I was pretty tired myself, I decided not to wait. So I want back to my room and crashed."

"So you never saw her in the room?"

"I did call her this morning but still couldn't reach her. That's when I let my imagination run wild about what may have happened to her. I called Ray and asked him to come with me to report my concerns."

Waterford stood up and walked around to the front of the desk. "And I appreciate that. My gut tells me this Lightfoot woman will show up today with a good reason why she stood you up. In the meantime, I'll have my men ask around and talk to the other band members to see if we can track her down."

"We'd appreciate a call back when you have infor-mation," Ray said before standing and offering Jordan a hand.

"Absolutely. I will tell you this. Although my men didn't find Miss Lightfoot, they did find something curious in her room." Waterford got up from his desk and moved toward the door.

He pulled his phone from his pocket, scrolled to a picture, and then handed it to Ray. He was silent as Ray and Jordan looked at the image of Arizona's coffee table, covered with poker chips. "This makes me wonder if she stayed out all night playing at the tables."

Again, he stared at Jordan, but this time she wasn't freaked out and answered, "You're probably right. She did say she loved playing blackjack."

Ray opened the door and walked through before turning back. "Thanks so much for listening to us. When you find her, tell her Jordan would still like to have that girl talk."

"Will do. Now, if you'll wait right here, I'll have someone escort you downstairs." Waterford turned and walked back into the room.

As soon as the door closed, Jordan turned to Ray. "That man is lying through his teeth."

"I know. The sixty-four-thousand-dollar question is why?"

14

Jordan met the rest of the gang at lunch and told them what had gone down the night before and then again in the morning in Waterford's office.

"Holy cow!" Victor said. "You were actually hiding in the room while two guys with guns ransacked it? You must have been terrified."

"Terrified doesn't even come close to explaining how I felt. I was behind the curtains and was so scared, I had to hold my hand over my mouth to keep from screaming."

"I can only imagine," Michael said before turning to Ray. "So what did the head honcho say about the poker chips that Jordan had in the pillowcase?"

Jordan glanced toward Lola, and when she nodded, turned to Ray. "Your lovely partner was kind enough to let me borrow the Vera Bradley bag you bought her as an early birthday present. She didn't want me to look like an idiot walking through the casino carrying a pillowcase. Hope you don't mind."

Winking at Lola, he said, "I thought that bag looked familiar, but no, I don't mind at all, although I'm not surprised. My Lola has the kindest heart of anyone I've ever met. Certainly, she let you borrow the purse."

"What did the guy say when he saw the chips?" Victor asked, impatiently.

"We didn't tell him about them," Jordan said.

"What? Why not?"

Ray swallowed the last of his iced tea before responding. "Not sure why. I just got a feeling in my gut and decided to hold onto that information for the time being."

"Your gut has always been your best asset, Ray." Lola's eyes twinkled with mischief. "Well, maybe not your best asset. And if you thought it was wise to keep that information from him, it was probably the right thing to do."

"There was something about Waterford," Ray continued. "First of all, how did he know it was Arizona that we were worried about even before we mentioned her name? We only said we were concerned about a member of the band. We didn't even say if it was one of the singers or even that it was a woman."

"Then how would he have known you were talking about Arizona?" Michael asked.

"Exactly," Ray said. "I have to say, by this time, all my cop instincts were on high alert. He saw where I was going with the questioning and explained that one of the other band members had already called about her. That could be true, but for some reason, I doubt it. According to George, most of the other band members, both male and female, disliked the woman, and I know of at least one who is probably thinking good riddance right now."

"And he said he sent his men to Arizona's room this morning after the first concerned call. Said his guys told him it looked pristine—like the bed hadn't even been slept in." Jordan paused before continuing, "I know for a fact that Arizona's room was not *pristine*. Not unless you call clothes strewn all across the floor and the couch and the mattress slit right down the middle *pristine*."

"Good point," Lola interjected.

"And there's more," Jordan added. "Waterford said his men found a bunch of poker chips in her room. Said she may have stayed up all night playing at the tables. Again, I can assure you there were no chips in there when I left last night and definitely none in there this morning."

"Look at you, Jordan," Victor teased. "You sound like a mini Ray."

Ray grinned from ear to ear. "Maybe a little of me has rubbed off on her. She has picked up her game."

"I don't know," Michael said. "Arizona playing the tables all night might be a logical explanation for why her bed wasn't slept in and why she had a slew of poker chips in her room."

"Michael, weren't you listening?" Victor scolded. "Jordan went back to Arizona's room this morning and said it looked like a tornado had blown through it. Why would he give the impression that the room was...wait. How did Waterford describe it? Oh, yeah, pristine."

"I forgot that part. My bad." Michael rolled his eyes. "So, Ray, what else did your gut tell you?"

"Unfortunately, nothing that led me to believe Waterford was telling the truth. There's always the possibility his men lied to him about the condition of the room, though." Ray took a deep breath. "Anyway, I thought it best to keep the chips a secret for now."

"What are you keeping secret?" Rosie asked, as she pulled up a chair next to Jordan.

"We'll fill you in later today. I don't want to talk about that now when we only get to see you for a few minutes at a time," Jordan said. "You look adorable, by the way, wearing that big hat and the cute apron with the restaurant's logo."

Rosie touched the chef's hat. "Thanks for the compliment. George said I could take these home as a souvenir." Her face lit up. "Wait until you taste the Margarita Cupcakes and the Blackberry Peach Margaritas we're serving in the parking lot for the actual Cinco de Mayo celebration."

"I can't wait to taste those cupcakes. Do you really make them with tequila?" Victor's eyes lit up. "What could be better than my favorite liquor mixed with a sugar-filled dessert?"

"You bet," Rosie said. "I knew you'd be excited."

"I adore Blackberry Peach Margaritas," Lola said. "Any chance you can party with us out there? I miss having you around."

"Maybe not for the entire time, but I did tell Morgan that I was going to spend some time with you guys today. Tonight's meal is tortilla soup with fajitas, refried beans, and spicy, Spanish rice. It's pretty basic, so they really don't need me all afternoon for the preparations. The soup is already made and they're grilling the fajita meat with my special homemade fajita seasoning. The beans and rice are a piece of cake, so I can spend a couple or hours out there with you all."

Victor looked at his watch. "Excellent. Let's not waste any more time in here since we only have our dear friend for a few hours." He nailed her with his eyes. "And what, my lovely Rosie, are we having for dessert tonight?"

Rosie laughed. "I don't think I know anybody with

a sweet tooth as big as yours. Just for you, Morgan is baking German Chocolate *Tres Leche* cakes as we speak. And we're adding your favorite, cookies and cream ice cream."

"That's my girl," Victor said, making a face at Michael, who was frowning at the mention of Victor and sweets.

Michael couldn't help himself and laughed at Victor's antics. He stood up and nudged his partner toward the exit. "I'll give you a pass all day since we are celebrating your heritage today."

"Bring on the tequila cupcakes," Victor said before adding, "Did you know that Americans drink more tequila than any other country in the world and spend almost three billion dollars on margaritas every year?"

"I'm sure we're responsible for a large part of that number," Rosie joked.

"Especially you, Victor."

"Ha! I hear someone calling you back to the kitchen, Rosie," Victor joked back.

"Mea culpa, my friend. You know I love you and wouldn't want you any other way."

"I know." He high-fived her as they all stood up and headed for the exit.

All of a sudden, Jordan felt a chill crawl up her back. She had the distinct feeling that someone was watching her. She did a 360 turn but saw nothing that confirmed her suspicion. It was probably just a combination of the things that had happened the night before and this morning sitting in Waterford's office while he intimidated her with his stare.

Still, she couldn't shake the feeling. Inching her way over to Ray, she caught up to him and linked her arm with his. She wasn't sure about a lot of things, but one thing she knew for certain was that this man thought of her like a daughter, and there was no way he would let anything bad happen to her.

THE NORTH PARKING lot was already sectioned off and filled with open tents, some with stages. All were decorated with red, white, and green streamers, balloons, and flowers, all the colors of the Mexican flag. Kiosks offering a variety of Mexican cuisine were strategically placed around the area, and the smells coming from them were enough to tempt Jordan, despite the fact that just minutes before, she had devoured a huge serving of Rosie's King Ranch chicken.

Suddenly, the lively sound of a mariachi band could be heard coming from one of the tents in the center of the cordoned off parking lot. Recognizing the lively sound, they headed in that direction.

"It's *Jerabe Tapatío*," Victor said. He nudged Jordan toward the music, then pushed her to the front to get a better look at a group of Hispanic dancers, who were now taking their places on the make-shift stage. When the rest of the gang caught up to them, Victor explained, "It's the National Dance of Mexico."

"Sounds like the Mexican Hat Dance to me," Ray observed after he moved closer to see.

"Exactly," Victor said. "Check out their outfits."

Jordan glanced at the eight women, decked out in multi-colors, all with bright red and green ribbons adorning the skirts and the white, puffy-sleeved blouses. Even their braided hair was decorated with the colorful ribbons.

After the women took their places on the stage, eight men dressed like *charros*, appeared and fell into step behind them. The Mexican cowboys wore black pants with matching jackets and white, long-sleeved shirts with red, white, and green neckerchiefs around their necks. All were wearing boots that kept up with the beat of the familiar song as they tapped away. Each was wearing a huge hat that matched belts woven with intricate designs.

"Holy cow!" Rosie said. "I need to find out where they shop. I love those outfits."

Jordan laughed. "Why am I not surprised? You're like a bug to a light when it comes to bright colors and sparkly bling." She turned to Victor. "I can see why they call it the Mexican Hat dance. Look at the size of those big hats."

"They're called sombreros, *chica*. They're integral to the theme of *Jarabe Tapatío*. The dance represents a man's courtship to a woman he's attracted to. Watch as they place the sombreros on the ground next to the woman they're dancing with. It's their version of asking her out on a date."

"How romantic!" Lola exclaimed. "You should get one of those sombreros and do a dance around me, Ray Varga."

Ray chuckled. "Oh, Lord. You've seen me dance, darlin'. It would be anything but romantic."

After a few more minutes of the lively dancing, the men threw their hats on the ground, just as Victor had predicted.

"Oh, my heavens! And they do that instead of just asking the girl out?" Rosie asked.

"You're missing the whole point. It's a mating ritual and is part of the culture. Next, we're gonna find out if the woman is interested in the dude. Watch what the gals do next," Victor explained. "If she dances around the brim of the hat, it's a yes."

"Pay attention, Jordan. When Alex pops the question, you might want to dance around his sombrero," Victor said.

Jordan giggled and punched him in the arm. "Shut up! Number one, Alex isn't going to pop the question anytime soon. We're just getting used to saying I love you. And number two, I've seen my FBI guy dance. No way I'm saying yes after that."

"Yeah, right." Victor turned to the south end of the cordoned-off parking lot when the mariachi music stopped and the sounds of salsa music got his attention. "Come on. It looks like Rafael Morales and his band are just getting set up at the last tent over there. Michael and I will grab one of those Blackberry Peach Margaritas for all of us and head that way. You guys find us a good table," Victor said.

"It's a little too early for alcohol for me," Lola said. "I could go for one of those pink lemonades I saw when we first came out here, though. I'll come with you to help carry the drinks."

"To each his own, girlfriend," Victor replied. "But remember, it's five o'clock somewhere. They even made a song about that."

Just then the band began playing a salsa tune that seemed perfect for the Cinco de Mayo celebration and had them all moving to the beat as they hurried to the last tent on the lot.

Victor, Lola, and Michael scurried off to one of the kiosks where they were making the margaritas, and from the looks of the line waiting to get one, a lot of people lived by that five-o'clock-somewhere mantra.

The rest of them headed in the direction of the loud music, but when they got there, all the front tables had already been taken. They were lucky and snagged the lone empty table in the back. Before they sat down, they "borrowed" two chairs from a couple next to them and squeezed the others around the table.

After they were all seated with drinks in hand, Jordan felt the music whittle away at the tension she'd felt earlier, and before long, she was moving to the lively salsa beat and keeping time with her feet.

The stage was decorated in red, white, and green ribbons and balloons like all the other tents. Even Rafael had put aside his leather pants and fringed jacket and stayed true to the Mexican tradition with white pants and a white sequined shirt, unbuttoned nearly all the way to his waist and covered by a green vest.

Like the first time they'd heard him, Rafael seemed to be singing to her, even from a distance. She didn't know why, but she felt the color creep into her cheeks, and she had to remind herself that she had committed to an exclusive relationship with a certain FBI agent when she'd repeated the "L" word back to him.

Thinking about Alex, she sighed. Today marked the third day that she hadn't heard from him. He'd gone deep undercover in the past, but it had never been this long before he called her, even if it was only to let her know that he was OK and that he loved her.

"Jordan, the guy's singing to you. The least you can do is give him one of your gorgeous smiles," Victor said, disrupting her thoughts about Alex. "Trust me. I would definitely be overjoyed if he sang to me." When Michael coughed, he added, "Although not nearly as overjoyed as when you look at me in that special way, Michael."

"Good recovery, Victor. One of these days Michael is going to take you seriously, and you're gonna end up in the doghouse," Lola warned.

"Someone needs to remind my handsome friend that a very beautiful singer has her eye on me," Michael teased back.

"Yeah." Victor laughed. "Too bad Arizona has dropped off the face of the earth, so you're stuck with little old me."

Everyone laughed. It was nice to sit around and tease each other like they did back in Ranchero. They knew it was all good, clean fun, and no one took it seriously. If you were teased, it was like being reassured that you were loved.

Jordan took a drink of her margarita, then looked up as Rafael made his way toward them.

"Here he comes, Jordan. Don't forget to smile," Victor said.

The salsa singer stopped directly in front of her and held out his hand. When she accepted it, he lifted her out of the chair and began to dance as he sang *La Bamba*. It was hard not to get caught up in the mood, and Jordan did her best imitation of dancing, although it was a skill she'd never really learned, having grown up with four macho brothers who thought dancing was for sissies.

When the song ended, Rafael kissed her hand, and made his way back to the stage.

His next song was a slow one, and although Jordan didn't speak Spanish, she knew enough to know what *amor* meant, and this song mentioned it over and over again in the lyrics.

"I'm not familiar with this one," Victor said. "But I'm almost positive it's a love song."

"You most definitely have caught his eye, Jordan,"

Michael noted. "He's probably singing this one to you."

She shook her head. "No, not me this time. He's got his eye on someone else, a lucky girl in the back over there." She pointed to one of the tables out of her view, feeling relieved that his attention was on someone else and off her.

The salsa singer continued to stare in that direction, his eyes filled with longing, as he sang to the other woman. Jordan's curiosity got the best of her, and she stood up to get a look at her replacement.

But there was no woman back there.

She'd been wrong in her assessment that Rafael *did* bat for the same team as she did.

Very clearly, he did not. He was not singing the beautiful love song to a woman, but to a man sitting all alone at a back table.

She moved to the left to get a better look and nearly spit out her drink when she saw who the other man was. She was mesmerized as she saw the familiar face smile at Rafael and mouth the words, "I love you."

Still not believing her own eyes, she moved closer. This time, there was no doubt. As she watched Rafael sing to the man who was obviously his lover, she realized that her friend George had not been mistaken.

Without a doubt, the man on stage was singing a love song to Jeremy Redding, George's husband.

15

When the set ended, Rafael stepped off the stage and walked toward them while the rest of the band gathered up the equipment. He grabbed a chair from one of the tables and sat down next to Jordan.

"Can I join you?" When she nodded, he added, "I just wanted to thank you for being such a good sport and letting me dance with you. The audience loved it."

Jordan stole a glance toward the back where Jeremy had been sitting, but his table was now empty. More than likely, he was playing it safe so that no one made the connection between him and Rafael.

"Love that last song you sang," Victor said. "I listen to a lot of salsa music, but I'm not familiar with that one. What was it?"

"*Amor a la Mexicana*," Rafael answered. "Translated, it means Mexican style love."

"It was lovely," Lola said. "Are you from this area?" she asked, changing the subject.

"No, doesn't my accent give it away? I grew up in Queens."

The light bulb went on in Jordan's head. George

had suspected that Jeremy's lover had followed him from New York. More than likely, he'd been right.

"What brought you to Oklahoma?" Ray asked.

"I was offered an opportunity to have my own gig," Rafael explained. "I was singing back-up with a fantastic Puerto Rican band at a small club in downtown Manhattan, but my goal has always been to go out on my own and to sing only the songs that I love. When the opportunity presented itself, I jumped at the chance." He stood up. "Well, I guess I'd better help the band so we can grab some lunch before the next set." He looked directly at Jordan. "Thanks again for being such a good sport."

"Did you meet Jeremy at the club where you sang?" Jordan blurted before her brain had time to close her mouth.

A surprised look crossed Rafael's face. He glanced away for a second then sat back down again. "Do you know Jeremy?"

"Friends with his husband." Jordan heard Rosie gasp, but she couldn't stop now. "Did you know he was married?"

The singer shifted in his chair, obviously uncomfortable with the question. "Not back when I first met him in New York. When I did find out, it was too late. I was already too invested in the relationship and had developed real feelings for him. He assured me that he and his husband have been at odds for the past few years and that a divorce is imminent after George goes back to New York."

"So you knew Jeremy was married, but you still came to Oklahoma with him?" Rosie asked, clearly annoyed with the whole cheating thing.

Rafael took a slow breath. "Although I don't have to answer to any of you people for the way I live my life, I will tell you this. Jeremy mentioned that his brother was the CFO of a new casino and if I came down here with him, he would get his brother to hire me as one of the casino bands. Like I said, it was an opportunity I couldn't pass up."

"And you think that qualifies as a good reason to break up a marriage?" Rosie narrowed her eyes. "It doesn't. It only makes you a home wrecker."

Rafael looked away. "I'm sorry, but I'm not ashamed of what I did or how I feel." Once again, he got up. "It was nice talking to you. Enjoy the rest of your day." He walked back to the stage and joined his band before heading off in the direction of the food court at the other end of the parking lot.

No one spoke for a few minutes until Victor finally broke the silence. "I'm stumped, Jordan. I can't figure out how in the world you knew he and Jeremy were lovers."

"The first clue was when I noticed that Raphael was no longer interested in singing to me and was making goo-goo eyes at someone in the back. My curiosity got the best of me. I nearly choked when I saw that he was singing to Jeremy. It didn't take a rocket scientist to put two and two together."

Ray laughed. "Dang, girl! I'm gonna make a sleuth out of you yet."

"I feel like you already have," Jordan said, smiling at her friend before getting serious. "All fun aside, what we have to decide now is whether or not we're going to tell George."

"Tell George what?"

Jordan looked like a deer caught in a headlight when she turned to George Christakis, who had appeared out of nowhere. No one spoke for a few uncomfortable moments before Ray stepped up to the front and faced the New York chef.

"As a man, I would want to know what was going on. I would expect my friends to be honest with me," Ray said.

"I appreciate that, Ray, but I think I already know what you're about to tell me." George's eyes glistened with unshed tears.

"You do?" Jordan walked over to George. "You know about Jeremy?"

George sucked in a gulp of air, then blew it out slowly. "I've known since early this morning after I had a telephone conversation with him about our relationship. You can't live with someone as long as I have and not know when he's lying. That, plus the fact that I heard Jeremy whisper to someone in the background, all while he was denying that he was cheating on me."

Jordan patted his arm. "I'm so sorry, George." She turned and stared at her friends, and after each one nodded their approval, she continued, "We think we know who that other man is."

George bent down and kissed the top of her head. "My sweet child, I so adore you and your group of friends. I appreciate that you really don't want to hurt me with the information, but I already know that Rafael Morales is Jeremy's lover."

"How did you find out?" Ray asked.

"After our conversation this morning, I went to the Human Resources Department and told them I needed to see all the personnel files. Naturally, the lady in charge refused. So I mentioned that Santiago had given his approval, and when the secretary in the CEO's office confirmed it, she handed over the files."

"Why would Santiago allow you to get a look inside those files?" Ray asked. "I thought that information was guarded as tightly as medical records are with the HIPAA rules."

"That's true, Ray. And rarely do I push my weight around, but before I went to human resources, I paid a visit to Santiago's office and told him a lie about my reasons for needing to see them."

"It must have been one heck of a lie. Still, I can't believe he gave his approval," Ray said. "I see that as a very obvious invasion of privacy. I'm pretty sure those records are protected. It might even be a felony to look at them without authorization."

George grinned. "It probably is, but I was like a crazed man this morning and would have done anything. I told Santiago that I was looking to hire temporary help for today and tomorrow in the restaurant and needed to go through the records to see if I could find qualified people to pull from other departments. Full disclosure—I might have mentioned that I would have to close the restaurant today if I didn't get more help." He paused. "Do you have any idea how much my restaurant has brought in this weekend so far for the casino?" He spoke directly to Rosie. "All thanks to you, my dear."

"You could have been a good cop, my friend," Ray said. "I hope I don't have to pull some strings if you get arrested. So why was it so important to get a look at those records?"

"Like I mentioned back in Ranchero, from the beginning of all this, I had a feeling that Jeremy's lover had followed him from New York. I knew when I went through the personnel files that I might find a long list of employees who came from New York to work here, but to my surprise, there were only two."

"Who was the other one?" Victor asked.

"The man who heads up the security department."

"Waterford? Now there's a name I recognize. A man I wouldn't trust with my dog, if I had one," Ray replied with a heavy dose of irony. "After talking to him for only a short time this morning, you can safely rule him out as anyone's lover, in my humble opinion. The man has zero personality and even less integrity. He looked me and Jordan right in the eye and outright lied to both of us."

"Never having met the guy, I'll take your word for it. But I went another route to verify that Rafael is the one. I have a private investigator friend who works with the NYPD and asked him to check out both men. Found out that Waterford was a seasoned New York cop with over thirty some years on the job."

"You have to wonder why a man with thirty years on the job would give up that kind of seniority and just up and move to Oklahoma," Ray said. "Surely, a guy with that much experience was on his way up to a higher-paying job, which would automatically mean a higher pension amount when he retired."

"You would think so," George said. "But you'll understand when I tell you what else my PI friend told me about Waterford." He paused and glanced around before lowering his voice. "Before he left his job to take this one, he was facing an internal affairs investigation for allegedly stealing cocaine from the evidence room."

"Oh, yeah, that's big. Is he still under investigation?" Ray asked.

"No. Since the Manhattan precinct couldn't prove any of the allegations, they dropped the charges when he put in his resignation."

"So, he came to Oklahoma to avoid being charged with stealing? How in the world did he get hired as head of security at this casino? Seems to me someone needs to keep an eye on him, rather than the other way around," Victor said, making a face. "Sounds like the guy is a real loser."

"I'm sure you're right," George said. "It will all make sense when you hear the rest of his story."

They all huddled closer as George again lowered his voice. "Apparently, about a year ago, his wife was diagnosed with early Alzheimer's. On top of the costly medications she needs for that horrible disease, they found out she has type I diabetes. I don't have to tell you how expensive insulin is these days."

"It's disgusting," Lola said. "I have a friend on Social Security who has had to give up a lot of things we all take for granted just to pay for that one life-saving medicine every month."

"I almost feel sorry for Waterford, knowing what he is facing in the future," Michael said. "I don't know how far along his wife's Alzheimer's has progressed, but at some point in time, he'll have to deal with paying for her care. I get calls on my radio show all the time from people complaining about the cost of a good memory care facility."

"So you can understand why he would even consider stealing from the evidence room. Worrying about future care for his wife and how he will pay for it must be daunting," George explained.

"Wow!" Ray said. "And they hired him at this the casino knowing all that?"

"They didn't know. I scoured his records, and there was no mention of the investigation at all. As a matter fact, he got a glowing recommendation from his precinct captain."

"How could that be?" Jordan asked.

"Here's where it gets dicey. Apparently, Waterford

was hired by Jeremy's brother, Terry Redding. Probably at Jeremy's request, because as it turns out, Waterford is Rafael's uncle. I suspect the glowing recommendation was fraudulent."

"I certainly didn't see that one coming," Victor said. "Not sure why the guy left a good job for here, but it makes me wonder if Terry is paying him an unbelievable amount of money to work here."

George shook his head. "According to his records, he's getting what I suspect is a relatively normal salary for a department head."

"That's weird," Victor said. "But back to Raphael. How can you be sure he's the 'other man,' even though the only other possibility is older than dirt and sounds like he might be scum?"

Rosie skewered him with her eyes. "Watch your mouth, Victor. Don't you know fifty is the new thirty?"

"Oh, sorry," he said. "But back to my original question, how can you be sure?"

George looked down at the ground. "I'm ashamed to say that I broke every rule of my own integrity and followed Jeremy out here today. Stayed out of sight and watched Rafael sing to him."

"We saw that, too," Jordan said. "We couldn't decide whether to tell you or not."

"That's because you all are such good friends and didn't want to hurt me, but like Ray, I would have been grateful for that information."

"I'm going to play devil's advocate here and ask why you're so positive that he might be Jeremy's lover. Having someone sing to you isn't proof positive that something is going on," Michael said.

"Yesterday and again today, Rafael sang to our girl Jordan here. No way they're romantically involved," Lola said. "Because I care so much for you, I would only caution you to tread lightly. It could be a relationship-ending disaster if you accuse Jeremy of lying, and then find out that he wasn't."

"I took a picture of Rafael and sent it to Henri." George sighed. "He confirmed immediately that Rafael was the guy he saw kissing his dad outside the apartment door."

"I'm so sorry, George," Jordan said. "As someone who has had to deal with a third person in a relationship myself, I know how hurt you must feel right now."

George's eyes glossed over with sadness. "You're right. I am hurting, but I'm also relieved to know the truth. Part of me wants to keep on believing that Jeremy would never lie to me, even though I know he is. Without actually seeing it play out with my very own eyes, the farce may have gone on far longer than it should have before the truth finally came out."

"So what will you do?" Rosie asked.

"For now, I'm going to pretend that I don't know about them. I've decided to file for divorce the minute I get back to New York."

"And then what?"

"Did I mention that Santiago loves the income generated by my restaurant?" His eyes narrowed. "When I go to him with my request, there's no way he'll refuse me."

"What request?" Jordan asked.

"I want Rafael Morales and Sam Waterford fired the minute the Cinco de Mayo celebrations are over and I walk out of this casino on Monday."

"And Jeremy?" Jordan asked quietly.

"He thinks he's going to run my restaurant after I leave. No way that will ever happen now. I can't wait to see the look on his face when I fire him myself."

16

Jake Parnell walked into Luis Santiago's office and marched directly over to the front of the CEO's desk. "I saw my dad being escorted to your office earlier. What did he want?"

Santiago stared at the younger man, who was dressed in jeans that hugged his body like a glove and a white shirt embellished with a red, white, and green scarf. He motioned for him to sit. "I never knew you had a little Hispanic in you."

"What? I don't. I'm just getting into the spirit of Cinco de Mayo." He touched the scarf. "Everyone wears green on St. Patrick's Day, and we all know that most of the people aren't Irish."

"Good point. Now back to your question, your dad wanted to talk about the terms of our land sale."

"How much does he know?"

"Just about everything. Apparently, someone is digging up part of his land. I can guarantee you that it's not the casino doing it." Santiago reached into a drawer, pulled out a file, and opened it. "Now your dad is questioning why he hasn't seen the rest of his money yet."

Jake took a deep breath. "I never meant for him to

find out any of this until it was too late to do anything about it."

"So you know about the digging?"

"I was the one who hired a company out of Tulsa to start the preliminary groundwork for fracking while it's still allowed. Thought it would be at least a year or two before they got to it."

"Does your dad know you're the one behind the drilling?"

Jake shook his head. "Although I really haven't spoken to him in about four months, I'm pretty sure he doesn't. I'd hoped to make enough money to get my life back on track, then shut down the site and let him raise his cattle, no more the wiser. Now it sounds like it's all going to blow up in my face."

Jake walked over to the counter and poured himself a drink. After he was seated in the chair facing Santiago, he took a long swig before asking, "How did he take it when you told him he'd have to wait on the rest of the money until the golf course was built?"

"How do you think he took it? He was madder than a wet hen and at one point, threatened to go to the Feds in Tulsa."

"That's not good. That could potentially expose all of us," Jake said. "If he said he would go to the Feds, I guarantee, that's exactly what he'll do. He's already asking questions. My friend in the police department in Encenada said his boss is looking into Jubilee Ranch and its holdings at my dad's request. This could turn into a disaster for all of us."

"For you, maybe, but Casinos International did nothing illegal. You're the one who got him to sign off on the deal, which was for us to get 2000 acres. Anything else is strictly your own wheeling and dealing." Santiago paused and stared at Jake. "For the life of me, I can't figure out how you coerced him into signing off on the sale, anyway. My company tried for over six months to get him to sell. We offered multiple incentives, including favorable stock options. The answer was always no and usually came with an expletive."

Jake lowered his eyes. "I'm not proud of what I did, but as you know, I had a bad run at the dog races. Ran up a pretty sizable debt."

"Casinos International had nothing to do with that. You know that, right?"

Jake glared at the CEO. "Maybe not for my debt, but you do have to bear some responsibility for at least part of what happened next. After I took a couple of pretty good beatings, one even landing me in the hospital for several days, you can imagine how quickly I jumped at the chance to have my debt paid off when your man approached me with an offer."

"What makes you think it was my man?"

"Oh, come on. Who else would have offered to pay the loan shark fifty grand without asking me to pay back one red cent? Who else would have guaranteed that I would be debt free under one condition—that I got my dad to sign on the dotted line?" Jake tsked. "So don't play innocent here. You have as much to do with this dilemma as I do."

Santiago was silent for a moment. "I suppose you're right. I'm still curious about how you got him to sign."

"Have you met my dad? After my mother died, he picked up a bottle and has never put it down. Getting him drunk was easy. Switching the papers after his lawyer had signed off on them was even easier."

"All I asked for was the additional 500 acres. It was really stupid of you to ask for another 500 for yourself.

Your dad would never have known about all this if you hadn't been so greedy."

"I know. That part's on me, but I thought I would make a lot of money, shut down the drilling, and get out before he even suspected anything was going on."

"And you thought your dad wouldn't look out the window and notice the huge equipment tearing up his ranch?"

"My dad's not interested in too much since he lost all his cattle. I thought the equipment would be long gone before he ever got sober enough to care about anything other than how much liquor he had left in the liquor cabinet. The man drinks himself to sleep every night and then wakes up and hits the bottle again in order to deal with the hangovers. I never dreamed he'd look out the kitchen window and discover what I'd done."

"I know he only agreed to the deal after he lost all his cattle. And was strapped for cash. How did you make that happen?"

Jake sighed. "Again, it's not something I'm proud of, but I was desperate. Fortunately, I was able to get rid of all the evidence before he discovered the cause of the lead poisoning. To this day, he has no idea where the cows got the oil that killed them all."

"You know what? If I had a son, I'd pray to the Man above not to send me one like you," Santiago said. "Now, if you'll excuse me, I have work to do to make sure your dad doesn't get into his truck and drive to Tulsa."

"This was my screw-up, and I'm going to fix it. I plan on driving out to the ranch today and telling him everything. He's not the kind of guy who forgives and forgets, but hopefully, he'll see that in a year or two, I'll have enough money to buy him as many cattle as he wants. I can promise him that after the drilling stops, I'll be in a position to deed back the land to him."

"No need to drive all way out to the ranch."

Jake looked confused. "Why not?"

"I gave your dad food and alcohol vouchers for the entire day plus a hundred dollars to gamble with. Security has had their eye on him from the moment he walked out of my office. The cameras show that he's never left the casino."

"You look like you could use some cheering up, George," Victor said. "Any chance of you hanging out with us for a few hours before dinner?"

George's lip spread into a smile. "That's the best offer I've had all weekend. Lead the way."

"Fantastic! I heard someone mention there's going to be a Chihuahua race in fifteen minutes," Victor said. "We have just enough time to get another margarita before it starts."

He led them to the tent where all the beverages were being served, and when he saw the long line, he groaned. "Guess everyone has the same idea as I do."

"Never mind, my friend. I have connections."

George waved to the man behind the counter serving the guests, then held up seven fingers. The man gave him a thumbs up, and within a few minutes, handed George, Rosie, and Victor seven margaritas.

After thanking the guy, George passed out the drinks, then with a silly grin covering his face, he said, "I met him my very first night here, and we became fast friends. He eats at the restaurant every night on me."

"Nice," Lola said. "So, Victor, where is this Chihuahua race going on, and can we bet on any of the dogs?"

Victor laughed. "Pretty sure there's no gambling outside the casino, but that shouldn't stop us from making insider bets. Let's go. I see a whole bunch of people heading over there." He pointed to a large tent on the side of the parking lot where it looked as if they had set up what could be a racetrack of sorts in the grassy area. "Hurry. I want to get a place up front."

"Seriously? Chihuahua races?" Jordan took a sip of her drink. "Another one of these and those puppies will all look like greyhounds to me."

"Slow down, girlfriend. And for your information, Chihuahua races have become a tradition in a lot of cities as part of the Cinco de May celebration."

"You're making that up," she said, jokingly.

"No. Seriously, some cities in Colorado and Arizona have them every year. I don't know about here, but in those cities, they collect donations before the show, and the proceeds go to the Chihuahua rescue operation." He snorted. "I've been told that in one city in Colorado, they even have a beauty contest and name a Chihuahua king and queen, kinda like at the prom."

"That's hilarious," Jordan said. "I can't wait to see it for myself."

"And they do all this on Mexico's Independence Day every year?" George asked.

"Not Independence Day, George. Like I told the others, Independence Day happened fifty years before anyone even celebrated Cinco de Mayo."

"Then what exactly are we celebrating?"

"Cinco de Mayo is sometimes called the Anniversary of the Battle of Puebla in honor of a military victory in 1862 over Napoleon's French forces."

"Why were the Mexicans fighting the French?" Lola asked, leaning closer to hear.

"Apparently, Mexico placed a moratorium on the repayment of foreign debts, and the British, Spanish, and French troops invaded the city. The Mexicans were able to hold off the English and the Spaniards, and they withdrew, but the French remained for another five years. It was really a big victory for the undermanned Mexican army against an enemy with more sophisticated weaponry."

"I'm impressed," George said. "And because of that we get to enjoy authentic Mexican food for the entire day."

"Not exactly. A lot of Mexican food we eat in the United States is not actually part of the true Mexican cuisine. Dishes like hard-shell tacos, nachos, and burritos are what we call Tex-Mex creations."

"Whatever you call it, it's fast becoming one of my favorite types of food. I can't wait to incorporate some of Rosie's recipes into the menu at Chez Luí." George turned to Rosie. "Only with your permission."

"Absolutely. One of these days maybe I'll make it to New York and see for myself how it all worked out," Rosie said, just as an announcer moved to the microphone to welcome them and to explain that the dogs were from Tulsa where they normally raced every year on this day.

"Oh good Lord! How unbelievably cute are they?" Lola exclaimed as eight Chihuahuas, all wearing tutus and mini tuxedos made of vibrant, festive-colored material and matching hats, were brought to the starting line. It sounded like a dog party with all of them yapping at once.

"Okay," George said. "If this doesn't cheer me up, nothing will."

They laughed as thirty-two dogs competed in four different heats. The noise was deafening as the crowds cheered for their favorites. First and second place winners of all four races were then lined up for the final race.

"This is it," Victor said. "The winner gets to wear a crown for the rest of the day and earns a big bone as a bonus. I've got my money on that little guy over there in the red, green, and white outfit. He smoked the competition in his heat."

"I'm going with the petite, girly one in the pink and white tutu," Jordan said. "She's gonna kick your boy's butt out there."

"Five bucks says you're wrong."

"You're on," Jordan said, just as her phone rang. She glanced at the caller ID, fully intending to ignore the call until she saw the name.

Natalie Moreland.

Why was Alex's mother calling her? An overwhelming sense of dread rushed through her body. Natalie almost never called and when she did, it was usually not to chitchat.

Jordan tapped Rosie on the shoulder. "This call is from Alex's mother. I'm going to find a spot where it isn't so noisy."

"You'll miss the final race," Rosie argued.

"I can't help it. I have to find out what she wants."

By the time she found a quiet spot on a bench away from the dog races, it was too late. The call had already gone to voicemail.

Without bothering to listen, she dialed Natalie and held her breath until she answered.

"Natalie, it's Jordan. Is everything all right?"

"Have you heard from Alex in the last couple of days?"

Jordan's heart sank. "No, but he told me on Wednesday that he was going deep undercover and would probably not be able to call for a while."

Please God, don't let her give me bad news.

"His handler called. They haven't heard from him, either. They're worried."

Tears welled up in Jordan's eyes. "Don't they know that sometimes he can't get to a phone without blowing his cover?"

"They do, but his handler said usually Alex is able to get a message to him somehow within a day or two. He said he's trying to reach Alex's partner, and even he isn't answering." Her voice broke. "I don't mean to upset you, dear. I was only hoping you'd heard from him. I know that if he was able to call anyone, it would be you."

Jordan tasted the tears that were now running down her face. She wanted so desperately to be able to offer some kind of hope to Alex's mother, but she couldn't.

"I'm sure he'll call in a day or so and tell us we worried for nothing. It's probably as simple as him not being in an area with cell coverage," she said, hoping her voice didn't give away that she was just as worried as both Natalie and Alex's handler.

"I hope so. I guess all we can do now is pray. I'll call you the minute I hear something, and you do the same." Natalie sniffed. "Again, I hope I didn't totally ruin your day. When I spoke to Alex on Wednesday night, he mentioned that you and your friends were going to spend the weekend at a new casino that was opening in Oklahoma."

"That's where I am now," Jordan said, holding back

her own sniffles. "I'll be here until tomorrow when we head back to Ranchero. I'll have my phone on me at all times, so call the minute you hear something. I'll do the same."

She hung up the phone and swiped at her eyes, wishing she believed what she'd just said to Natalie. She leaned back on the bench, not ready to rejoin her friends. Not ready to have to tell them about Natalie's phone call.

"Mind if I sit here?"

Jordan looked up at an elderly man who had appeared out of nowhere. She recognized him as the guy she'd seen on her first night at the casino being manhandled by four security police officers trying to force him to leave. Eventually, they'd succeeded, but not before he'd given them a run for their money and left all four of them gasping for air.

She patted the seat next to her on the bench. "No problem. I'm only going to be here a little longer, anyway, and you can have the entire bench to yourself."

The man sat down beside her and took off his hat before swiping the sweat from his forehead with his sleeve. "I saw you crying and wanted to find out if there was anything I could do."

She shook her head, unsuccessfully trying to smile to reward him for his thoughtfulness. "I'll be all right in a minute."

"If you don't mind, I'll just sit quietly with you." He offered his hand. "I'm Quincy Parnell, by the way."

17

"Jordan McAllister," she said, shaking his hand. "I just got some bad news and needed to be by myself to wrap my brain around it."

"Today's supposed to be a day of celebration. I'm sorry your news isn't good." Quincy stood up. "I'll leave if you want me to, but it's been my experience that most of the time when I'm saddened by something, it's always helpful to have someone beside me, even if neither of us talks."

Jordan sized him up. He looked to be in his late fifties, early sixties with blue eyes that were filled with compassion. Ordinarily she didn't open up to strangers, sometimes not even to her friends, but there was something about this guy that made her feel safe.

"Sit, Mr. Parnell. I could use the company."

He sat back down. "Call me Quincy. I promise to be quiet."

"My boyfriend might be in trouble," she said, suddenly.

"Might be? So there's a possibility that he isn't?"

She thought about that for a minute. Her head told her this man might be right. Alex could be on his way back to Ranchero right now with a plausible explanation why he hadn't called. Her heart told her a whole different story, though, as the ominous feeling of dread rushed back into her body and more tears began to flow down her cheeks.

Why hadn't she told Alex she'd loved him more often before he'd left? There had just been that one time she'd said it, and that was only after he'd said it first. Why did she feel compelled to go slowly with him?

She didn't have to think long and hard for the answer to that question. She knew she'd built a wall around her heart after giving it completely to Brett for so many years, then watching him break it to pieces when he dumped her for another woman. She'd made sure that wall was solid brick now, hard to penetrate.

But Alex wasn't Brett. She knew that—had known that from the very first time she'd met him. So why was she holding back?

Quincy gave her hand a squeeze. "I've upset you. I'm sorry. It's hard knowing that someone you care about might be in trouble and there's nothing you can do to help."

She glanced up at him and saw tears welling up in his own eyes. "It's that not being able to do anything about it that's killing me." She dabbed her eyes with the handkerchief he pulled from the back pocket of his overalls. "Until I know something for sure, I need to try to stay positive, keep hope in my heart, and pray."

Quincy gave her a half-shrug. "That's a good mantra for me, as well."

She couldn't stop herself, and even though she knew it was none of her business, she said, "I saw the security cops throw you out of the casino the other night. Is that why you're worried?"

"I could have kicked all four of their butts if I'd really wanted to." He looked away for a second before responding. "No, that's not it. Like you, I'm worried about someone close to me."

"Why didn't they want you in the casino? Are you one of those card counters? I know they frown on people who do that."

"Nothing like that. I sold part of my land to them a little over a year ago, and I have yet to see all the money. The CEO gave me some BS about waiting until they began construction on a golf course before they made the next payment." He rolled his eyes. "Ha! That may take five years or longer. I can't wait that long. I'm out of reserve cash and on the verge of losing my ranch. I thought if I made a big enough stink in the lobby, I'd force their hand, and they'd give me my money just to shut me up."

"And did it force their hand?"

He laughed out loud. "It forced their hand, all right. You saw the results. They threw me out. It seems that when I signed the deed of sale, I didn't read the fine print." He paused for a minute, as if to collect his thoughts. "I still can't believe that happened. I even had my lawyer look over the paperwork before I signed anything, and he gave it his stamp of approval. Somehow, I was duped, but I just can't figure out how they did it."

"Is your signature forged?"

"No, it's definitely my handwriting. I came back today to try again to get my money. Like I said, I'm running out of cash, and there's a good chance I'm going to lose the ranch that's been in my family for generations. Thought when I told them why I needed the money so desperately, they'd figure out a way to give me at least some of what I'm owed out of the goodness of their hearts."

"And did they?"

"What do *you* think? My first mistake was assuming that Santiago—that's the CEO— had a heart to begin with." He pulled out the vouchers. "He did give me free food and a little gambling money to appease me. Like that's gonna save my ranch."

"That's rough," Jordan said. "As much as I feel for you, I hate to admit it, but hearing about your problem has made me forget about mine, at least for the moment."

He grinned at her. "Then at least something good has come out of all this. I'll figure it out and when I do—"

"There you are," Victor said, suddenly appearing at her side. "Rosie said you got a phone call from Alex's mother." He stopped talking and stared at her face. "You been crying?"

"Natalie got a call from his handler. They've lost contact with him and his partner."

"Oh no." Victor bent down and kissed the top of her head. "Sweetie, you know as well as I do that this isn't the first time Alex has gone off the radar. He's FBI. He knew the risks when he took this assignment, but he's always managed to come back to you." He turned to Quincy. "Who's your friend?"

"Sorry. I'm so busy thinking about myself that I forgot my manners. Quincy Parnell, this is Victor Rodriguez, my very best friend in the entire world."

Victor narrowed his eyes. "I know I've seen you before but I can't remember where."

Jordan patted Quincy on the shoulder. "You're looking at the man who took on four security guards the other night in the lobby."

A flash of recognition crossed Victor's face. "Oh, yeah." He shook Quincy's hand. "Nice work, my friend."

They chatted for a few more minutes before they heard Lola calling them in the distance. After saying their goodbyes to Quincy, Jordan and Victor headed in that direction. The gang was all there except Rosie who had gone back to the kitchen to oversee the preparations for the night's dinner menu.

Lola ran up to Jordan and hugged her, then held her at arms' length and studied her face. "Is everything all right?"

Jordan decided to take Quincy's advice and not let what hadn't happened—and might not ever happen—spoil the last day at the casino for everyone. "I'm okay. I'll tell you all about it later. For now, I'm really thirsty and need something cold and non-alcoholic."

"They're already closing down the tents," Lola said. "Guess the party out here is over. I'll run and get you one of those pink lemonades I had earlier before they shut that one down. It was hand-squeezed and delicious."

"Did Victor tell you he owes you five bucks?" Ray asked.

Jordan thought about that for a second before his meaning sunk in. "So my little girl in pink beat his macho boy in the final race?"

"Yep," Ray said. "Knowing Victor, he probably would never have told you."

"I was waiting for the right time," Victor said, with a grin. "Your little fireball ran circles around my Chihuahua." He pulled out his wallet and handed her a five-dollar bill.

Jordan reached for the money. "You have no idea

how much I needed this today. Beating you and taking your money warms my heart."

"Glad to oblige," Victor said. "Now let's go get one of those margarita cupcakes before they tear down that tent. Then we should probably get cleaned up for dinner before we head over to listen to the James Brothers."

"Good idea," George said. "I've already secured backstage passes for all of you. I think it's gonna be—" He stopped talking when Jeremy ran up to him, clearly out of breath and distraught about something.

"Where've you been? I've been looking for you for over an hour."

George was silent for a moment, probably fighting with his emotions after having caught Jeremy lying about having a lover. Probably trying to save all his rage for tomorrow when he fired him. "Well, now you've found me. What's got you so upset?"

"My brother's missing."

"What do you mean missing?" George asked.

"I've been trying to call him all day. His phone goes immediately to voice mail, and he hasn't answered any of my texts."

"Have you called Marilee?" Jordan asked.

"You know his wife?" When she nodded, he turned to George. "She's not answering, either. I talked to the head of security. He's been trying to reach him since early this morning." His voice caught. "I'm really worried that something has happened to both Terry and Marilee."

"Maybe they decided to do something fun with the family," George suggested. "His CFO duties have been keeping him pretty busy these past few months."

Jeremy shook his head. "I don't think so. Last week, Terry and I had a long talk about what's going on in our lives. He said he was thinking about contacting a lawyer about a divorce."

"Did he say why?" Ray asked. "Doesn't he have three kids?"

"Yes, but he said he was no longer in love with Marilee." Jeremy turned to George. "You've got to help me find him."

"Did you talk to the security chief? It's my understanding that all the executive offices are close together on the upper level. Maybe someone saw him leave and knows something," Ray offered.

Jeremy's eyes turned defiant. "My brother would never leave without letting someone know where he was headed. This is opening weekend, for goodness sake. He told me he's been living on site here to make sure everything goes well. Said he set up a bed behind the wine room upstairs."

"That's got to be hard sleeping there with all the noise," Lola said.

"The entire upper level is soundproofed," George said. "It makes sense for him to stay close to his office in case there's any kind of problem this weekend."

"My point, exactly," Jeremy said. "He would never leave like this without telling someone where he was in case of an emergency."

"And you said you've tried to call Marilee, too?" Lola asked.

"Yes. I even paid one of the security cops to drive out to their house and see if Terry's there."

"And what did he find?" Ray asked.

"Nothing. Nobody answered the door, and there were no cars in the garage that he could see when he looked through the top window. Said the house looked deserted."

"That might give credence to George's suggestion

that maybe he and his family are on an outing. It is Saturday, you know," Ray said.

"I wish I believed that." Tears filled Jeremy's eyes. "Once when I was visiting them from New York, we were playing Sequence or some other board game, and out of the blue, the conversation turned to men cheating on their wives."

"You think Terry's cheating on his wife?" Ray asked, even though they all knew the answer to that question.

"If he is, I don't know about it. Anyway, Marilee straight out said she'd kill him if he ever cheated on her. Said if she couldn't have him, nobody would." Jeremy tapped his fingers on the side of his pants nervously.

"That doesn't sound good," Lola said.

Jordan had to bite her tongue to keep from informing him that Terry was definitely having an affair with Arizona, and worse yet, Marilee knew it. After confronting the singer at the pool yesterday morning, Terry's wife said she wouldn't stand by and allow any woman to take her man from her, no matter what she had to do to prevent it from happening.

"I'm going up to Waterford's office now to see if he's heard anything. Maybe he'll let me go over the security tapes to see if I can find Terry on one of the screens." Jeremy blew out a long, slow breath. "I have no idea what I'll be looking for, but I can't just sit around and do nothing. Not when my gut tells me that Terry is in trouble."

"Ray's a retired cop, Jeremy. Maybe he could go with you upstairs," George said.

Jeremy turned to Ray. "Would you?"

"Only if Jordan can come with us. She and I need to follow up with the chief on another matter."

"Okay. Can we go now?"

Ray reached for Jordan's arm. "Come on. Hopefully, this won't take too long and we can find out about Arizona."

"What about Arizona?" Jeremy asked, suddenly interested.

"She's missing, too. Jordan was supposed to hook up with her after the show last night for a little girl time. Arizona stood her up."

Jeremy lowered his eyes. "I probably shouldn't tell you this, but I lied earlier. Terry had a thing for Arizona. You don't think the two of them have run off somewhere, do you?"

Jordan shrugged. As far as she knew, only she and her friends knew about the poker chips she'd found in Arizona's room, and she wasn't about to tell Jeremy. Nor was she going to tell him that they were just as worried about Arizona as he was about Terry.

"It's possible, but Arizona went missing last night. You said you talked to Terry this morning, so it's highly unlikely the two of them have run off together." Ray grabbed Jordan's arm. "We'll follow you to the upper level and see if we can get some answers."

"I'd go with you," George said, "but I need to get down to the kitchen to put out any fires they may have." He grinned. "Pun intended."

"I'll call you if we find anything." Jeremy blew George a kiss.

Without acknowledging it, George turned and headed into the casino, leaving Jeremy standing there dejected.

Ray and Jordan followed Jeremy to the concierge desk where he told the man about his dilemma. Before long, they were on their way upstairs and then seated in Waterford's office.

After hearing Jeremy's concerns, Waterford told them that although he hadn't talked to Terry since earlier that morning, he was more inclined to think he was just somewhere without cell coverage and more than likely would show up before the big performance in the concert hall that night. He did agree to look over the security tapes, though, and promised to call Jeremy if he found anything.

When Jeremy turned to leave, Ray said, "You go on. Jordan and I need to talk privately with Waterford."

After Jeremy was gone, Ray faced the security chief. "Any news about the missing band member?"

"Matter of fact, there is. When I talked to Terry this morning before his so-called disappearance, he said Arizona left last night after the show and took the red-eye to California. Said her old boss called and made her an offer she couldn't refuse." He sat down behind the desk. "So, that's one problem solved. Hopefully, Terry will show up, and we can get on with the rest of the weekend."

A look passed between Jordan and Ray before Ray thanked him. They were silent on the ride down the escalator. When they were in the casino, Jordan pulled him aside.

"Now I'm really worried about Arizona."

"You thinking like me—that the story about her was a lie?"

"I know it was a lie." She narrowed her eyes. "Remember that talk I had with her around the pool yesterday?" She didn't wait for his answer. "She told me her boss in Los Angeles was a psychopath who physically abused her so badly that she had to spend over a week in the hospital. She ended up suing him and got a pretty hefty settlement. Then she made sure his name and what he'd done to her got front page coverage in all the LA newspapers. No way he'd offer her a job after that, and absolutely no way she'd go back to him."

"Any idea where she might be?" Ray asked.

"No, but I can tell you, that man up there is lying through his teeth, just like the first time we talked to him."

"He said Terry told him."

"Which is probably another lie. Marilee said Terry was obsessed with Arizona, and according to Jeremy, his brother was thinking about divorcing his wife. I find it hard to believe he'd just nonchalantly tell Waterford that Arizona had gone off to California when he was in love—or at the very least in lust—with her. I think one of them, or possibly both, are definitely hiding something."

"And once again, my question to you is why?"

18

"You're unusually quiet tonight, dear. Is everything all right?" Lola asked when the dessert arrived.

Jordan glanced toward Ray before speaking. "The head of security told us that Arizona went back to California. I just can't quit thinking about that."

"At least it has your mind off Alex and whether or not he's in trouble," Victor said.

"Victor!" Michael exclaimed. "Why would you say something like that, knowing it might upset her all over again?"

Victor turned to Jordan. "Sorry, kiddo. Sometimes my mouth doesn't wait for my brain to catch up."

"Sometimes?" Jordan fired back at her friend. "More like all the time. But I'm not upset. I decided that worrying about Alex isn't helping anything. I thought about calling his mother to see if she's heard back from his handler, but at the last minute, I changed my mind. I know she would have already called if she had. Besides, it's our last night here, and I don't want to be a Debbie Downer."

"That's my girl," Lola said. "Whatever happens, know that we'll be right by your side."

"Thanks, Lola. Let's finish our dessert and gamble for the next two hours before we see The James Brothers in concert. I can't wait to hear them."

"Me too," Rosie said as she grabbed a chair from the table beside them and pulled it over next to Jordan.

"Well, hello, stranger. Are you here to tell us that you can spend some time with us tonight before the concert?" Ray asked.

"I'm all yours for the rest of the trip. As of this moment, my kitchen duties are over. Starting tomorrow, Wild Card Steak and Ribs goes back to its regular menu."

"That's terrific. You get to decide what we all do for the next few hours." Michael gave her shoulder a squeeze. "It's so good to have our Rosie back with us."

"I've always wanted to learn how to play blackjack but never had the opportunity." Rosie patted Jordan's hand. "I'm hoping Jordan and Ray will teach me."

"You bet we will. We'll have you playing like a pro in no time."

"That's great. It will take her mind..." Victor stopped when everyone glared at him. "I mean it will take *your* mind off of all the work you had to do this weekend."

"That it will," Rosie said. "And don't forget, I made a bundle of money doing what I love, so I can afford to lose a little while I learn."

"With Jordan teaching you, that's probably a good thing," Victor teased.

Everyone laughed, even Jordan. "You're such an idiot."

"I know. That's part of my charm." Victor took a bite of his cupcake. "Yum! Eat up. We've got some serious money to win, right, Rosie?"

She high-fived him. "I so missed you all, but I wouldn't trade that experience for anything. Morgan dubbed me an honorary chef and said I could come back anytime and cook with her." She stood up. "Come on. Let's go win some money."

They left the restaurant, all talking at once, and when they reached the center of the casino, Michael, Victor, and Lola went in the directions of the slot machines, and Ray, Rosie, and Jordan found a blackjack table with three empty seats. Ray sat down at the number one spot and Jordan and Rosie took two end ones next to a nice-looking, older gentleman.

The minimum bet at all the tables had changed from five to ten dollars when the after-dinner crowd rolled in. Although, Jordan hated betting that much, she decided what the heck. It was their last night and she was still up about fifty bucks. Plus she was excited to be able to teach Rosie the game. Her only hope was that her friend would walk away a few bucks richer.

The older gentleman pulled out three black, hundred-dollar chips from a man-purse in front of him and placed his bet, before turning toward them. "I'm Pete. You ladies play blackjack often?" Although he spoke to both of them, he kept his eyes on Rosie.

Jordan looked at her friend and swore she had just fluttered her eyelashes at the attractive older man. Somewhere in his late fifties or early sixties, Pete was wearing a Western shirt with a bolo tie around his neck. Jordan knew without even looking at Rosie that she was intrigued.

Then Jordan saw the wedding ring on his left hand and wondered if Rosie knew he was married.

Time to end the conversation.

"Not really. We came here with a friend for the

weekend," Jordan said, hoping that would discourage any further chit chat.

"Me neither. This is probably the first time in over ten years that've I've been to a casino. Usually, I play the slots, but I decided to try my luck at blackjack."

Thankfully, the chatting stopped when the dealer began to deal the first cards. Like before, the first cards were all dealt face down. On the second pass, Ray got a seven while Pete got a six, and Jordan a nine. They all laughed when the dealer dealt Rosie an ace, and she turned over her hidden card to show the blackjack, squealing like she'd just won a new car.

"Beginner's luck," she said when she gathered up her fifteen-dollar winnings.

"Good on you," Jordan said. When the dealer turned over a six, she leaned closer to Rosie and whispered. "Now watch how this plays out."

For the next few minutes, she explained that the likelihood of the dealer busting with a presumed sixteen was high, and that's why everyone at the table whose cards totaled under twelve should stay and not draw another card. They all did, except Pete who ended up drawing a face card to his fifteen and busting. They all cheered when the dealer busted, even Pete, who after reaching into his bag, placed another three hundred dollar bet on the table. Once again, he busted when he ordered another card with a seventeen count.

The next few minutes were played in silence except for Jordan's occasional instructions whispered to Rosie. When the dealer stopped to shuffle the cards, she was up another fifty dollars and Rosie had eighty extra bucks.

"Nice haul," Pete said. "I haven't done so well." Again, he reached into the leather bag and pulled out eight one-hundred-dollar chips and placed them on the table.

Jordan had to bite her tongue to keep from saying he hadn't done so well because he really didn't play so well. Why someone who hadn't played blackjack in over ten years would be willing to part with that kind of cash baffled her. She scolded herself for being so judgmental like she was with Violet on their first night at the casino. It was none of her business how this man wanted to spend his money.

Still, her curiosity nagged at her and she leaned toward Pete. "What do you do for living, if you don't mind me asking?"

"Retired now, but I used to be a schoolteacher." He placed another three black chips on the table for his next bet. "Both my wife and I taught high school kids for over thirty years."

Rosie narrowed her eyes. "Is your wife here with you?"

He shook his head. "She died about ten years ago, God rest her soul. I live with my daughter and her family now."

Jordan saw the sparkle return to Rosie's eyes. A widower who lived with his family, still wore his wedding ring even after his wife had been gone for so many years, and apparently had money, definitely piqued her interest. Throw in a cowboy outfit, and she couldn't resist.

For the next hour, they made small talk while they played.

Then Jordan glanced at her watch and stood. "I'm going to the powder room, Rosie. Play my cards for me."

"Really? You trust me with your money?"

"Absolutely. You're a natural."

Jordan headed toward the restrooms in the center of the casino, thinking how much fun she was having with Rosie and looking forward to the concert. When she came out of the restroom, she noticed Quincy, the man she had met earlier during the Cinco de Mayo celebration outside in the parking lot. He was sitting backwards on the stool at one of the slot machines and staring at the door that led to the upper-level escalators.

When she walked over and touched his shoulder, he jumped. "Sorry. I didn't mean to creep up on you like that. I'm Jordan. Do you remember me from outside earlier?"

"Of course, I do. Who could forget someone as beautiful and kindhearted as you?"

"What are you doing here? Did you hit the jackpot and now you're waiting for someone to come down and cash you out?"

"Nothing like that. I saw my son go through that door about a half-hour ago, and I'm waiting for him to come back out. I have some issues I want to talk over with him."

"You never mentioned you had a son. Does he work here?"

"I don't know." Quincy choked back a cry. "We haven't spoken in over four months. I need to find out if he knows anything about the money the casino owes me."

"Why don't you just walk up there and ask him?"

"Can't." Quincy pointed to the concierge. "I'm almost positive they've all been instructed to keep an eye out for me so I don't harass the CEO again."

"They can't keep you from talking to him, can they?"

"They can, and they will. I'll just have to wait for Jake to come back down."

"Can you say you want to talk to the head of security about a problem?"

"He's probably the one who's keeping me from Santiago, the CEO."

"And you said you have issues with your son?"

"Yeah. Santiago suggested I talk with Jake about a problem with my land sale. He hinted that Jake might be responsible for part of that problem." Quincy lowered his eyes. "I hope it isn't true. I just really need to talk to him and find out, one way or another, even if I have to sit here all night."

"Well, good luck. I hope you're able to get some answers." Jordan started to walk away, then turned back. "I just got an idea. Not sure if it will work, but it's worth a try."

"What is it?"

"I'm going to go over to the concierge and tell him I need to speak to Waterford. He's the security chief that I spoke to earlier. I'm gonna lie and say I have new information about the girl who went missing last night."

"A girl went missing?"

"No time to tell you about that now. Let's see if we can get you up the escalator for a heart to heart with your son."

Quincy raised his eyebrows. "So you'll get up there. How's that gonna help me?"

"Once I get the concierge to open the door, I'll follow him. You be ready and sneak in behind us before the door closes."

Quincy considered that for a few minutes. "You know. That just might work." He chuckled. "Beautiful, kind-hearted and smart. I might have to introduce you to my son, Jake."

"Not sure my FBI guy would take too kindly to that. But I'd love to meet him."

"Then, let's do it."

The plan worked like a charm, and soon Jordan was on her way up the escalator with Quincy right behind her. As soon as they reached the top level, the concierge directed Jordan to Waterford's office, giving Quincy just enough time to slip behind one of the men monitoring the cameras, his back turned away from the path to the escalator.

When the concierge was on his way back to the first level, Jordan quickly pointed toward Waterford's door and waited for Quincy to walk that way.

"That was amazing," he said when he joined her in front of the office marked SECURITY. "Santiago's office is over there." He pointed farther down the hall.

Jordan blew out a breath. "Okay. If you're good now, I'm going to leave and go back downstairs. My friends are probably wondering what happened to me."

"Can't you stay a little longer? I'd really like you to meet my son."

After giving that some thought, she decided a few more minutes wouldn't hurt. Rosie and Ray were probably so busy playing blackjack they didn't even notice she hadn't come back yet.

"Okay, but then I really have to go before my friends call in the SWAT team." She pointed to Waterford's office. "Do you think he's in there?"

"No idea. I don't hear anything."

"My friend mentioned that this entire area up here is sound proofed. I guess the only way to find out if he's there is to march right in and confront him."

"Good idea. If Santiago comes out and catches me out here, there's no doubt that I'll be booted right down the escalator...and thrown out the doors, probably for good."

"Then we'll avoid the CEO's office and just check out this one to see if your son's in there in a meeting with the chief of security." She grabbed the door handle before turning to Quincy. "You stay here just in case Security has been alerted and Waterford recognizes you." She giggled. "I can see your face on one of those Most Wanted posters now. Guess that makes me your partner in crime."

Just as she was about to open the door, there was a commotion around the monitors in the front. When she moved closer and peeked around the corner to see what was going on, she nearly fainted.

Quincy, who was right behind her, almost knocked her over when she stopped abruptly. "What?" he asked, as he steadied her.

"See those men over there?" When he nodded, she whispered. "I think they're bad guys."

Quincy looked at the men, both tall and slender, both wearing dark suits. The older one was barking orders at some poor computer techie, who apparently, wasn't pulling up the video feed fast enough for him.

"Why would you think that? They look like part of the security team to me."

"Most likely, they are, but I had an unpleasant encounter with them yesterday." When he looked confused, she continued, "Do you remember that missing girl I told you about?"

"Yes, but what's that got to do with those two suits?"

"It's a long story, but I was in her room waiting on her when these two thugs came in, apparently to rob her." She shivered. "They both had guns."

When the younger of the two men turned around

to talk to one of the men watching the casino floor through the window on the other side of the room, both she and Quincy quickly backed out of sight.

"Let's go have a talk with the head cop. He'll know how to handle this." He grabbed Jordan's arm. "Follow me."

As quietly as they could, they made their way back to Waterford's office and without knocking, opened the door and walked in. Jordan fully expected the man to scream at them for not making an appointment before they barged in. To her surprise, the room was empty.

"What do we do if those two big slugs come in here?" Jordan asked.

Quincy did a quick scan of the office. "It looks like that closet over in the corner is big enough for both of us to hide in if it becomes necessary. Hopefully, we're worrying about nothing, and those two guys will get what they need from the surveillance feeds and leave."

Just then, they heard a noise and glanced up at the door that was still cracked a little. As a man walked past, they rushed over to the closet to hide, just in case.

Quincy pulled the door open, and both of them jumped back when a man fell forward and landed on the carpet in front of them.

Jordan nearly passed out when she realized she was looking at a very dead Sam Waterford.

19

A horrified look covered Quincy's face. "Who is that?"

Jordan stared at the body, then pointed to the name plate on the desk. "It's Sam Waterford, the security chief." She couldn't take her eyes off the corpse. "I just talked to him this morning."

"About the missing girl you mentioned earlier?"

"Yes, that and another issue. My friend's husband was upset when he couldn't reach his brother, who's the CFO here."

Just then, whoever had walked past the door earlier, walked back toward the front where all the cameras were located. Both of them froze.

When she thought it was safe again, she whispered, "Oh no! Do you think they looked at the screen and saw us come back here?"

"No way of knowing. But just in case they did, we might want to stay out of sight for a while in case whoever did this decides to come back." Quincy bent down and tugged at Waterford's body until he had it back in the closet. Then he closed the door and met her eyes, now widened in fear. "Now what?"

"I don't know. I wish my friend Ray was here. He's an ex-cop and would know exactly what to do."

Quincy walked over to the door and peeked out. "It doesn't look like anyone's in the hall right now. You stay here, and I'll sneak out to the front to see if those two big guys we saw earlier are still out there. Hopefully, they got what they needed and left because we need to find a way to get back downstairs quickly to alert the security guards."

"How can we be sure the security cops aren't involved in the murder?" Jordan asked, moving closer toward the door—and Quincy. "You said yourself those two guys out there looked like part of the casino security."

"I did, didn't I?" Quincy pulled out his phone, then looked down at Jordan. "No coverage with my cell service. Check yours."

Jordan reached into her back pocket, then remembered she'd left her phone back at the blackjack table with Rosie. "I'll use the landline on his desk and see if I can get the operator to call the local cops." She ran back to the desk but even before she got there, she stopped in her tracks. "The wire's been cut." She picked up the phone anyway, hoping the receiver still had enough charge for her to make the call, but it was dead, the battery nowhere in sight. "Whoever did this went to a lot of trouble and thought this out. No doubt this was premeditated."

"Sounds like someone had it in for him."

She was about to walk back over by the door with Quincy when she noticed a folder with her name on it lying in the middle of the desk. "What the..."

Quincy was beside her in a minute. "What is it?"

Jordan pointed to the file. "Why would Waterford have a file on me?"

Quincy picked up the file and opened it. After a moment, he handed it to her. "Apparently, he's been watching you."

"What? I barely knew the guy." She forced herself to look down at the picture of her entering Arizona's room the night before. She squinted in deep thought. "So, if he knew I'd been in the missing woman's room, why didn't he just ask me about it? Why all the secrecy, and why did he tell us she'd gone back to California when I knew she hadn't?"

"I have no idea what you're talking about," Quincy said. "How well did you know this guy?"

"I only talked to him twice. Both times were about the missing woman, like I said. But I can tell you this, there was something screwy about him that made my skin crawl. That, plus he lied straight to my face, and not once but twice."

"A guy like that probably had a lot of enemies, which makes me even more worried that one of them may come back to make sure he's still in the closet." He stepped out into the hallway. "Stay quiet. I'll be back in a flash."

The five minutes it took for Quincy to return seemed like hours to Jordan. The only good thing about the wait was that now that the body was back in the closet, she didn't have to stare down at the lifeless eyes.

She jumped when Quincy appeared suddenly in the doorway.

"Come on. Those two guys are still out there. My guess is that one of them is probably the killer, and I don't think it's a good idea for us to be in here if they decide to come back."

"Okay." She was on her way to the door, then walked back to the desk and picked up the file with the picture of her in it. Off to the side of the desk, she spied Waterford's ID badge on a lanyard and picked that up as well. She held it up for Quincy to see. "We might need this to open doors."

"Good idea. Now, hurry."

Quickly, she followed him down the hallway, away from the front and the possible killers.

Quincy pointed to an office with LUIS SANTIAGO, CEO in bold letters on the door. "Let's go in here." He tried to open the door, but it was locked. Reaching behind him, he grabbed Waterford's ID badge from Jordan.

She held her breath as she watched him insert it into the door, praying that it worked. When it opened, she let out a relieved breath as a little hope returned. Surely, the CEO would be able to get on the horn to call the local police before the bad guys found them.

She rushed past Quincy and walked into the office.

"No," he exclaimed, reaching for her arm and pulling her back toward the door. "Nobody's here, and I can see that his phone line has been cut, too. That tells me we probably don't want to get caught in here, for sure. If whoever killed Waterford took the time to cut off Santiago's phone, they've probably already done something to him—or are planning to. Either way, we need to find another hiding place."

"I just remembered that Jeremy, that's my friend's husband, said his brother has been spending the weekend in a small room behind the wine room. That might be a good place to hide out until help arrives." A frightening thought made her cry out. "What if help doesn't come?"

"Be assured help will come. When your friends realize you haven't gotten back to them, they'll come looking for you."

"They have no idea I'm up here. I only said I was going to the restroom."

Just then they heard a noise, and when Quincy looked out, he turned to her, almost in a panic. "The two big guys just went into Waterford's office. We need to get out of here fast."

Jordan followed him out of Santiago's office and around the corner, until he came to a stop in front of a room with no signage on the door.

"Do you think this is the wine room?" Quincy asked.

"Probably. Use the ID thing, and we'll find out. Hurry, though. Those two guys are terrifying me."

Quincy did as instructed, and the door opened into a huge room with eight or nine rows of metal racks that stood all the way to the ceiling. Each one was loaded with boxes holding what Jordan assumed was wine and liquor.

"There's no good place to hide," Quincy said. "We might be better off back at Santiago's office in the closet."

"No," Jordan said. "There should be a room in the back where Jeremy's brother sleeps when he stays overnight." She headed toward the back and found the room but was disappointed that it was locked.

Grabbing the ID badge out of Quincy's hand, she inserted it and almost cried when it opened into a room about a third of the size of the outer liquor area. It was sparsely furnished with only a small desk, a single bed, and what looked like a small bathroom off to the side. One tiny closet was adjacent to the bed and had a large black trunk with wheels and a handle, similar to a piece of luggage in front of it, and was clearly labeled SERENDIPITY.

The closet was a perfect place to hide.

Before she had time to question why a box that obviously was used to transport the equipment for the casino band was stored in the tiny bedroom, Quincy tapped her on the shoulder. "Come on. Help me move this big box away from the closet in case we need to get in there fast."

He bent down and tried to pick it up and groaned when he couldn't.

"This is probably what the band uses to transport their costumes and gadgets after a show." Jordan reached for the handle. "Here. Try using—" She clapped her hand over her mouth to keep from screaming when she saw a piece of red sequined material hanging out of the side.

"What?" Quincy was beside her in no time. "Are you okay?"

She pointed to the piece of red material peeking out of the trunk. "If I'm correct, we're looking at the dress the lead singer for the casino band wears for her closing number, Tina Turner's "Proud Mary." The singer I'm talking about is the woman that went missing last night."

Quincy looked confused. "Don't jump to conclusions, Jordan. You said it yourself that this was probably used to transport the band's outfits to a safe place instead of keeping them backstage."

Jordan dropped the handle. "I don't think it would be this heavy if it were only clothing."

Quincy frowned. "Are you thinking what *I'm* thinking *you're* thinking?"

Jordan nodded, then touched the lock. "As much as I don't want to open this, I have to find out. Hopefully, we'll find lots of heavy instruments in there."

When she lifted the lid, all her fears were realized as the smell of decomposing flesh hit her nostrils.

Inside the box, still completely clothed in the red shimmering outfit, Arizona Lightfoot lay squished into the black box, staring lifelessly up at her, almost as if she was begging for help. The front of the red dress was dark with what appeared to be dried blood.

Jordan couldn't stop her eyes from tearing up. Arizona Lightfoot had not been the nicest person on the planet, but no one deserved to be murdered and then stuffed into a seven-foot box.

"We might be in a lot more trouble than we thought," Quincy whispered.

"What should we do now?" Jordan asked. "We definitely shouldn't stay..." She stopped when she heard a muffled sound coming from the bathroom.

Quincy put his finger to his lips to silence her. "We need to find some kind of weapon," he whispered.

Jordan scanned the room, but there was nothing they could use until a check of the night stand beside the bed uncovered a half-empty bottle of tequila. "Lame, I know, but it's all we got." She handed the bottle to Quincy. "You lead."

She followed closely behind him as they slowly walked toward the half-opened bathroom door. The muffled sounds grew louder, and when the door was finally opened, Quincy looked inside and gasped.

Sitting on the shower floor with his hands and feet duct-taped was the man Jordan had seen on her very first night at the casino. It was the guy who'd bumped into her in the lobby and then helped her pick up the contents of her purse that had spilled out all across the marble floor. His mouth was taped shut, and dried blood covered one side of his face from a nasty wound above his left eye. The floor was covered with shattered glass, more blood, and puddles of what smelled like liquor.

Quincy rushed over to the man and pulled the tape from his mouth. "Who did this to you?"

"Sam Waterford."

Quincy grabbed a shard of glass and cut through the gray tape on the young man's hands and feet, then reached for his arm to help him stand up. When he stumbled, Jordan grabbed his other arm, and together, they walked out of the bathroom.

When they had the man seated on the edge of the bed, Quincy examined the head wound. "It needs stitches, but otherwise, I think you're okay, thank the Lord."

Jordan saw Quincy's eyes filling up with tears that threatened to overflow. "Do you know this man?" she asked.

"This is my son, Jake."

Quincy's son tried to smile but couldn't quite pull it off. "We've met—well, sort of."

"You said that Waterford did this to you. Why would he do that?" Quincy asked.

Jake's shoulders slumped under his father's questioning gaze. "I have a lot of explaining to do. I'm the reason you're losing your ranch."

Quincy's entire body stiffened. "You? What did you do, son?"

Jake lowered his head and took another deep breath. "I screwed up so badly, I just couldn't get out from under all that money I owed. After several beatings, including one that landed me in the hospital, the loan shark offered me a way out."

"You should have come to me," Quincy said.

"That's just it, Dad. I couldn't, not after I made sure you had lost most of your money. They wanted your land, and you wouldn't budge. I was told if I didn't force your hand, they would kill both of us."

Quincy stepped back from the bed. "You're responsible for what's going on with my ranch? What did you do?"

Tears trickled down Jake's face. "I'm so ashamed. After Mom died, I hated you for not helping me out with money—"

"Get to the point, son. What did you do?"

Jake couldn't look at his father. "I poisoned your cattle so you'd have to sell some land to save the ranch."

"Dammit, son. That was my livelihood."

"I know, but I was desperate. When you agreed to sell the casino 1500 acres, they decided they wanted more. After your lawyer signed off on that deal, I got you liquored up one night and exchanged the paperwork to say you were selling them 2000 acres. You signed without even reading it again."

"Because I trusted you. I can see that was a grave mistake." Quincy paused for a few moments before continuing, "And the casino is the one digging up my backyard?"

Again, Jake lowered his head. "No, Dad, that property belongs to me. Mostly me, I should say. The casino helped me through an off-shore account for a third of the profits. Using a shell corporation, we were able to set up an oil lease and hire the drilling company."

"You're Jubilee Ranch?"

Jake stared down at the floor, unable to meet his father's eyes. "I thought I would make a lot of money with fracking for a few years, then we could use that profit to turn the property back into a productive cattle ranch."

"Your mother must be turning over in her grave right now."

"I know, but I'm going to fix it. I promise. That's why I came to see Waterford today. I told him I was planning to tell you everything. He wasn't real happy with that but laughed and said it was too late. What was done was done, and there was no going back."

"How did you end up in here with your head cracked open?" Jordan asked.

"While I was talking to Waterford, two of his security officers came in with bags of hundred-dollar chips. I knew that the CFO and not the head of security handled all the books and the cash, and when I questioned Waterford about it, two more cops walked in with more bags of chips. I guess it hit me then that Waterford was somehow up to no good."

"How do you know the bags were full of hundred-dollar chips?" Jordan asked.

"Because the cop didn't see me standing in the back of the room and spilled the contents of the bag all over Waterford's desk."

"And you think that's why he did this to you?" Quincy asked.

"Yes. Apparently, he suspected that I was putting it together in my mind, but before he could ask me anything, his phone rang. I could only hear his end of the conversation, but it sounded like he was angry and said he'd be waiting in his office to resolve the issue. That's when he brought me in here and led me into the bathroom. Then he said he'd be back to finish the job and clobbered me with a bottle from the liquor room."

"You said he had bags of hundred-dollar chips." Jordan's mind began to race. "I knew there was something going on. Arizona had some—" She stopped talking when the door opened, and Terry Redding walked in.

"What's going on here?" He did a 360 around the room before focusing on the black box by the closet. "Did you bring that here?"

"No, it was already here and we walked in. There's a dead body in it," Jordan said. "We need to call the local police and let them know about it. Also, we think some of the casino security might be involved in a poker chip scheme."

"What makes you say that?" Terry moved closer to the head of the bed.

"Because Waterford had bags of the chips delivered to him by his security team," Quincy said. "Give me your phone. I'll call the local police now."

Terry reached under the pillow and pulled up something wrapped in a white towel. "That's not gonna happen," he said, as he unwrapped a gun and pointed it directly at Quincy's head.

20

"What the hell are you doing?" Quincy asked.

Terry ignored him and turned to Jake. "What's with that nasty cut on your head?"

"Compliments of your friend, the security chief." He took a step forward but stopped when Terry turned the gun on him.

"Come any closer, and you're a dead man."

"Were you in with Waterford on the poker chip scheme?" Jordan asked, stepping up to stand between Quincy and Jake, hoping she could distract Terry and somehow get the gun out of his hand.

"There was no scheme. It's my job to keep track of all the poker chips in the casino. Waterford has nothing to do with them, so why would you think that?"

"Well, guess what? The guy who was hired to keep all the bad guys in check is probably a bad guy himself," Jordan said. "You already know he's the one responsible for Jake's head wound. My guess is he may even be responsible for the dead body in that trunk over there." She pointed to the black Serendipity band box.

"If there's a dead body in there, why would you

think Waterford had anything to do with it?"

"Because he was planning to kill Jake, too. Who knows what his motive was? Maybe he was having a thing with her and was jealous. And correct me if I'm wrong. I happen to know that Sam Waterford was being investigated in New York City for allegedly stealing from the evidence room. Bet your boss didn't know that when he hired him." Jordan glared at Terry.

The CFO threw back his head and laughed. "Why do you think he was hired in the first place?"

Jordan's eyes widened. "The casino bosses knew he might be a problem and still made him head of security?"

Once again Terry laughed out loud. "They didn't hire him. I did. And to answer your question, I considered his willingness to skirt the law as his best qualification for the job." The smile faded. "Now, back up before I'm forced to hurt one of you."

"You don't want to do that, Terry. You're the last one the cameras picked up coming into the wine room. How do you think it's gonna look if you make good on that threat?" Jordan fired back.

"You've got a point. I'll have to figure something out." He faced Jake. "How do you know these two anyway?"

"Quincy's my father, and I just met Jordan today when they rescued me. Waterford brought me back here at gunpoint, right after he got a phone call that he said was urgent. That's when he knocked me unconscious and apparently taped me up. For sure, he would have come back and finished me off if someone hadn't killed him first."

Terry narrowed his eyes. "How do you know he's dead?"

"Because we saw him in the closet in his office,"

Jordan said. "Now, can you put the gun away so we can call for help?"

Terry considered that for a moment. "Good idea, but first we need to get our stories straight. You said Waterford was probably running some kind of poker chip scam. Do you know how he was doing that?"

"No, but after I found several thousand dollars' worth of chips in Arizona Lightfoot's room last night, I started noticing how many people were betting big at the blackjack table—and playing badly, I might add. I stood behind an elderly woman who I had seen lose a bundle and watched her cash out almost twelve hundred dollars. That got me thinking that something fishy might be going on. I didn't put it together until just now when Jake mentioned the chips he saw in Waterford's office."

He pointed to the black box. "So you think that's what this is all about? That Waterford killed Arizona because of the chips, then brought her here?"

Jordan froze. "How do you know it's Arizona in there? We never mentioned who was in the box."

Terry's facial expression changed into that of a kid who'd just been caught in a lie, then just as quickly, he recovered. "I assumed it was Arizona. You said there was a dead body in there, and since no one has seen her since last night, it was a good guess."

"My gut tells me you killed her," Jake said. "You were so obsessed with her that you couldn't even see straight. You even asked me to pretend like I was the one having a fling with her to keep the heat off you. So what did she do? Break up with you?"

"Think about it. Why would I kill her if I loved her so much?"

"You tell us," Quincy said. "I'll bet you even used the gun you're pointing at us to do her in."

Anger flashed in Terry's eyes. "You don't know crap about anything. I would never kill Arizona." His voice cracked. "I was going to marry her after I divorced Marilee."

"Then who did kill her?" Jordan asked before a wild thought suddenly popped into her head. "It was Marilee, wasn't it? She told me she would never let Arizona steal her man."

Terry looked stunned. "When did you talk to my wife?"

"Yesterday at the pool. I was sitting with Arizona when Marilee confronted her about sleeping with you. Then when I ran into her today, she said she was going to have a 'come to Jesus' talk with your mistress after the show, and this time she'd let her know that continuing with the affair wasn't an option. She wanted her to break things off with you because she said you were too weak to do it yourself."

"Not weak. Like I said, I loved Arizona, and I grieved when Marilee shot...." Immediately, he stopped talking when he realized what he had just said.

Jordan caught her breath. "So, I was right. Marilee did kill her. How did she end up in a box here in your sleeping quarters?"

Terry blew out a breath. "Marilee walked in on Arizona and me in her dressing room. We were going at it hot and heavy. She went all wacko on me and started shouting obscenities, which she's never done before."

"Geez, let me think about that," Jordan said sarcastically. "The woman walks in on her husband and his lover making out, and she starts spewing cuss words. Call me crazy, but I would have done more to you than just hit you with a few swear words."

"She never swears—won't even let me cuss around her or the kids." He put his head down before he continued, "Anyway, before I could calm her down, she pulled out my gun, which she'd apparently gotten from the safe in our bedroom. I didn't even know she knew the combination."

"Is that the same gun in your hand?" Quincy asked.

"She had a look in her eyes that I've never seen before when she pointed the gun at both of us. Then Arizona tried to disarm her, and when I grabbed Marilee's arm to try to take the gun away from her, it went off. Arizona fell to the floor, bleeding like crazy from her chest. I tried to give her CPR, but she was gone." Terry stopped and took another deep breath. "What was I to do? I was between a rock and a hard spot. I have three kids. I couldn't let their mother go to jail because I knew there was no way I could ever raise them on my own. On one hand, I hated my wife for killing the love of my life. On the other, I had to defend her for my kids' sake."

"So you stuck Arizona in that box and brought her up here?" Jordan asked, thinking the longer she could keep him talking, the better their chances were of someone finding them before he killed them.

"Had to. Then I drove Marilee and the kids to her mother's house in Oklahoma City. Told her to take a shower and throw away her clothes in case the cops came around. That way they wouldn't find any gun powder residue on her hands or any of Arizona's DNA on her body. She was a mess and wouldn't stop crying. Her mother thought I had beaten her or something, when in fact, I was the one who had actually saved her from having to face the police. I told her not to mention what went down to anyone. Said if the police questioned me, I would say I was the one who shot Arizona in self-defense." He paused to gauge their reaction.

None of them were buying the good husband story. The man could talk until his lips turned blue, but they all knew he'd only done those things for his own benefit, and no one else's.

"I just got back a few hours ago and planned to wheel the box out of the casino so I could dump it somewhere in the boonies near the Texas border. I figured if the body was ever found, the police would suspect Serendipity's backup singer, who had a thing for Kenny, the drummer—who had a thing for Arizona." He smirked. "Quite a love triangle, don't you think?"

"Sounds like you had a good plan. What went wrong?" Quincy asked.

Terry pointed to Jordan. "You're the one responsible for today's drama."

"Me? What did I do?"

"If you had just left those chips in Arizona's room, none of this would have happened." He lowered his eyes. "Well, Arizona would still be dead, but nobody would know about our poker chip scam."

"Our scam? You were in on it?" Jordan asked.

Terry blew out a puff of breath. "And you thought you were so smart. Who do you think is the brains behind this little operation? Not Waterford, that's for sure. The guy couldn't even steal a few kilos of cocaine from his own police station without getting caught. I'm the one who came up with the idea, and I'm the one who made sure the books didn't reflect the four hundred thousand bucks that we planned to steal from the casino this weekend."

"How did you hook up with Waterford?" Quincy asked. "I would think an investigation into his illegal activities would not be public knowledge, especially to a nobody in Oklahoma."

Terry grinned. "Here's where it pays to know people. My brother Jeremy called me one day and told me about his new boyfriend, then mentioned how said new boyfriend had an uncle who was in trouble with the NYPD for possibly stealing right under their noses. My mind snapped into high gear since I'd already met Arizona when she interviewed for a job about a month before. It was love at first sight, but as we got friendlier, I knew she wouldn't come cheap. Like I said, I was so in love with her, I would have done anything to keep her."

"Seems like you had it all worked out," Jordan, said, thinking she needed to convince Terry they were sympathetic to his predicament.

She knew it was critical to make him believe they'd all collaborate his story and put the blame for the poker chip scheme squarely on Waterford's shoulders and convince the police that one of the band members was responsible for Arizona's death. Pulling off this lie was their only chance of getting out of there alive—if there even was a chance, which looked more doubtful by the minute. At this point, Terry had nothing to lose and might figure his chances were much better if there were no witnesses.

"It was a perfect plan until Waterford got greedy."

Jordan detected a hint of regret in Terry's voice. "You should have realized that a known thief wouldn't change his colors, especially when the reason you hired him was to steal again," she said, unable to hide the sarcasm in her voice.

So much for trying to stay alive.

"I did know that, but like I said, you came along and ruined it for everyone." When Jordan wrinkled her eyebrows, he explained. "Waterford sent his men to Arizona's room to get rid of the evidence so that nobody would get suspicious about why she had that many chips in her possession. When they couldn't find them, Waterford went straight to the video feeds and saw you going into her room. Unfortunately, he also saw me throwing out the clothes in the Serendipity equipment box in back of the stage and shoving Arizona's body into it. The cameras even picked me up in the service elevator when I brought the body up here."

"So now he had something on you," Jordan said, sneaking a peek at her watch and wondering how much longer it would take for someone to notice that she hadn't returned from the restroom and send up a red flag.

"He thought he could make me pay through the nose. Me, the one who brought his thieving self here from New York. His cut for the poker chip thing was twenty percent to my eighty percent since I was the one paying off the people involved, but he insisted I jack it up to a fifty-fifty cut. I stopped by his office today hoping to reason with him before I moved Arizona's body."

For the first time Jordan understood how this had all played out. "You're the one who killed him and shoved him into his closet, right?"

"Had to, and unfortunately, I've said too much already. I can't take the chance of any of you repeating what I've just said to the police. I'm thinking I'll say Waterford killed all of you when you discovered his poker chip scheme, and that I killed Waterford when he tried to kill me as well." He turned to Quincy. "Let's start with you, old man."

Quincy moved toward Terry to try to grab the

weapon, but just before the gun went off, Jake stepped between them. With a look of disbelief in his eyes, the younger Parnell crumpled to the floor, blood pouring from a shoulder wound. For a minute, Terry seemed stunned that it was Jake on the ground, and Quincy lunged for the gun, knocking it out of Terry's grasp. The weapon clattered to the floor, Jordan scrambling for it as Quincy bent down to give aid to his wounded son.

She beat Terry to the pistol, then aimed it right at him. "Back up, or you're gonna join your lover in that box." She was surprised at how in control she felt all of a sudden. It was a given that the weapon in her hand had a lot to do with her new-found bravado.

Just then there was a commotion coming from the wine room. No one spoke for fear that it might be Waterford's men coming to finish the job Terry had started.

They stood silently, holding their collective breath, as the door to Terry's room slowly opened. Jordan aimed the gun in that direction, hoping she could fire it if she had to.

When she recognized one of the voices, she ran toward the door. She got there just as it swung open, and she came face to face with Ray.

"Oh my God! You have no idea how good you look right now."

"The feeling's mutual," Ray said as he took the gun out of her hand. "When you didn't come back to the blackjack table, Rosie and I went looking for you, and when we didn't find you, we recruited the entire gang for a manhunt. We were so worried and assumed the worst had happened to you. Rosie and Lola wouldn't stop crying, and even Victor was bawling like a baby."

"It's a long story," Jordan said. "One I'll tell you

later when we're with the others. Right now, we need to deal with bigger things." She pointed to the Serendipity box. "Arizona's in there."

"Who killed her?" Ray moved aside so the police officer behind him could get a better look.

Jordan glanced at Quincy, and he nodded his head slightly, almost as a signal that he knew what she about to say and that he gave his approval. "He did." She pointed to Terry. "He also killed Waterford and was planning on killing us, too."

"Waterford's dead?"

"You'll find his body in the closet in his office. Forensics will also prove that the bullets that killed him and Arizona came from the same gun—the one in your hand right now."

"Sonny, call 911." Quincy barked the order to the officer from his position kneeling next to Jake on the floor. He grabbed a pillow from the bed and used the case to put pressure on his son's shoulder wound. "Jake's been shot, and although I don't think his wound is life-threatening, he's lost a lot of blood. The sooner we get him to the hospital, the better his chances are of making a full recovery."

Jake was conscious now and tried to sit up. Quincy put his hand on his chest and gently pushed him back down. "Be as still as you can, son. Help will be here soon."

Jordan studied the police officer, wondering how Quincy knew his name. Since he was wearing a uniform and not the suits that the security cops wore, she figured he must be from the local police station.

"Is that ambulance on the way?" Quincy asked, impatiently.

The man Quincy had called Sonny checked his

watch. "It should be here any minute, Quincy. Keep holding the pillowcase tightly against the wound."

So they did know each other. That was comforting to Jordan, and she felt her body relax a little.

Ray saw Jordan staring at the officer and explained, "This is Sheriff Peterson from Encenada. I called him when we couldn't find you."

The officer walked behind Terry and ordered him to put his hands behind his back. When he was handcuffed, he glanced down at Quincy. "Do I even want to know how you got involved in all this?"

"That's a story for later. Right now, all I care about is getting Jake to the hospital."

"Okay. I'll come by the hospital to interview both of you after we take care of business here." Peterson frowned. "There hasn't ever been a double homicide since I've been sheriff, and the only murder we've had in the entire county since I was elected was when old man Williams shot a man trying to steal his horses. I may need to call in more experienced officers."

"Don't use the casino security force," Jordan warned. "Terry was running a poker chip scheme with Waterford before he killed him. I'm positive that at least two security cops, and probably more, are in on it."

"I knew it!" Ray exclaimed. "I didn't trust Waterford from the minute I laid eyes on him. Thankfully, once a cop, always a cop, and my instincts kicked in when we couldn't find you. I knew Waterford lied to us about the poker chips you found, and I worried that he'd done something to you, so I called the local authorities instead of using the casino security team. Glad I did."

"A poker chip scheme. I believe that would make

this a federal offense, and I should be able to get the Feds in here to help." Peterson looked relieved.

"Did Waterford figure out you had Arizona's chips?" Ray asked Jordan.

"Yeah, but that's not why I'm here. I came with Quincy to confront the CEO about money he was owed for the sale of his land to the casino."

"And how do you know Quincy?" Ray asked.

"Another long story," Quincy said just as two EMTs wheeled a gurney into the small room and went to work on Jake. When they had him strapped on the gurney with an IV running wide open into his arm, they headed for the door.

"I'm going with him," Quincy said, his voice daring either of the two medical technicians to say no.

When Jake was on his way downstairs and to the ambulance, the sheriff opened the door wide and said, "I'll need you all to step into the outer area. This room is now a crime scene, and the forensic team is on the way."

When they were all in the other room, the sheriff closed the door. Before he could ask any questions, Jordan faced Ray. "So how did you find me?"

"It wasn't easy. After we looked everywhere we thought you could have gone, and there was no sign of you anywhere, I knew I had to get help. Like I said, I called in the local police since I didn't trust the casino cops. It was a good decision since I needed the sheriff here to help me get a look at the video feeds to figure out where you were. I knew they wouldn't just hand them over to me, but when he arrived, they refused him as well, citing client privacy."

"Yeah, like we gave a good horse's butt about client privacy at this point," Peterson added. "I let them know in no uncertain terms, that unless I was granted access to their feeds, I would evacuate the entire casino and begin a room-to-room search for the missing woman."

"That freaked them out, and they put in a call to the CEO, who quickly instructed them to allow us access." Ray glanced at the sheriff. "That was good thinking, by the way." He focused back on Jordan. "We sped through the video feeds from all over the casino before we saw you going into the wine room with a man behind you. At first, I thought it was someone who had abducted you, but Sheriff Peterson recognized his friend almost immediately."

"I was only helping Quincy out." She held back the part about lying to the concierge to trick him into letting her and Quincy up to the second level to see Santiago. "Since we also didn't trust the casino security, we decided we needed to find a good hiding place after we found Waterford's body."

For the next hour, Jordan answered so many questions, she thought she'd lose her voice. Although she didn't outright lie about how Arizona was killed, she didn't offer up the truth that Marilee was the one who had brought the gun to the casino and was the one holding it when it went off. Terry had said that both he and Arizona lunged for it, so hopefully, if there was video it wouldn't prove beyond a reasonable doubt who had actually fired the gun. Jordan felt sure that was a moot point since there probably wasn't a video at all. Terry had said that Marilee had confronted him and Arizona in her dressing room, and more than likely there wouldn't be cameras in there, anyway.

Although Jordan felt a little guilty about withholding that information, she felt it was the right thing to do. Even if Terry changed his mind and pinned the singer's death on his wife, it would be his word against hers. He'd already instructed her on what to say to the cops so they wouldn't arrest her.

Jordan felt a wave of sadness wash over her. Despite the fact that Terry Redding was actually a cheating scum-bag and was going to divorce her and marry his mistress, Marilee still loved the guy. She and her children would suffer enough with Terry in prison, so why make it worse for them? Why should the innocent kids end up without a father *and* a mother because their father was unfaithful? If she was wrong about her decision not to implicate Marilee, she'd have to live with it.

"You OK?" Ray asked when the police were done questioning her.

"Yes. All I want to do now is go to bed. When I wake up tomorrow, it will probably hit me hard that I almost died tonight."

Ray reached for her hand. "No worries, princess. You're like a cat with nine lives, and according to my count, you have more than a few left."

She rewarded him with a smile then linked her arm in his. Together, they walked out to the front and down the escalator, where the entire gang, including George, was there to greet her.

"Holy crap, Jordan," Victor said, with tears still running down his face. "You made us miss the James Brothers."

Ordinarily, Jordan would have fired back some insult to her best friend, but she was so glad to see him, she grabbed him and hung on for dear life.

"Geez! I can't wait to hear what happened to make you ignore my obnoxious remark and give me a hug."

She shook her head. "Not today. I love you all, but right now, I've got a date with my bed. Tomorrow is soon enough."

21

Jordan was awakened by a knock at the door. Rubbing the sleep out of her eyes, she sat up in bed and watched Rosie throw on a robe and walk to the door. When she returned, she had a tray of food and placed it across Jordan's lap.

"Here you go, sweetie. Thought you deserved a little pampering after all you went through last night."

Jordan rubbed her hands together, anticipation covering her face. "You're a doll. You know how much I love breakfast in bed." When she lifted the cover from the plate, she saw a huge cinnamon bun and an equally huge piece of chocolate cake.

"I know that Hostess HoHos are your drug of choice for just about everything, but they didn't have any in the kitchen. George came to the rescue and had Megan make a version of it with a recipe he got off the internet. She calls the creation a Wild Card HoHo cake."

Rosie poured a cup of strong coffee for herself and one for Jordan. "Be careful not to spill it. It's really hot."

"I truly don't know what I would do without you and the rest of the gang. I will never stop counting my blessings for that day when I blew into Ranchero, beaten down by rejection with no place else to go. That was when I met all of you, and you welcomed me with open arms. I still consider that as the luckiest day of my life."

"Aw, honey that was our blessing, too." Rosie's face turned serious. "I can't believe we almost lost you last night."

"Ray told you all about Terry and Waterford?"

"A little," Rosie said. "We're meeting everyone at lunch today before we head back to Ranchero, and he said you'd fill us in on all the details then."

"That's good. Then I'll only have to tell what happened one time. After that I can work on trying to forget about it." She finished the last bite of chocolate cake, then licked her lips. "Morgan could give Hostess a run for their money. She's hit a home run with this cake. I swear it tastes just like my HoHos."

Rosie looked pleased. "That was her primary goal, but she's so talented, I knew she wouldn't let you down."

When Jordan finished the last of her cinnamon roll, she took one final drink of the coffee before she pushed the tray away. "I think I'll take a shower and get ready for the day."

"Oh no, you don't. We're not meeting up with the rest of the guys for a few hours. I'm gonna use all that time to pamper you before we have to pack up to go home." She picked up Jordan's tray and set it outside the door.

When she returned, Jordan had already climbed back underneath the covers. "You've convinced me. Another hour of sleep sounds fantastic since I have a feeling today is going to be hectic."

"Good idea." Rosie crawled in beside her. "Another

hour is just what we both need. I'm so used to getting up early to prepare for the day's menu, I almost forgot how much I enjoy sleeping in."

"I love you, Rosie," Jordan said before she closed her eyes.

"Back at you, kiddo. Now get some sleep."

~

At exactly one o'clock, Jordan and Rosie got off the elevator on the first floor and couldn't believe it when they saw the long lines of people waiting to check out.

"Guess news about the murders traveled fast," Jordan deadpanned.

Rosie grabbed her arm as they maneuvered their way around the crowd and headed for the restaurant. The rest of the gang was already there when they arrived, and Victor rushed over to give her a bear hug.

"You're squeezing me to death, you big dork," she said. When he released his grip on her, she swiped at a lone tear that had made its way down his cheek. "Seriously, I'm okay, dude. I need the sarcastic Victor back to make me laugh, though."

He tried to smile and almost accomplished it before his lower lip quivered and he fought to control his emotions. "That can be arranged, girlfriend, but don't yell at me when I overdo it."

She reached for his hand. "Like that would be a new thing. You always overdo it."

The gang laughed, and everyone relaxed a little. "What's on the menu for lunch? Rosie didn't feed me, and I'm starving." She sat down and wiggled her brows comically at her roommate.

"We're back to the regular menu," George said when he appeared out of nowhere and pulled up a chair at the table. "Rumor has it that Morgan has cooked a chocolate cake just for you, Jordan."

"Already had a piece," Jordan said. "And I can tell you it was excellent. My compliments to the chef."

"So you lied about Rosie not feeding you? Why am I not surprised?" Victor asked.

"He's back," Rosie said. "No more Mr. Nice Guy."

"Hush, Rosie," Victor said, making at face at her. "Your sense of humor, or lack thereof, can't dampen my expectations for that chocolate cake, but first I want the biggest cheeseburger they have along with a plate of crispy French fries covered in cheese. I'm ready for some high-carb American food."

Michael started to comment, but after Victor shot him a look, he closed his mouth. "I'll have that as well," he said, prompting Victor to blow him an imaginary kiss.

"Me too," Jordan said. "Let's eat first, and then I'll tell you all about last night over dessert."

After they had all ordered, George patted Jordan's hand. "You're my new hero, you know that?"

Jordan tried to keep her emotions in check. "Thanks, George. You all can't even imagine how happy I was to see Ray's face when he—"

"What's going on, George?"

They all looked up to see Jeremy beside the table, staring down at George, his face scrunched in anger.

"Hello, Jeremy. I would invite you to sit down, but as you can see, there's no room."

"I guess you know that Rafael was fired," Jeremy said. "He's my friend, the singer from one of the bands here. Santiago sent him a text saying you had something to do with it. Why would you do that?"

"You heard correctly. I definitely did have something to do with it," George said. "And the reason was because I felt like his qualifications for the job should have been more about his talent, instead of who he was sleeping with."

Jeremy's eyes widened in surprise. "You know?"

"I've known for a while. I also know that you've been seeing him as far back as a few months ago in New York and lied right to my face when I asked you about it." He reached for his iced tea and took a long drink while Jeremy stood silently waiting for an explanation.

When one didn't come, Jeremy said, "He's going back to New York, hoping he can get his old job back."

"That's probably a good idea," George said. "You should consider doing that yourself."

"What do you mean?" Jerry face showed his surprise. "I'm staying here to run the restaurant after you leave tomorrow."

"First of all, I'm leaving tonight. I miss Henri, and I can't wait another day to be with him. Secondly, you most certainly are not going to run the restaurant when I leave. I agreed to sell it to Morgan, and she wants no part of you working here. So, I'm delighted to say that as of this moment, you're fired."

Stunned by those words, Jeremy just stared, apparently unable to believe this was happening.

When he turned to go, George said, "Oh, and by the way, my lawyer will get in touch with you sometime this week to talk about the divorce."

Jeremy turned back and pleaded with his eyes. "We can work this out, George. Rafael was just a fling."

George's eyes filled with contempt. "Save it. We're through. When you find another place to live, text me the address, and I'll have your things sent over. And Jeremy, don't even think about joint custody of Henri." He turned back to the people around the table, totally dismissing his ex. After Jeremy walked out of the restaurant he sucked in a deep breath. "That felt good."

"I'm so sorry, George," Jordan said. "I know even though it's probably the right thing for you to do, it still must hurt."

George waved his hand, dismissively. "Enough about me. Now tell us all about what happened to you last night."

Just then the food arrived, and for the next fifteen minutes, nothing more was said about Jordan's escapade. As they waited for their dessert, she began to talk. For the next thirty minutes, she told them everything about her scary night, pausing only to scarf down the chocolate cake.

"You never told us how you met Quincy in the first place, honey," Lola said.

"Remember when I left you all at the dog race to answer Alex's mother's call?" When Lola nodded, she continued. "Quincy saw me crying and sat down next to me to comfort me."

"I like him already," Michael said.

"He's the best," Jordan responded. "When I saw him at the casino trying to figure out how to get upstairs, I had to help. And that's how it all began."

"Sheesh! Who would've thought that Terry Redding, who I had pegged early on as a Casper Milquetoast kind of guy, is actually a killer," Lola said, before turning to George. "And what's with you selling the restaurant, my friend. You love this place."

"I do, but after all that's happened this weekend, I realized that I don't need any more excuses for not spending more time with my son. Chez Luí keeps me busy enough already, and truthfully, I only agreed to open a restaurant when Jeremy begged me. I now know his real motivation for the ask."

"So Morgan will run the place?"

"Yes, but I have more news. The casino's corporate office executives flew in late last night and promptly fired Santiago. Even though he didn't do anything illegal, they decided as CEO, he was responsible for hiring both Terry and Waterford and had to bear some responsibility. The Feds also arrived, and it didn't take them long to officially arrest Terry for the three murders."

"Three murders. Who else besides Arizona and Waterford did he kill?"

"Well, they can't prove it yet, but when the autopsy of an elderly woman who they initially believed had fallen in her room and fractured her skull showed that she'd been drugged, Terry became their primary suspect."

"Why would Terry want Violet dead?"

"You knew her?" George asked.

"Not really, but I sat next to her at the table, and I can verify that she lost a boatload of money," Jordan said before asking, "She seemed like a really nice lady. Why in the world would Terry want to kill her?" Jordan repeated.

George leaned in and lowered his voice. "I'm not supposed to know this and definitely shouldn't be telling you, but one of the good security cops told me that apparently, the woman was one of the forty or so elderly people, all on social security, that Waterford hired for his scheme to steal large amounts of money from the casino. He supplied them with thousands of dollars in chips to gamble with. They were supposed to gamble a little, then cash in the rest of the chips and bring the money to him. With Terry cooking the books, no one would be the wiser."

"But why kill her?" Jordan probed.

"Apparently, your sweet Violet decided that what she did for them was so important that they should double what they were paying her. Threatened to call the cops if they refused. They were already thinking about cutting her loose because she was losing way more than she was supposed to."

"I knew it!" Jordan exclaimed. "I saw her lose a ton of money then cash out for nearly eight grand at the cashier's window."

"A pretty good scheme if they could have gotten away with it. They'd use nine or ten people in the morning and a new set of nine or ten in the evening. They expected to make—I should say steal—close to two-hundred thousand dollars every night this weekend."

"Wow! The plot thickens," Victor said.

"Indeed, it does, my friend. Now that the Feds have opened up a full-fledged investigation into nearly all the security team here, they're closing down the casino for as long as it takes to find answers. I was told the corporate guys are okay with that since it will take at least a month to bring in a new CEO, CFO, and an entirely new security force to take over here," George said.

"We saw all the people checking out," Rosie said. "The lobby is a real madhouse right now."

"I know, but you'll be glad to know that I cleared it with the concierge so that you all are good to go. No standing in line."

"Thanks. That's a relief," Rosie said. "What about you? You're heading out today as well?"

"I'm booked on a flight tonight back to New York.

That will give me enough time today to oversee the transfer of the restaurant to Morgan. She's going to do a good job."

"So that means we won't be seeing you around these parts anymore?" Victor asked.

"Not as a restaurant owner, but I'm sure I'll drop by Ranchero every so often. Good friends like you are hard to come by. Plus, one of these days after my life settles down, I'm going to bring you all to New York to see how the other half of the world lives."

"Sounds terrific," Rosie said. "I guess this is goodbye then."

"For now." He stood up. "I've got a lot to do before tonight, so I'll be in touch."

When he was gone, Ray glanced at his watch. "It's two thirty. We wanted to be on our way to Ranchero by four. Can we make it?"

"Yes, but I, for one, have some packing to do. I'll see you all in the lobby at four," Victor said.

"Ray, do you think we can make a quick stop at the hospital in town so I can run in and check on Jake and say goodbye to Quincy?" Jordan asked.

"Absolutely. I feel like we owe him a lot for taking care of you."

They met in the lobby right at the scheduled time and packed up the Suburban when Ray drove up to the front door. By then, most of the casino customers had already checked out and the parking lot was only half-full. Using the GPS, Ray drove to Ensenada General Hospital, and the gang waited in the car while Jordan ran inside.

After getting Jake's room number from the woman at the front desk, she got on the elevator to the fifth floor. As soon as she knocked on the door to his room, Quincy opened it and hugged her.

"How's Jake?"

"Ask him yourself."

She walked over to the bed and checked him out. He had an oxygen tube in his nose and an IV running into his arm, but otherwise, he looked good. He gave her a half-smile.

Quincy pulled a chair over by the bed next to his, and she sat down. "I can't stay long. Everyone is outside waiting in the car, and we want to get home before dark."

"I'm glad you stopped by. It gives me a chance to say how grateful I am that I met you yesterday. My entire life has changed in one day."

"For the better, I hope."

"Definitely." Quincy patted Jake's hand. "He and I had a long talk this morning after they pumped two units of blood into him. We're going to get my lawyer to file a lawsuit against the casino, saying Jake was being threatened and I was incapacitated when I signed the contract, thereby making it invalid."

"And you'll get your land back?"

"Hopefully, but I decided I really don't need that much land. I'm an old man now and after last night, I'm ready to enjoy the little time I have left on this earth and renew my relationship with my son."

"Quincy, that's great news."

"Jake and I are going to let them continue with the drilling long enough to build a nest egg for the future. I'm pretty sure the casino will make another offer to buy my land for the golf course, but this time it will be on my terms."

"So you can go into the cattle business again?"

Quincy looked at his son and grinned. "Jake has loved horses all his life. I've decided that I'll have a head of cattle—just enough to help with the bills—and

Jake will have his horses. He's agreed to move back home until we can build him his own place on the property. Eventually, the cattle ranch will be known for the horses that Jake will train rather than for cattle." He gave a thumbs up to his son. "And maybe we'll have a few little Jakes running around and keeping me entertained."

"That's great." Jordan stood up. "I have to go, but here's my number. Call me anytime."

"I've already checked out the local AA meetings. I'll need a clear head to help Jake eventually take over the reins." Quincy reached for the note and then, with watery eyes, he said, "Thanks again, Jordan. I will never forget you."

"Nor will I forget you." She waved goodbye and headed to the car to begin the drive back to Ranchero. She felt happy and sad at the same time. Happy for Quincy and still a little sad for George.

~

LIFE IN RANCHERO seemed to go on as usual, but not for Jordan. A week had gone by since they'd returned from Oklahoma, and she still hadn't heard a word about Alex. She'd broken down and called his mother several times, but there was no new information.

On Friday that week, the gang was meeting to continue the weekly game night and potluck dinner at Rosie's. They were all there when she arrived with Max, who made the rounds with wet sloppy kisses before he plopped down on the couch next to her. Everyone steered clear of any mention of Alex, knowing it would only remind her that he might be hurt–or worse–somewhere and unable to get to a phone.

Tonight, instead of Rosie cooking, they decided to order pizza, and when the doorbell rang, Jordan assumed it was the delivery guy. Rosie ran to the door, and screamed, calling Jordan's name.

When Jordan saw who was at the door, she was unable to stop the tears. "Alex, I was so worried about you. I thought—"

He grabbed her and kissed the top of her head. "Come here. The time for talking about what each of us has been through will come later. Right now, all I want to do is hold you."

"You know about the murders at the casino?"

"My mom told me that when Victor called to ask about me, he told her what happened to you." Alex held her at arm's length and stared into her eyes. "I can't believe I almost lost you."

Then he dropped down onto one knee. "I just got into town today and came right here. I wanted to surprise you, but I had no time to go shopping." He reached for her hand. "Jordan McAllister, I can't even imagine life without you. Will you make me the happiest man in the world and marry me?"

Jordan was so overwhelmed, she couldn't even speak for a few minutes. When she found her voice, she said, "Yes, but don't ever scare me like that again."

He stood up and grabbed both her arms. "You'll be happy to know that I turned in my resignation this morning, fully expecting to leave the FBI, but they made me an offer I couldn't refuse."

"What kind of offer?" Victor asked, moving over to stand next to Jordan.

"You're looking at the new liaison between the Dallas Police Department and the FBI office. Rocco will be my assistant, and we'll coordinate any investigation that involves both agencies."

"And no more undercover for either of you?" Jordan's eyes pleaded with him to say that part of his life was over.

"No more. The good news is they've given us a month to recover from our ordeal. So, my lady, you and I are going ring shopping, and then I'm going to book us on the next flight to Hawaii. We both need a vacation."

"I wanna go," Victor whined.

"Oh no," Jordan said. "I love you, but you're the third wheel here, and only two of us are getting on that plane."

Everyone laughed while he pouted. When the pizza came, they all pigged out and were about to enjoy Rosie's version of the HoHo cake when Jordan's phone rang.

"Hey Mom, what's up?" she answered, excited about telling her mom that she was now engaged. Her mother loved Alex and would be just as happy as she was that he was going to be part of the family.

"Danny's in trouble."

"What kind of trouble?" By now the entire gang had formed a circle around her and waited for an explanation. *My brother*, she mouthed.

Sylvia McAllister's voice cracked. "Apparently, he got a little tipsy at the cowboy honky-tonk on the outskirts of town and met up with a woman that he brought back to his apartment."

"That's not unusual for Danny," Jordan said, remembering his reputation as a big party guy.

"I know, but this morning, when he woke up beside her, she was covered in blood with a steak knife in her chest. He tried to revive her, but she was already dead."

"Oh my God! What did he do?"

"He called the police, but he couldn't remember anything beyond dancing the Texas two-step with her at the bar. Because his DNA was all over the woman and the knife that he'd pulled out of her when he attempted CPR, the police arrested him and threw him in jail. Your father is still in London on business, and I didn't know where to turn. Your brothers are down at the police station now trying to get Danny released on bail."

"Oh, Mom, that's awful. What can I do to help?"

There was silence on the other end before Sylvia McAllister responded. "I hate to ask this, especially after what you've been through, Jordan, but I need you here. You've always been able to calm your brothers down, and right now I'm worried that with their tempers, all three of them are going to end up in jail with Danny."

Jordan glanced toward Alex, seeing the beaches of Hawaii fading away in her mind. But it didn't matter. This was Danny, the brother she adored.

"Give me tomorrow to clear this with my boss and see if I can work from there. I should be able to be there either Sunday or Monday."

Her mother's voice cracked. "I knew I could count on you."

Jordan hung up, then faced Alex. "We're going to have to delay our Hawaii trip for now. Danny's in trouble, and my mom needs me."

"So you're going back to your hometown?" Victor asked.

"It's Danny. I have to. I'll leave for Amarillo as soon as I can talk to my boss about it."

"I'm going with you," Alex said. "Maybe I can be of some help to him."

"You don't know how happy that makes me. Danny's accused of murder, and we could use your expertise."

"Murder? Then I'm coming, too," Ray said. "I still have some expertise left in me, as well."

"Me too," Rosie and Lola both said at the same time. "No expertise to speak of, but we can definitely be there to support you," Rosie added.

"You all can't go without me," Victor said. "My antique shop will do just fine if I'm gone for a few days."

"I'll try to make arrangements with the radio station, but I can't promise anything." Michael said, his face showing his regret.

"It's okay, Michael. Victor will make sure I don't get into trouble." She surveyed her friends, noticing the love on every one of their faces. "Okay, then. We'll head to Amarillo as soon as we can. Since my brothers are all married except for Danny, you all can stay at my parents' house. There are four empty bedrooms, and my mom will love the company."

"Road trip to Amarillo, nicknamed The Yellow Rose of Texas," Victor said, gleefully, until he saw Jordan's face. "Oh, sorry. I know you're worried about your brother, but honestly, with Alex and Ray on the case, what kind of trouble could you possibly get into?"

"Hello," Alex said, with a grin. "Have you met my fiancé?"

BLACKBERRY PEACH MARGARITAS (4 LARGE OR 6 SMALL)

Compliments of https://suebeehomemaker.com/about-me/

For the Blackberry Margaritas

4 ounces tequila

2 ounces orange liquor

3 ounces fresh lime juice

1 ounce simple sugar - more if you like a sweeter drink. (Buy a bottle or see recipe below)

2 cups frozen blackberries

3 cups ice cubes

For the Peach Margaritas

4 ounces tequila

2 ounces orange liquor

3 ounces fresh lime juice

1 ounce simple sugar - more if you like a sweeter drink. (Buy a bottle or see recipe below)

2 cups frozen peaches

3 cups ice cubes

To Serve

Additional simple sugar optional

Kosher salt to line the rims or use store-bought margarita salt

Fresh lime wedges

Fresh blackberries

Well in advance, make a quick simple sugar syrup by combining an equal amount of sugar and water in a small saucepan. Bring to a boil and then simmer until sugar is dissolved. Store in the refrigerator to cool.

Prepare 4 large or 6 small margarita glasses by rubbing lime along the rims and dipping them in a bowl of kosher salt/lime zest (or use store bought margarita salt.)

Squeeze limes to make 6 ounces of lime juice.

Place all ingredients for the blackberry margaritas in a blender. Puree until smooth. Pour into prepared glasses so that half the glass is full.

Rinse blender and place all ingredients for the peach margaritas in the blender. Puree until smooth. Pour on top of the blackberry margaritas.

Serve with fresh blackberries and a lime wedge.

To prepare the margaritas in advance, you can store the blackberry margaritas in a container and the peach ones in a separate container. Keep them in the freezer. At party time, remove from freezer and spoon into glasses. Let them sit for a few minutes to make them on the slushy side.

JALAPEÑO POPPER DIP

Dip

2 (8 ounce) cream cheese softened

1 cup of mayonnaise (not Miracle Whip)

1 cup of Mexican blend grated cheese (Monterrey Jack and Cheddar)

2 cans (4 ounces) chopped green chilies

1 can (4 ounces) chopped jalapeño peppers (See instructions.)

1 cup grated Parmesan cheese (in bag not can)

Topping

4 tablespoons butter, melted

1 cup Panko bread crumbs

½ cup grated Parmesan cheese (in bag not can)

Preheat oven to 375° F. Mix first 6 ingredients in a food processor. Add the diced jalapenos a little at a time to get as spicy as you like. I use less. Pour into a 9 X 13 inch baking dish. Mix the melted butter with the other two ingredients and spread on top of the dip mixture.

Bake for 35-40 minutes until cheese is bubbly. Serve hot with tortilla chips or crackers.

Fajita Seasoning

2 teaspoons chili powder

1 teaspoon paprika
½ teaspoon ground cumin
½ teaspoon garlic powder
½ teaspoon onion powder
1 teaspoon dried oregano
1 teaspoon salt
1 teaspoon sugar
¼ teaspoon cayenne pepper

In a small bowl, combine all the ingredients. Use as needed (2 tablespoons per recipe.)

You can double this recipe but remember to store in an air-tight container in a cool, dry area in the pantry or on a shelf in the kitchen that doesn't get too warm. This will keep for up to 6 months.

SPICY GREEN ENCHILADAS

Serves 10

½ cup salted butter
    ½ all-purpose flour
    4 cups chicken broth
    1 (16 ounce) sour cream
    4 tablespoons diced jalapeños (or you can use fresh chopped jalapeños.)
    15 (6 inch) corn tortillas
    2 cups chicken, cooked and shredded (use crock pot chicken or rotisserie)
    4 cups grated Monterey Jack and Colby cheese mix
    ¾ cup onion chopped and sautéed in 3 tablespoons of butter.

Preheat oven to 400° F. Lightly grease a 9 X 13 inch baking dish. Melt butter in a large saucepan over medium heat and add flour slowly, stirring until smooth. Cook 1 minute, stirring constantly. Gradually add broth and cook, stirring constantly until thickened and bubbly.

Remove from heat and stir in sour cream and jalapeños.

Mix shredded chicken with 3 cups of cheese and sautéed onions in a large bowl.

Pour ⅓ of the sour cream mixture into prepared baking dish: set dish aside.

Heat tortillas in the microwave for approximately 30 seconds (5 at a time)

Spoon 2-3 tablespoons of chicken mixture down the center of each tortilla, Roll tortilla up and place seam down in prepared dish. Pour remaining sour cream mixture over the enchiladas.

Bake in preheated oven for 25 minutes. Sprinkle remaining cheese on top and bake an additional 3-4 minute or until cheese melts. (I always add more because I'm a cheese addict.)

For cheese enchiladas, use 5-6 cups shredded cheddar cheese instead of the chicken.

For beef enchiladas, cook and stir 2 pounds of ground beef. Drain grease. Use 2 packages of taco seasoning and cook as directed. Use this mixture instead of the chicken.

CROCK-POT SHREDDED CHICKEN

3 pounds chicken breasts (about 4 large breasts)
    1 cup chicken broth
    1 teaspoon salt
    1 teaspoon pepper
    1 teaspoon garlic powder
    1 teaspoon onion powder

Place chicken breasts in the bottom of crock pot.

Pour chicken broth and seasonings over chicken.

Cook on low for 6-8 hours or high for 3-4 hours.

Remove chicken from crock-pot and shred with two forks. Add

BBQ sauce to any leftovers for yummy BBQ sandwiches.

Spicy Spanish Rice

Serves 6-8

4 strips bacon (Reserve the bacon grease)
    1 tablespoon butter
    1 onion, finely chopped
    1 small green pepper, finely chopped
    2 cloves garlic, minced
    1 (10 ounce) can Ro-tel brand original diced tomatoes and green chilis, drained (or hot if you prefer)

2 (4 ounce) cans diced green chilies
1 cup chicken broth
1 cup long grain rice

Fry the bacon in a skillet until crispy. Remove from heat, drain the strips on a plate with a paper towel, then crumble and set aside. Reserve the bacon grease in the skillet.

Melt the butter in the skillet with the reserved bacon grease and add the onion, green peppers and garlic and sauté until the onions are translucent.

Add the Ro-tels, green chilies and chicken broth and simmer for approximately 20 minutes or until rice is cooked.

Sprinkle the crumbled bacon bits on top of the rice and enjoy! You can make this less spicy or more spicy by adding a tablespoon of diced jalapeños.

ROSIE'S KICK BUTT CHILI

Serves 8-10

1 ½ pounds ground beef
   1 ½ cups chopped green and red peppers (3/4 cup each)
   1 cup chopped onions
   2 teaspoons minced garlic
   2 (15 ounce) cans tomato sauce
   1 (14 ½ ounce) can petite diced tomatoes
   1 (15 ounce) Hunts chunky chili tomato sauce
   1 (15 ounce) pinto beans w/jalapeños
   1 (15 ounce) regular black beans
   1 package Taco seasoning
   1 (10 ounce) package frozen corn

Brown hamburger, peppers, onions and garlic in a Dutch oven. Drain grease. Add everything else except the corn. Bring to boil and reduce heat. Simmer uncovered for 1 hour. Add the corn and continue to simmer for about 30 minutes. Serve with jalapeno cornbread. (see recipe below)

Mexican Corn Bread

½ cup melted butter
   ¾ cup white sugar
   4 eggs
   1 (15 ounce) cream-style corn
   4.5 ounce can of diced jalapeños, drained
   ½ cup shredded Monterey Jack cheese

½ cup shredded cheddar cheese
1 cup all-purpose flour
1 cup of yellow cornmeal
¼ teaspoon salt
4 teaspoon baking powder
Preheat oven to 300° F. Lightly grease a 9 X 13 inch baking pan.

In a large bowl, beat together the butter and sugar. Beat in eggs one at a time. Blend in cream corn, jalapeños, and both cheeses. In a separate bowl, stir together flour, cornmeal, baking powder, and salt.

Add flour mixture to corn mixture and stir until smooth. Pour into prepared pan and bake in preheated oven for 1 hour or until a toothpick inserted into the center of the pan comes out clean. (You can cheat and buy the packaged jalapeño corn bread mix or just buy the jalapeño corn bread already made. I'm all about easy.)

Frozen Blue Moscato Margaritas

Serves 4

1 tbsp. granulated sugar
1 tbsp. kosher salt
Lime wedges
7 c. ice
1 c. moscato
3/4 c. blue Curaçao
1/2 c. tequila
1/4 c. triple sec
2 tbsp. lime juice
Fresh blueberries, for serving

1. In a small dish, combine sugar and salt. Rim mason jars with lime wedge then dip in sugar-salt mixture.
2. Combine Moscato, Curaçao, tequila, triple sec, and lime juice in blender. Add ice and blend until smooth.
3. Divide mixture between 4 glasses. Garnish with lime wedges and fresh blueberries.

For sugar/salt mixture, ad ¼ cup salt, ¼ cup sugar, zest of one lime, and zest of ½ lemon.

PECAN PIE BROWNIES

Serves 12
Ingredients

1 box Brownie mix for 9 X 13 pan.

Pecan Pie Filling

1 cup sugar
1 ½ cups light corn syrup
4 eggs
¼ cup unsalted butter
1 ½ teaspoons vanilla extract
2 cups pecans, roughly chopped

Preheat oven according to brownie package instructions. Grease a 9 X 13 inch
Baking dish.

Mix brownies according to package instructions, pour into greased baking dish, and bake for 20 minutes.

Mix the sugar, corn syrup, eggs, butter, and vanilla in a small saucepan. Cook over medium high heat, stirring constantly for about 15 minutes.
It should have thickened enough to coat a spoon.

Add the pecans and continue to cook for another 2-3 minute. It should be loose enough to pour over brownies but not totally liquefied.
When the brownies have finished pre-baking re-

move from the oven and pour the pecan pie filling over them, completely covering them.

Place them back in the oven for another 25-30 minutes or until the pecan mixture is set.

Let brownies cool completely before cutting into squares and serving.

LIZ'S FABULOUS BEEF ENCHILADAS

Serves 8-10

2 pounds ground beef
    1 (15ounce) tomato sauce
    1 can Ro-tel brand diced tomatoes and green chilis
    ½ cup water
    2 packages Chilo mix or another brand chili mix
    1 cup salsa
    1 can Wolfe brand chili *without* beans
    1 pound Cheddar cheese, grated
    1 package burrito-sized flour tortillas
    2 whole onions, chopped (optional-see note below)

Brown and drain ground beef.

Add everything except cheese and onions.

Simmer about 30 minutes.

Preheat oven to 350° F. Put meat sauce on bottom of 9 X 13 pan just like you would do for lasagna. Warm tortillas one at a time for 20-30 seconds in microwave to soften. Fill with meat sauce, onions (optional) and cheese just like you were making a taco. Save some of the meat mixture for the top of the enchiladas. Roll and place in a baking dish seam side down. It usually takes 4 big rolled tortillas length-wise and one half of another across the bottom to cover the dish.

Cover entire dish with rest of meat mixture, then onions (optional), then cheese.

Bake long enough to melt the cheese. (About 20 minutes.)

Serve with refried beans and rice. My sister-in-law Merci, a second generation Mexican, taught me an easy way to make the beans. Empty any brand of refried beans into a skillet with a little oil. Warm over medium heat, turning once to make sure all the beans get hot. Cover entire skillet with grated Mexican (cheddar and jack) cheese. Yum! You can buy the taco rice packet to make for a great tasting and easy rice dish or use the Spicy Spanish Rice recipe I've provided. Enjoy.

ROSIE'S KING RANCH CHICKEN

Serves 8-10

12-13 soft corn tortillas
    1 can (14.5 ounces) chicken broth
    4 tablespoons butter
    1 cup chopped onion
    ½ teaspoon minced garlic
    1 (16 ounce) container sliced mushrooms
    1 medium green pepper, chopped
    1 (16 ounce) container sour cream
    1 tablespoon flour
    1 tablespoon corn starch
    1 can (10 ounces) Ro-tel brand diced tomatoes and
green chilis
    1 package taco seasoning
    3 cups chicken, cooked and diced (approximately 3
large breasts)
    Cooking spray
    24 ounces of Colby/Monterey Jack cheese mixed

Preheat oven to 350° F. Place the tortillas in the chicken broth for 10 minutes, (Do not cook.)

In a large skillet, sauté the onion, garlic, mushrooms and green peppers in the butter.

Add the sour cream, flour, and corn starch, heating until smooth and bubbly.

Add the Ro-tel, taco seasoning, and the diced chicken and mix.

Spray a 9 X13 casserole dish with the cooking spray. Cut the tortillas into 6 pieces each. Layer ½ of these on the bottom of the prepared baking dish. Next layer ½ of the chicken mix and then ½ of the cheese mix. Salt and pepper each layer. Repeat, ending with the cheese.

Bake for 30 minutes or until cheese is bubbly.

ROSIE'S TORTILLA SOUP

Serves 8-10

1 onion, diced
    4 tablespoons olive oil
    1 can (14.5 ounces) petite diced tomatoes
    ½ bunch cilantro, finely chopped
    2 cloves garlic, minced
    1 teaspoon red pepper flakes (more or less as you like)
    1 teaspoon ground cumin
    2 cans (4 ounces each) diced green chilies
    1 bag frozen corn (I use a can of Southwest kernel corn for a nice bite)
    48 ounces chicken broth (I always add more to taste, so buy extra)
    28 ounces of water
    2 chicken breasts cooked and cut into bite-sized pieces. (I use a can of chicken)
    Lots of salt and pepper to taste.

Garnish
    Avocados cut into bite-sized pieces
    Corn tortilla strips (find these where croutons are sold)
    Monterey Jack cheese, grated.

In a Dutch oven, add olive oil, onions and diced chilies and cook until the onions become translucent.

Add cilantro, tomatoes, garlic, cumin, chili peppers and stir-fry for 3 minutes.

Add the chicken broth, corn, water, salt and pepper, and chicken, and cook on medium heat for 1½ hours. You can cook for just an hour but the longer it cooks, the better it tastes.

Once fully cooked, serve in soup bowls and add the desired amounts of garnish.

Add more chicken broth for leftover soup that has thickened. I usually freeze two bags of this.

TACO SPAGHETTI

Serves 8-10

12 ounces spaghetti, broken into thirds
    1 pound ground beef
    1 package taco seasoning mix
    2/3 cup of water
    1 (10.5 ounce) can cream of chicken soup
    1 (12 ounce) can evaporated milk
    1 (10 ounce) can Ro-tels brand diced tomatoes and
green chilis
    1 (8 ounce) package Velveeta cheese, cubed
    1½ cups grated Mexican style cheese (I use more
because I'm a cheese freak.)
    1 box store-bought frozen taquitos

Preheat oven to 350° F. Lightly spray a 13 X 9 inch pan with cooking spray. Set aside.

Cook pasta according to package directions.

In a large skillet, cook ground beef over medium to high heat until no longer pink. Drain fat.

Add taco seasoning and water and stir to combine. Cook for 5 minutes.

Stir in soup, milk, Velveeta, and Ro-tel's. Cook on low until cheese melts, stirring constantly.

Stir in spaghetti and pour into greased baking dish.

Bake for 30 minutes or until heated through.

Serve with store-bought taquitos cooked as directed on package

If you make this the night before and cook the next day, allow a little extra time in oven to heat throughout.

GERMAN CHOCOLATE TRES LECHE CAKE

Yields 10-12 servings

1 box chocolate cake mix
    1 can (14 ounces) sweetened condensed milk
    1 can (12 ounces) evaporated milk
    1½ cups heavy whipping cream
    ¼ cup rum
    3 tablespoons confectioner's sugar
    ½ cup sweetened shredded coconut, toasted
    ½ cup pecans, finely chopped
    Chocolate syrup (optional)

Preheat oven to 350° F. Prepare and bake the cake according to directions on the box. Pour into a greased and floured 9 X 13 baking dish. Cool on a rack after toothpick inserted into the center comes out clean.

In a large bowl. Whisk the milks, ½ cup of the cream and the rum. With a wooden spoon, poke holes in the cooled cake about ½ inch apart. Slowly pour milk mixture over cake, allowing it to absorb into cake. Let stand for 30 minutes, then cover and refrigerate at least 8 hours or overnight before you make the icing.

In a small bowl, beat remaining cream until it begins to thicken. Add confectioners' sugar and beat until stiff peaks form. Spread over the top of cake.

Sprinkle with coconut and pecans. If desired, drizzle servings with chocolate syrup.

Store leftovers in the refrigerator.

MARGARITA CUPCAKES

Makes 16 cupcakes

For the Cupcakes
    1 box white cake mix
    ⅓ cup lime juice
    ⅓ cup tequila
    ⅓ cup buttermilk
    ½ cup vegetable oil
    3 large eggs
    1 tablespoon lime zest
    1 tablespoon tequila for brushing the tops

For the Icing
    8 ounces cream cheese, softened
    ½ cup unsalted butter, softened
    2 cups confectioners' sugar
    2 tablespoons lime juice
    1 tablespoon tequila
    ½ tablespoon lime zest

Garnish
For sugar/salt mixture, add ¼ cup salt, ¼ cup sugar, zest of one lime, and zest of ½ lemon.

Preheat oven to 350° F. Line a muffin tin with foil cupcake liners. Spray the liners with nonstick spray.

In a large bowl, mix the dry cake mix, lime juice, tequila, buttermilk, oil, eggs, and the lime zest and beat with hand mixer until just combined.

Fill each foil cupcake liner about 2/3 full (approximately 3 tablespoons) and bake for 14-17 minutes. Remove from oven and let cool to room temperature.

Brush the tops of each cupcake with the reserved teaspoon of tequila. Refrigerate the coated cupcakes for 30 minutes before frosting.

While the cupcakes are cooling, make the frosting by whipping the cream cheese and butter together until completely smooth. Add in the remaining ingredients and whip until combined. Frost each cupcake.

Place the sugar/salt mixture in a small bowl. Carefully roll the edges of each cupcake in the sugar to achieve the margarita sugar rim effect. Be sure and refrigerate leftovers.

ALSO BY LIZ LIPPERMAN

As Liz Lipperman

Jordan McAllister Mysteries
Liver Let Die
Beef Stolen-Off
Murder for the Halibut
Chicken Caccia-Killer
Smothered, Covered & Dead
Enchi Lotta Bodies

Romantic Suspense
Can't Buy Me Love

As Lizbeth Lipperman

Garcia girls Mysteries
Heard it Through the Grapevine
Jailhouse Glock
Mission to Kill
Rock Around the Corpse

Stand-alone Romantic Mysteries
Shattered
Mortal Deception

Sweepers Inc. Romantic Thriller
SWEEPERS: A Kiss to Die For

SWEEPERS: Die Once More

ABOUT THE AUTHOR

Liz Lipperman started writing many years ago, even before she retired from the medical field. Wasting many years thinking she was a romance writer but always having to deal with the pesky villains who kept popping up in all her stories, she finally gave up and decided since she read mysteries and obviously wrote them, why fight it? She has two mystery series--the Jordan McAllister Mysteries (formerly the Clueless Cook Series) and The Garcia Girls Mysteries (formerly A Dead Sister Talking Series)which are available in all formats. You might also want to check out her romantic thrillers, Mortal Deception and Shattered and a romantic short titled Can't Buy Me Love. Also, be watching for the debut of a new romantic suspense series titled SWEEPERS coming sometime next year. She wants readers to know that her G rated cozies are written as Liz Lipperman and her R rated, grittier mysteries as Lizbeth Lipperman. Check out her web page for a more detailed listing of her books along with reviews and trailers. www.lizlipperman.com

She lives north of Dallas with her HS sweetheart hubby. When she's not writing she spends her time doting on her four wonderful grandchildren.